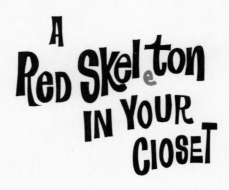

A Red Skelton IN YOUR CIOSET

A Red Skelton IN YOUR CIOSET

Ghost stories—gay and grim— selected and edited

by Red Skelton

Publishers GROSSET & DUNLAP New York

For permission to include copyrighted material, the editor wishes to extend his appreciation and to acknowledge the following:

TO STARCH A SPOOK by Andrew Benedict. Copyright © 1965 by Grosset & Dunlap, Inc., and printed here for the first time by permission of the author.

MY DISPLACED GHOSTS by John West. Copyright © 1965 by Grosset & Dunlap, Inc., and printed here for the first time by permission of the author.

THE SPOOK UPON THE STAIRS by Andrew McCullen. Copyright © 1965 by Grosset & Dunlap, Inc., and printed here for the first time by permission of the author.

THE OPEN WINDOW by Saki (H. H. Munro). From *The Complete Short Stories of Saki,* copyright © 1930, 1957 by The Viking Press, Inc. Reprinted by permission of The Viking Press, Inc. Also from *The Bodley Head Saki,* reprinted by permission of The Bodley Head, Ltd.

THE SUPERSTITIOUS GHOST by Arthur Guiterman, from *The Mirthful Lyre* (1918). Reprinted by permission of Mrs. Arthur Guiterman.

IN A DIM ROOM by Lord Dunsany, from *The Fourth Book of Jorkens.* Copyright © 1948 by Lord Dunsany; by permission of Arkham House.

THE HAUNTED TRAILER by Robert Arthur. Copyright © 1941 by *Weird Tales* under the original title of DEATH THUMBS A RIDE. Reprinted by permission of the author.

O UGLY BIRD! by Manly Wade Wellman. Copyright © 1946 by Fantasy House, Inc., for *The Magazine of Fantasy and Science-Fiction.* Copyright © 1963 by Manly Wade Wellman; by permission of Arkham House.

THREE GHOST STORIES FOR CHRISTMAS EVE by Jerome K. Jerome, from *Told After Supper.* Reprinted and abridged by permission of Miss Rowena Jerome.

MR. WHITCOMB'S GENIE by Walter R. Brooks. First published in *The Saturday Evening Post.* Copyright © 1945 by The Curtis Publishing Company. Reprinted by permission of Brandt & Brandt.

THE WONDERFUL CAT OF COBBIE BEAN by Barbee Oliver Carleton. Copyright © 1956 by The Curtis Publishing Co. Copyright © 1957 by Holt, Rinehart and Winston, Inc. Reprinted by permission of Holt, Rinehart and Winston, Inc.

THE WONDERFUL CAT OF COBBIE BEAN was originally published as "Was Cobbie Bean Bewitched?" in the October, 1956 issue of *Jack and Jill.* Copyright © 1956 by The Curtis Publishing Company.

HE WALKED BY DAY by Julius Long. Reprinted through the courtesy of Mrs. Mary F. Abel, executrix of the estate of Forrest G. Long.

THE WATER GHOST by John Kendrick Bangs, from *The Water Ghost and other Stories* by John Kendrick Bangs, Harper & Brothers.

Of Course I Believe In Ghosts

DOESN'T EVERYBODY?

Sometimes, just before I go on stage, the ghost of the greatest pantomimist of all whispers in my ear. His name was Grimaldi and even though he lived a couple of centuries ago, he tells me funny things to try and do. And you should hear him laugh when I don't do it just right.

Grimaldi is a fun ghost. But then, most ghosts are nice and friendly, and only try to scare you when you bother them or hurt their feelings. I must admit that now and then I've been plenty scared. Maybe I accidentally stepped on their toes or something.

I remember the very first time I was scared and thought I was about to meet my first ghost. I was just a little boy back in Vincennes, Indiana and had saved up enough pennies to go to the movies to see "The Phantom of the Opera." It was a real spooky picture with lots of shivers. When I started for home afterwards, down the dark street, I heard a sound following me—crunch—crunch. With each step, I walked faster and looked behind me. Nothing was there but the sound, right with my footsteps, crunch—crunch—crunch. I just had to start running, but there it was, even closer, keeping time, crunch—crunch—crunch—crunch—crunch, following me right up the steps at home and into the lighted hallway. I stood there, out of breath—to not a sound.

It wasn't until I started to move, and heard the sound again as one leg passed another . . . from my new corduroy pants! My mother had given them to me that afternoon and in all the clamor of the day I had never heard their sound until the quiet of the night.

Afterwards, I think I was disappointed. Maybe if I had stood perfectly

still on that dark street, a friendly ghost would have whispered in my ear
—"It's just your new corduroy pants."

Whenever you feel that wonderful shiver run up and down your back,
or the wind is whispering in the trees, or dark shadows seem to waver all
about you—just stand perfectly still. Maybe a friendly ghost will tap *you*
on the shoulder and say a comforting word. If you act scared or run, he'll
probably just go away and won't even say hello.

Those of us who believe in ghosts, or even just think that maybe we do,
sooner or later find our favorite ghost stories. It was back there in Vincennes
in grammar school that I first started collecting my favorites.

In one grade—I don't remember exactly which one it was, I was never
good at grades—we had a teacher named Miss Marsh. She was a fine, old
fashioned teacher. I mean she was strict! She kept us hard at work except
for once a week when story time came. That was the one thing about
school we looked forward to.

One day Miss Marsh brought out a book and said to us, "We live in
Indiana."

Right away I gave her 100 for geography, because we certainly did.
Vincennes, Indiana. But I didn't say anything because she didn't like to
be interrupted.

"Indiana's greatest poet," Miss Marsh went on, "is James Whitcomb
Riley. Today we are going to read one of his poems. It is called "Little
Orphant Annie."

That didn't mean anything to me. I'd never heard of "Little Orphant
Annie." Of course, today everybody knows the Orphan Annie in the newspaper comic strips, but this was a different one.

Then Miss Marsh started to read. The whole class sat without a wiggle
or a squirm until she had finished. I can still remember the delicious chill
that went through me as Miss Marsh repeated the lines at the end of each
verse:

> *An' the gobble-uns'll get you*
> *Ef you*
> *Don't*
> *Watch*
> *Out!*

Maybe you've read the poem. Or better still, had it read to you in front
of an open fire with the wind howling outside. If you haven't, I've included
it in this book because it was my first introduction to the thrill of a ghost
story. And if you've read it, it's worth reading again.

That was the first time I ever realized that to be just a little bit scared, in
a harmless way, could be fun.

For the rest of the term, whenever Miss Marsh asked us what we'd like
her to read at story time, someone was likely to suggest "Little Orphant

Annie." But Miss Marsh was too good a showman to keep on repeating herself. She gave us more of James Whitcomb Riley's poems, and she read us stories about fairy princesses, brave dogs who saved their masters from drowning, and things like that.

Her next big hit, though, came when she read us Oscar Wilde's wonderful story, "The Canterville Ghost." We all laughed aloud at the poor ghost's troubles with the pesky twins. And when the story was over, I'd made a new discovery. Ghost stories could be funny! They could be scary-fun and they could be funny-fun. Either way I enjoyed them.

And I have enjoyed them ever since. Here in this book are a selection of my favorites.

Some of these stories are very funny. At least, they made me laugh. Others are just scary enough to be fun.

You'll find such enduring comic masterpieces as "The Canterville Ghost" by Oscar Wilde and "The Ghost Ship" by Richard Middleton, along with such grand spoofs as "The Legend of The Moor's Legacy" by Washington Irving and "Three Ghost Stories For Christmas Eve" by Jerome Fox Jerome. There's also the weird modern folk story "O Ugly Bird" by Manly Wade Wellman and Lafcadio Hearn's almost fairy tale "The Boy Who Drew Cats." Plus——

Ah, Grimaldi! He says I am talking too much—to let you get on with the stories. Happy reading.

RED SKELTON

Hollywood, California
1965

CONTENTS

10 Contents

The Spook
Upon The Stair

ANDREW McCULLEN

The Spook
Upon The Stair

I met a spook upon the stair;
   He was a haunt who had no hair.
In fact, he didn't have a head
   (Which made me think he might be dead).

     His head I saw beneath his arm,
        Safely tucked away from harm,
     But still to me it spoke, and said,
        "Before you go on up to bed,
     Please let me say you should not stare
        At ghosts you meet upon the stair."

          Thus spoke that spook, I do not lie,
            Before I could quite pass it by.
          "The thoughtful, gentle thing to do,"
            It said to me, as I say to you,
          "Is act as if they were not there,
            And never, never, never stare,
          Even though beneath an arm
            Their heads they carry, safe from harm.

"However frightful they may be,
  Act as if you did not see,
And if you did, would not have cared.
  Above all, *never* show you're scared."

  This spook he spoke so plain and fair,
    I heeded him, right then and there.
  I hurried on up to the top,
    And as I went I heard a pop.
  I turned—and there was nothing there.
    The spot the spook had been was bare.

My Displaced Ghosts

JOHN WEST

The D.G. problem is getting very serious these days. Never heard of the D.G. problem? Well, then, here it is. . . .

My Displaced Ghosts

YOU PROBABLY haven't heard of the D.G. problem yet. It's just begun to develop, but it's getting bigger all the time. If you come home some night and find your neat little split-level ranch-type house occupied by a strange spook, don't be surprised.

You won't like it, of course. But neither will the ghost. A ghost likes privacy as much as people do. Maybe more. But the way things are going, if a ghost does show up, you're going to have to live with it.

D.G. simply stands for "Displaced Ghosts." All over the country, big old houses, many of them empty and rundown, are being wrecked. These are the kind of houses ghosts like to haunt. In their place are being built acre after acre of small, compact, three-bedroom jobs. Ghosts hate small houses. But with the big houses being torn down every place you turn, where else

is there for the ghosts to go?

I stumbled onto the D.G. problem because I owned a big, rambling, rundown old house north of Los Angeles, California. It was a fine old Spanish-style mansion built along the crest of a ridge that gave it a wonderful view of the hills. It was one of a group of six, all pretty much alike, with big stables and out-buildings, built back about 1880 by six rich men from the East, who decided to spend their days in California and wanted to stay together.

They liked privacy, so they built a long way from anybody else. They had enough money to buy up the land around them, and they imported servants, so for a few years they lived in grand style.

Well, times changed. Since the war, money has been tight and servants scarce, and the descendants of the original six found the location too lonely for them.

One by one, the big houses were deserted. The only reason I lived there was because I had inherited one of the houses from an elderly uncle. And I'm a writer. I don't make much money. I needed a place to live and the big old mansion was a roof over my head.

In the beginning, I just sort of camped there, and it was pretty lonely. Then I learned my house had a ghost in it. The ghost waited for about six months before letting me see him; then, one night when I was at my typewriter, he materialized slowly in the air in front of me.

I won't go into the details. I mean about my hair standing on end, and feeling cold chills and all that. Because none of it happened. The truth is, I was feeling so lonely at the moment, that even a ghost was welcome. I jumped up and tried to shake his hand, but all I could manage was the feel as if I had touched a wet fish very fast.

But that was all right. He understood. He was the ghost of a Spanish grandee named Don Esteban y Garcia, who had been killed in a duel on that spot two hundred years before. A real gentleman. Gentleghost, I should say.

He had been haunting the house ever since it had been built. He'd never caused any trouble; most ghosts don't, you know. They're rather considerate people. I mean, phantoms. It's only the unhappy ghosts, or the ones with bad consciences, that go around moaning and groaning and scaring people.

Many was the night, Don Esteban told me, that he had attended a big party in the house without ever being suspected. He merely moved around unseen, breathing the aroma of the gentlemen's cigars, sniffing the fragrance of the ladies' perfume, occasionally inhaling a deep whiff from a glass of brandy, and thoroughly enjoying himself. He would have been ashamed of himself to have alarmed anyone.

Don Esteban had only shown himself to me because he could feel I was lonely. Also, I was getting a bit desperate about my writing. No sales; no money. He hoped I might forgive him. He only wanted to help if he could. Maybe a little company—even ghostly company—would cheer me up.

As soon as I got used to the idea, I began to appreciate his thoughtfulness. It gave me somebody to talk to, you know. A writer needs to talk. He likes to try out his plots. Esteban was willing to listen to me all night.

The trouble was, he didn't like my material. He kept shaking his head.

I should write about real people, he told me. For instance—and he started off on a tale of his ancestors who had come exploring in California with the early missionaries.

Adventure? Romance? It was the real thing, and I knew it. I wrote it down, making only a few changes, and rushed it off to New York. A couple of weeks later I got my first real check, and I decided to throw a party to celebrate—after using most of the money to pay up my back taxes.

There weren't any people living close enough to come to a party, so I decided it would just be for Don Esteban and myself. I set the table in the big old dining room with the panelled walls. Real linen tablecloth, real silver, real crystal wine glasses—I'd inherited them all from my late uncle, but never had a use for them before.

When everything was ready, I poured some wine, lit a fine cigar, and let it burn in an ashtray. Then I lit the candles and called Don Esteban. I had to call several times, and when he finally did materialize, he only half made it. I mean, he materialized from his waist up, and floated there, looking at me sheepishly.

"Don Esteban!" I said. "It's a party! Come on! Shape your essence and sit down! Sniff the cigar—imported from Spain. And the champagne. France's best!"

With an effort he finished himself as far as his knees. He couldn't seem to manage his legs and feet. Perhaps because the polished boots he wore were rather hard to materialize.

"What is it, Don Esteban?" I asked. He wasn't himself at all. "Something wrong?"

"I have a confession to make, amigo," he said, in a very small voice. Of course, ghosts seldom have really loud voices, but this was just a whisper.

"A confession?" I couldn't imagine what he was getting at. "What kind of confession?"

"There are others of us present," he said. He held himself erect, like a true Spanish grandee. "I—I have abused your hospitality, amigo. This last week or so I have been giving refuge under your roof to a number of D.G.'s."

"D.G.'s?" I stared at him, baffled. "I've heard of D.T.'s but what are D.G.'s?"

"Displaced ghosts," Don Esteban said sadly. Then he went on to tell me about the displaced ghost problem. I've already filled you in on the details. Big houses being torn down, resident ghosts with no place to go—Well, the long and short of it was that Don Esteban had allowed a few of them to come to haunt my house.

"I realize I shouldn't have done it, amigo," he said. "It is, after all, a matter of pride with us never to haunt in groups. Sometimes, in the case of castles, we may allow two or even three ghosts to haunt it, but a house such as yours—No, I have done wrong! I humbly apologize. I will send them away."

"Now wait a minute, Don Esteban," I said. I was feeling good about the sale I had just made. "This is a big house and another ghost or two—I probably won't mind it. Why don't you just introduce your friends and let's talk this over?"

"Very well," he said. "Let me introduce Senorita Marguerita Velasquez. Unfortunately caught in a landslide up in Santa Barbara in 1851. Her home, a big one, is but one of many that have just fallen into the hands of the wreckers."

The senorita materialized about three feet off the floor and gave a curtsy. She was—I mean, she had been a very good-looking senorita.

"I thank you, senor," she said in a charming almost-voice, "for giving us sanctuary. And my mother thanks you. My father thanks you. My two brothers thank you. My sister thanks you."

"Tell them they are welcome, when you write," I said grandly. "They're back in Spain, I suppose?"

"Oh, no." I had the positive feeling she was trying to blush, but it is very hard to tell when a ghost is blushing. I mean, a blush is caused by blood rushing to the surface of the skin and ghosts don't have any blood You can see the problem. But as I say, she tried.

"They are here with me, senor. We were all caught in the same landslide."

And like those Japanese paper flowers you put in a glass of water, just tiny pellets that bloom into full-sized flowers, her whole family materialized in front of me . . . Papa, mama, sister, and two great big brothers, all of them aristocrats.

Now instead of just Don Esteban, I had seven ghosts in the house with me. I was beginning to feel a little crowded.

"Don Esteban"—I gave him a look that made him disappear from the waist down—"I'm beginning to understand what you mean by the D.G. problem. All these folks—phantoms, I mean—are displaced ghosts?"

He nodded, slowly materializing his lower half again. This time he managed his feet, polished boots and all.

"All from Santa Barbara," he said. "Unfortunately, a whole group of old houses there are being torn down by the developers. However, amigo, these are all. Absolutely all—unless you count the players."

"Count the players?" I asked. "You sound like someone selling a baseball program! Buy a program and count the players! What the deuce do you mean, the players?"

"I mean the theatrical troupe, the traveling actors—players, as they were formerly called. You see, there were two stagecoaches together going through a pass in Santa Barbara that year. One carried Senorita Marguerita Velasquez and her family, the other carried the players, bound for San Francisco. Alas, the same landslide took them all, without partiality. I will introduce them!"

I took a glass of the wine I had poured, to steady my nerves. After all, ghosts are ghosts. I mean nothing to be scared of, but a whole roomful can make you nervous. I hate crowds, anyway.

"Sir Anthony Trembleau," Don Esteban said, like an announcer at a big party. "Lady Trembleau. The Right Honorable Anthony Mainwaring. Miss Cynthia Lovelace. Richard Trent. Howard Lamb. John and Will Jameson . . ."

With every name he spoke, a new spook appeared. Some stood on the floor, some floated in the air. Sir Anthony Trembleau was a fine-looking gentleman with flashing eyes. His wife was a very strongwilled-looking lady. The others—well, they were all actors. They were all dressed in full Shakespearean costumes. For *Hamlet,* I believe. Altogether there were eleven of them. Plus the other seven. Eighteen ghosts in all.

I took another glass of wine hastily.

"You're positive this is all?" I asked Don Esteban. He nodded, then disappeared up to his chin. As he materialized I realized he was hiding something from me.

"All right," I sighed. "Where are the others?"

"Oh, not in the house, amigo," he said. "Come to the window."

I went to the window with him. We both leaned out. Don Esteban put his fingers between his lips and gave a ghostly whistle.

Then out of my garage, which had once been the stables for the big house, came a ghostly stagecoach, pulled by four phantom horses. Behind it came a second coach, larger and pulled by six equine spooks. The two coaches marched around the back yard and returned to the stables.

"The coach, the coachmen and helpers, and the horses, amigo," Don Esteban said. "Naturally, they have to haunt the stables."

He felt me looking at him, and he sighed.

"I am sorry," he said. "It was very necessary. The D.G. problem is becoming acute and this house is so suitable."

I took some more wine. My nerves were steadier but my knees were feeling wobbly.

"Don Esteban," I said, being very stern. "Send them away. There are five other empty houses in this group. All big. All empty. All echoey and dark and spooky. Send your friends to haunt those houses and you can visit them, nights."

Don Esteban vanished all the way up to his eyes. He was embarrassed. And suddenly I knew the truth.

"Don Esteban!" I yelled at him. "Have you gone and filled those other houses with displaced ghosts, too?"

Slowly he reappeared and nodded.

"All," he said. "There are cowboys and Indians, dudes, several fine folk who became ghosts during the San Francisco fire of 1906, gold miners, hunters—I don't know who all. Some of them are rough diamonds. Their manners are not of the best. I invited only the quality ghosts to your residence, amigo."

I took another glass of wine. Then I fainted.

I have no doubt that it was a faint. I came to on my own bed, fully clothed, next morning, and assumed Don Esteban and his friends had managed to carry me there. I had a splitting headache. The result, of course, of realizing that I not only harbored eighteen ghosts in my home, but was surrounded by other empty houses jammed to the rafters with ghost refugees.

Why, I couldn't take a step now without feeling watched. I kept stopping and stepping aside, feeling I was about to bump into some unseen ghost. I didn't dare sit down for fear of sitting on a phantom.

I couldn't write any more. I couldn't eat. Soon I was a wreck, a mere shell of my former self.

Don Esteban tried to talk to me a few times, but I couldn't bear the sight of him any more. I began to feel—yes, I actually began to feel prejudiced toward ghosts! Cold chills ran up and down my back and my hair stood on end when Don Esteban approached.

It wasn't my fault. I couldn't help myself. Eighteen ghosts in one house are a lot of phantoms to have to live with. Especially after they started to quarrel. About who was going to haunt which room and at what hours. The whole house was filled with ghostly footsteps, ghostly bangings and stampings, sighs, groans, moans, and other assorted phantasmal sound effects.

If I'd had the money, I'd have gone some place else. Any place else.

Then the State Highway Department came to my rescue.

You probably know that California has more people than any other state in the Union. Also more automobiles. Also more roads. California is constantly building new roads for new people with new automobiles. In California they are called freeways. And all the freeways are jammed. No matter how many new ones are built.

Well, one day some engineers came through my region, surveying. They told me a freeway was going right smack through the spot where my old house stood. The house would have to come down. I'd be paid for it, of course. I could have kissed them on the spot. But I didn't. They wouldn't have understood.

Now that I knew I could unload that old house for a good price, I became cheerful again. I even stopped resenting Don Esteban and his phantom friends. I stayed up evenings and let them haunt me.

We had some nice chats. The Shakespearean troupe of players did a complete version of *Hamlet* in the library. Hamlet's father's ghost played by a real ghost was a wow. They did *Macbeth,* too. That has a ghost in it— Banquo's ghost. Of course, having a ghost play a ghost is type casting, but it certainly was effective. I applauded for five minutes, while they took bows. They all felt better than they had for years, they told me.

Actors are actors, dead or alive. They yearn for applause.

Naturally, I kept the news about the sale of the house to myself. In a way

I felt badly that the house was going to be demolished and all my D.G. boarders were going to be displaced still again. Now that I had got to know them better, I actually began to like them. They had a spooky sort of charm. But it was too late to do anything about it anyway.

When a State Highway Department decides to build a road, that's it. Anything in the way comes down. And besides, I'd already signed the initial papers and the other houses had been happily unloaded by their absentee owners.

Since the ghosts never stirred before nightfall, they weren't aware of all the activity. Don Esteban didn't learn what was about to happen until the day the Project Chief and his assistant came to the house to have me sign the last papers.

They were delayed and didn't get there until after dark. I should have realized that this could mean trouble, but I didn't. I was looking forward to getting that nice fat check from the Highway Department.

I tried to hurry the Project Chief and his assistant, a young chap named Harry, through the details, but they weren't in any rush. We had to sit in the library and smoke cigars while they talked about what the new freeway was going to mean to the state.

"Just think," the Project Chief said, letting his gaze roam around the room. "All these old houses will be cleaned out and a lovely eight-lane highway will run through here. Eight lanes of the finest concrete, with the most up-to-date road markers on it, capable of carrying—" He turned to his assistant. "How many cars will it carry, Harry?"

"Ten thousand cars an hour, peak load," Harry said. "Figuring an average speed of sixty miles an hours, that is."

"Ten thousand cars an hour, all doing sixty, right over this spot. It certainly must make you feel good to think about that," the Project Chief said happily. "All those people, going from one place to another, and then going back again. And it's us—Harry and me and the others—who make it possible. I tell you, sir, it warms our hearts to meditate upon it."

"Well, now, I see your point," I told him. "You'll probably want to be running along, to get yourself a motel before it's too late. I would invite you to stay here, but I haven't any sheets, blankets, things like that."

"Yes, I guess we'd better go. Come along, Harry," said the Project Chief, and they rose.

"It's been a pleasure to do business with you, Mr. West," he said to me. "You can leave any time now—officially, this house now belongs to the state. I estimate we'll have it torn down in six weeks. I wouldn't waste too much time getting anything you want to save out of it."

He let his eyes roam over the fine old redwood panelling.

"Shame to have to rip out all this fine old woodwork," he murmured. "But that's progress for you."

That's when Don Esteban y Garcia appeared. Standing beside the fire-place, fixing me with a haunting stare. He looked ghastly. I mean, ghostly. No, I don't know what I mean. Just that he looked awful. If a ghost could turn pale, Don Esteban had turned pale. His eyes glared.

"Good heavens!" the Project Chief cried. "What's that?"

Don Esteban faded out, all except his eyes, which fixed me with one last accusing stare before they, too, disappeared.

"Nothing," I said. "Nothing at all."

I had my first premonition of trouble coming. The way Don Esteban had looked at me—you'd think I'd stabbed him in the back or something. I decided on the spot not to stay in that house one more night. Not with so many ghosts who, it suddenly occurred to me, might be resentful.

"Gentlemen," I said, "I believe I'll come with you. To the motel. My car is being fixed so if you can give me a lift—"

They were glad to. I was packed and out of there in five minutes. As I went, I had the feeling of being watched. By unseen shapes. All of them furious at me.

It was a relief when the Project Chief's station wagon started down the private road that connected the six old houses.

"Yessirree!" he said, looking around him as he drove. "Eight lanes of pure concrete running right over this spot! It'll be the finest road in the country when it's finished. Take the traffic pressure off the Coast Highway."

He'd hardly said that when my worst fears were realized.

I'd guessed Don Esteban would try something, but I thought if I could get away soon enough, I'd fool him and the others.

Obviously he'd been too fast for me.

Down the road straight for us at a dead gallop came an old-fashioned stagecoach, drawn by six horses. Chasing the coach was a band of mounted Indians, giving out shrieks to curdle the blood. Every last one of them a ghost, you understand. I recognized the coach. It came from my stable. The Indians must have come from the next house. Don Esteban had rounded them up fast.

The coach came careening toward us. It was filled with the Shakespearean acting troupe. They all leaned out the windows, registering extreme terror.

The Project Chief saw the coach about to crash into us and just gave a moan. He let go the wheel and covered his eyes with his hands. The car swerved off the road and overturned in a ditch just as the phantom stage-coach rushed past us, followed by the whooping Indians.

Luckily we hadn't been going more than ten miles an hour. We were jarred and jolted, but when we unscrambled ourselves and crawled out, we weren't hurt.

The Project Chief and his assistant looked numb. Dazed.

I didn't blame them. I was pretty shaken myself.

"What . . . was . . . that?" the Project Chief, a large, portly man, asked, spacing his words.

"I saw a stagecoach, chased by Indians, coming down the road at us," Harry, the young man, announced. He wiped his upper lip. "They ran right through us," he said.

"Good heavens, they're coming back!" the Project Chief cried.

He ducked behind the overturned station wagon. We joined him.

The coach came rushing back at us. Now the six phantom horses were breathing fire, a little touch someone had thought up in the interval.

So were the horses of the Indians. All breathing fire.

Even though I knew it was just a lot of ghosts play-acting, I couldn't help feeling sorry for the Project Chief and Harry.

The Indians caught the stagecoach directly in front of us. They dragged out the ghostly Shakespearean troupe inside. They scalped every one of them while we watched. Of course, all the actors were wearing wigs. I saw Sir Anthony Trembleau wink at me as his Indian scalped off his wig.

After the performance was over, the whole scene just faded from view.

I helped two badly shaken men back to my old house—actually the state's old house now—and gave them something to revive them. It was half an hour and several revivals later before they could speak clearly. Then they demanded to know what the—well, anyway, what was going on around there.

While I was trying to answer, Sir Anthony Trembleau materialized in front of us. Still in costume as Hamlet's father, you understand. But for a little added touch he was carrying his head under his arm. These actors! They'll do anything for an effect.

"Sir Anthony Trembleau, at your service, gentlemen," he said and made a bow. The effect of the bow was sadly marred by the fact that he dropped his head. The Project Chief staggered backwards. Harry, his assistant, caught him and they fell into a chair together.

"I am here in the public interest, sir." Sir Anthony now was talking directly to the Project Chief, in his best acting voice. "To save you from making a sad mistake. Do you not know that this ridge upon which these houses sit is known as—" he lowered his voice to a sepulchral whisper— "Haunted Hill?"

"H-H-Haunted Hill?" The Project Chief was stuttering now. As I have said, he was a big man and every inch of him quivered.

"Did you say H-H-Haunted H-H-Hill?" squeaked Harry, like a stuttering echo.

"Haunted Hill. The valley down below, where all the trees are, is known as Spooky Hollow."

As he said this, Sir Anthony Trembleau gave a ghostly laugh. The Project Chief swallowed three times before he could speak.

"You're ghosts? You haunt this property?" he asked.

"We are spirits, sir, lady and gentlemen spirits. And we inhabit this property. If you wish to call it haunting, you may do so," Sir Anthony replied with—I almost said spirit.

The Project Chief sat up. He pushed Harry off his lap and Harry got his own chair. The Project Chief was beginning to recover himself. You have to be a tough man to be a Project Chief of a big highway development program. Any man who dispossesses real living people every day to get room to build new roads isn't going to be stopped by a mere ghost or two.

"My friend," he said, "this house is coming down. You will soon find a beautiful eight-lane freeway of the finest American-made white concrete, guaranteed to last fifty years, running where this house is. Then what will you and all the other spooks do? You won't have any house to haunt any more."

"Then, sir, we will haunt the freeway," said Sir Anthony with dignity. "It will be known as the Haunted Highway. We will have stagecoach races nightly, followed by Indian attacks, and then by battles between cowboys and Indians. From dusk until dawn we will romp on your beautiful eight lanes of white concrete for a distance of two miles in each direction."

"You couldn't!" The Project Chief turned a ghostly off-white himself. "You wouldn't!"

"We could and we would!" said Sir Anthony. "Permit me to introduce you to my fellow spirits. First, Lady Trembleau!"

Lady Trembleau materialized. Then the rest of the Shakesperean troupe, each one bowing to the pop-eyed Project Chief and his assistant. Then Sir Anthony started materializing the family of Senorita Velasquez. He was starting in on the Indians and cowboys when I slipped from the room.

I went to my own room and called: "Don Esteban! Come here! Show yourself!"

Slowly Don Esteban materialized, right down to the pointed toes of his shiny boots. He seemed reproachful, yet self-satisfied.

"Amigo," he said, "I thought you were our friend. To think you would do this to me—to us! Sell the house to be torn down and make D.G.'s out of us!"

"I didn't do anything," I told him. "Listen, when a highway department gets a mad passion to push eight lanes of nice new concrete across your property, nothing human is going to stop them."

"We're not human," Don Esteban said. "We are spirits. We are making our last stand in this world of progress, and we intend to fight with every weapon. We will haunt that new highway until frightened drivers by the hundreds pile up their shiny new cars and join us. It will be worse than a battlefield. It will be—catastrophe!"

"What's happened to you, Don Esteban?" I demanded. "You told me when we first met that ghosts are shy, that they don't like trouble, that they only show themselves when they have to!"

"It is the influence of the players, of Sir Anthony Trembleau and his company," Don Esteban said. "Every actor wants an audience, even if he is just a ghost of an actor. The little scene we staged outside an hour ago was directed by Sir Anthony, with some help from you."

"From me?" I cried. "How did I help?"

"Those trashy historical adventure stories you were trying to write when we first met," Don Esteban said. "They gave me all the material I needed to help Sir Anthony work out an impromptu script."

"Well!" I stared at him. An idea was beginning to come to me. "Listen, could you do it again, any time you wanted? That stagecoach chase? And others like it?"

"All night long," Don Esteban said, "if we had an audience. Sir Anthony and his troupe are turning us all into hams, I'm afraid."

"Then," I cried, "if you'll just play along with me—all of you—I may have the solution."

And I went back into the library, where the Project Chief and Harry were staring, eyes popping, lips trembling, knees shaking, at a roomful so packed with assorted ghosts that some of them were being squeezed into the fireplace and sucked up the chimney by the natural draft.

"Okay, boys, break it up," I said briskly. "I want to talk business to these gentlemen."

Don Esteban made a sign and the ghosts all vanished.

I poured a strong dose of revival medicine for the two men.

"Gentlemen," I said, "you have a problem. If you build this highway, it will be known as the Haunted Highway. Every evening will see a scene of carnage and massacre unrivaled since the sack of ancient Troy. And you—*you* will be blamed for engineering an unsafe highway. Because who will believe the drivers are being scared off the road by ghosts?"

"It's true, Chief," Harry groaned. "We'll be blamed for building a death-trap."

"Last year I won the National Safety Award for building the world's safest highway," the Project Chief cried. "It's only a mile long and doesn't go any place and no one drives on it so there weren't any accidents, but that's beside the point. I'm known for building safe highways. I can't have a thing like this on my record."

"We'll move the freeway!" Harry said. "We'll put it the other side of the hill. Mister West, you can have your house back."

"Now wait a minute," I said. "If you do that it'll cost several million. You'll have to explain why you changed the plans. What will you say? Have you thought of that?"

"Yes, Harry, what will we say?" the Project Chief echoed.

"We'll say we did it to avoid some ghosts who—No." Harry gave a long sigh. "That won't work either. Frankly, Chief, I don't know what we'll say."

"Gentlemen, if I may make some suggestions, I think I can help you out of your problem," I said.

And then I began to talk.

At first they said no.

They said no a second time.

Then they thought of their reputations as highway engineers, and they finally said yes. We drew up the agreements on the spot.

So the Highway Department, instead of tearing down the six fine, if run-down, old buildings, carefully moved them a quarter-mile downhill into a nice, spooky sort of hollow, with trees and a brook. They built a good exit and entrance road to the spot from the splendid new, eight-lane freeway they then built where the houses had been.

They threw in a fence around the property for good measure, and, of course, made sure I had clear title to the land down in Spooky Hollow— as I renamed it—and to the houses.

We are now busy on the final stages of my scheme.

We're going to be open nightly, from sunset to sunup. We'll put on ghostly stagecoach races, phantom combats between spectral cowboys and Indians, scenes from Shakespeare for the culture lovers, and a lot of other inspiring entertainment that Sir Anthony Trembleau and his cast of hundreds of stage-struck ghosts are busy rehearsing.

Yes, sir, when you come out this way next, you'll be able to see the spirit world integrated into the world of progress. We're licking the D.G. problem, anyway, at the local level.

I predict we will be a major tourist attraction, right up beside Disneyland and Marineland. As there is almost nothing to do in California at night, except for a few night baseball games, and we will be open all night long right beside a modern freeway, I anticipate fabulous business.

Look for our signs next time you're out this way.

What are we going to call our enterprise?

Why, GHOSTLAND, of course.

What else?

In A Dim Room

LORD DUNSANY

It was only logical. If the story was true the person telling it simply had to be a ghost!

In A Dim Room

It is some while now since I have recorded any unusual experience that has come the way of my friend Jorkens. The fact is that I incurred a certain amount of odium in one house by bringing him into it. It was not my fault, nor do I think it was his. What happened was that a certain friend of mine said that his children liked thrilling tales, and I told them a few tales of lions and tigers, which had quite failed to thrill them. It suddenly occurred to me that there is something a little unusual in some of Jorkens' experiences amongst Asian or African carnivora, so that any tale of his might be likely to succeed where those that I told had failed. So I said to my friend's three children that I knew an old hunter of big game whose experiences were more out-of-the-way than mine, and asked my friend if I might one day bring him to tea.

I had no idea that there would be anything frightening about one of Jorkens' tales; nor did I think that the three children, ranging between ten and twelve years old, would be easily frightened. The permission to bring Jorkens was readily given, and the children unfortunately asked him for a thrilling tale, in those actual words, and Jorkens began at once as soon as they asked him. Now it is all blamed on me. I can only say that they asked for it, and they got it.

It should be borne in mind that they had never seen Jorkens before, and had only his own word for what kind of man he was; and then children can be very credulous. Well, here is the story, which he told almost as soon as he was seated in a comfortable chair, with the children standing before him, two boys of ten and eleven and a girl of twelve.

31

It was all about a tiger. But I was counting on his telling a straight story, such as I have so often heard him tell to grownups, and did not expect him to vary his style to suit his audience, if "suit" can be the proper word for the alarming effect he created.

"The tiger," said Jorkens, "had spotted me and was following me quite leisurely, as though it did not want to run in the hot weather, and knew perfectly well that I couldn't. My story may serve as a convenient warning to you, when you grow up, never to go near an Indian jungle unarmed, and never to think as I did that just for once, on that particular morning, and for only a short walk, it wouldn't matter. It mattered more than I think you can possibly guess. The tiger was there, and he was coming slowly after me, and I was walking away, and the tiger was walking a little faster than I was. Well, of course I realized that, if he was only doing five yards in a hundred faster, I had no chance of escaping by walking. And I knew that running would only make it worse."

"Why?" asked the children.

"Why?" said Jorkens, "Because if I started a new game the tiger would play it too. At walking he was only gaining five yards in a hundred, but at running he would have gained fifty. That's why I preferred walking, but it wasn't any better really, because it would end the same way. Unfortunately it wasn't actually in the jungle, but on some rocky land outside it; and there was no chance of a tree, because I was walking away from the jungle."

"Why?" asked another child.

"Because the tiger was between me and it," said Jorkens. "The tigers go outside the jungle at night and go back in the very early morning, when the peacocks are waking and screaming. All this was in the early morning, but the sun was well up and I thought that the tigers would all have been back long ago. So I went for that walk unarmed, and, of course, I was quite mistaken."

"Why were you taking the walk?" asked the girl.

"You should never ask anyone," said Jorkens, "why he did anything that leads to disaster; because all such things are done for the same reason, which one does not like to admit. But there it is, they are all for the same reason, pure foolishness."

"Did it lead to disaster?" asked she.

"You shall hear," said Jorkens. "Well, I think I told you I was on rocky land; it was hilly, too; and the tiger was getting nearer. And then I saw a cave in the rocks, near the top of a little hill. Of course, to go in there would cut off my retreat; but my retreat was doing me no good, and there was nowhere better to go. It seemed to me that the small cave might get smaller, till there was no room for the tiger, or it might get larger and have ramifications amongst which I might dodge him. There were just two small hopes and nowhere else to go. So I stooped and went into the cave, and the tiger came in, too.

"He was still some way behind me, and I saw the light go out as he entered, for he just about filled the entrance. The cave did get smaller, and soon I was on all fours. Still the tiger did not hurry. If it got smaller still, I might still conceivably squeeze on where the tiger could not. And it did get a little smaller, but not small enough. We went on over the smooth gray stone, and it got darker as we went, till I could no longer see the color of the floor, and the tiger seemed to absorb the whole of the daylight.

"A faint hope came to me from a story of a skeleton of a mouse, which had been found in a wall of a cathedral with the skeleton of a cat behind it. He had got where the cat could not follow, but it didn't do him much good. I hoped that, if ever I found such a refuge, the tiger would have more sense than that cat. But still the cave ran on, without getting as small as all that. Still the tiger wasn't hurrying, and that seemed to me to make the situation even more desperate. It seemed to show that the tiger was so sure. Of course, I could smell him behind me, for he was still gaining; but the smell seemed almost too strong for a tiger nearly thirty yards behind, and the awful thought came to me that this cave which I hoped might shelter me was the tiger's own lair. That is very much what it seemed to me.

"Then came the hope, after going some distance, that the cave might soon come out through the little hill, though I don't know what good that would have done me. Still, absurd though it may seem, logically it seemed better to me to lose five yards in a hundred when walking in the open, if ever I could get there again, than what I was losing by going on all fours in a race with an animal to whom that sort of walking is natural. And then the uncertainties of the other side of the hill seemed better than those around me, as they often do in such cases, and I though I might find a tree. But there was no draught in my face; there was only the smell of the tiger in the darkness, and I realized I should never come to the open air."

I glanced at the children's faces to see if Jorkens was holding their attention any better than I had done. They were certainly listening intently, though I could not see that they were showing much more interest than they had shown in my poor story. The idea came to me, which may have been quite unjust, that the sympathies of the girl, so far as she felt any, were on the side of the tiger. But that, of course, may only have been my fancy. I should perhaps say that it was in the autumn, and no lights had yet been turned on, and the room was growing dim. I repeat that it was no fault of mine: I had no idea what was coming.

"The tiger was gaining rapidly," Jorkens continued, "and the perfect smoothness of the limestone floor had made it quite clear by now that it must have for long been polished by soft feet, the large feet of a heavy animal; there was no roughness left on any edge upon which I had put my hand. And then the smooth floor came to a sheer smooth rock without crevice or crack in it, and no turn to the left or right. The cave had ended. I turned round in the dark and smelt, rather than saw, the tiger."

"What happened then?" asked one of the boys.

"He ate me," said Jorkens. "It is a ghost that is speaking to you."

And all the fuss that happened in that dim room was blamed entirely on me.

The Wonderful Cat of Cobbie Bean

BARBEE OLIVER CARLETON

Luckily for Cobbie Bean, he was no ordinary animal. He was, in fact, a very special cat. . . .

The Wonderful Cat of Cobbie Bean

IN THE early days of this country there lived by the sea a ne'er-do-well lad named Cobbie Bean. In those days witches were said to be abroad in the land. So strange things happened by night and by day, and this is how it was.

From his cornfield on the hill, Cobbie could look out over all the world. He could see the village of Salem, with the forest dark on one side and the harbor bright on the other. He could see the fine ships of his cousin, Captain Bean, who was as fat as a pudding.

Now, the captain was a getter. He got and he got. Already he had got himself a fleet of ships and a wharf and a warehouse; and day by day he got more and more.

And Cobbie could see the handsome house of his other cousin, the famous Deacon Bean, who was as thin as a bone. The deacon was a doer. He did and he did. He wrote deep books that nobody understood. He preached dark sermons that frightened folk half to death. So the deacon was the most famous man in all of Essex County, just as the captain was the richest.

As for Cobbie Bean, he had done nothing, and he had got nothing. Yet, he had the sun at his head and the world at his feet and the merriest heart in the county. He had it all for keeping a cow and a patch of corn. "Nothing to it," said Cobbie Bean.

But one night something happened. It was twilight, and the air was sweet with lilacs and the twittering of birds. Happy as a clam at high tide, Cobbie sat on his doorstep eating his supper of porridge.

Then he saw two figures on horseback, moving with purpose up the hill. One was as fat as a pudding. One was as thin as a bone. And they looked grim, even from a distance.

Cobbie sighed. "I wish my cousins would move to China!" he told himself. Then his Conscience bothered him.

"They only want you to make something of yourself," said his Conscience.

"I doubt it," said Cobbie. "The less I am, the bigger they feel."

"How can you think such a thing!" said his Conscience. "Especially when you didn't lay a hand to the hoe all day."

"I did so," said Cobbie uneasily. The cousins were getting nearer.

"You did not," argued his Conscience. "All morning you lay on your back on the top of the hill and watched the clouds go by. Whistling, at that!"

Cobbie said, "Well, I was wondering· . . ."

"Wondering what?" demanded his Conscience. "How to grow a corn crop?"

"I was wondering where the wind goes. . . ."

His Conscience sniffed. "That is all very well. But here come your cousins. Let's see you whistle your way out of this one, Cobbie Bean."

Solemnly, the deacon and the captain hitched their horses to Cobbie's gate. In all their finery, they swept into the cottage and sat stiffly on the two rude stools.

The deacon wrinkled his long, thin nose, as if he smelled something unpleasant. "Well, Cobbie Bean, I see that things are as bad as ever with you."

"Better than ever, Cousin," grinned Cobbie. "Spring is here!"

"Spring!" The captain snorted so loudly that all his five chins jiggled. "Look at those rags you wear, Cobbie Bean. Look at this hut you live in. Look at that cold porridge you eat for your supper." The captain shuddered.

"But I'm happy the way I am," Cobbie said timidly.

"That," hissed the deacon, "is the whole point. Happiness is a sin! If you are happy, Cobbie Bean, it is because you are bewitched!"

Cobbie's eyes popped. "B-bewitched?"

"Bewitched!" thundered the captain. "Your cousin and I agree that the time has come to tell you."

The deacon leaned forward and pointed his bony finger. "Cobbie Bean," he said darkly, "a strange thing happened at your christening. Just as the minister spoke your name, a large, gray cat leaped upon the window ledge. She wore a black cloak and a high-crowned hat, and her eyes glittered like ice! Then she spoke in the voice of the wind, or of the sea, and it filled the meeting-house: 'Cobbie Bean . . . Cobbie Bean . . . I give thee the gift of happiness. . . .' "

Cobbie turned as red as joe-pye weed. The deacon had always taught how sinful it was to be merry. The captain had told all over Salem that men who got ahead had no time for happiness.

" 'Gift of happiness,' indeed!" The deacon's long lip curled. "The cat was a witch, of course! As we tried to seize her, she disappeared in a sizzling chain of lightning!"

"And a thunderclap that made us all but deaf!" added the captain in a shaking voice.

"If you would have gifts," preached the deacon scornfully, "you should have the gift of doing. Look at me. I've done and I've done, and now, behold! I am the most famous man in all the county of Essex!"

"How about the gift of getting?" shouted the captain. "I've got and I've got, and look at me now! The richest man in the county!"

"But I had no choice," said poor Cobbie. "I was only a baby!"

"You're not a baby now," snapped the deacon. "You are a do-nothing, living off a cornpatch."

Hopefully, Cobbie said, "Yesterday I did something. I took some fresh herbs down to the jailer, who has the mumps."

The two cousins laughed aloud. "And, pray," said the captain "what did this great deed get you?"

Cobbie bit his fingernail. "Just made us happy, me and the jailer."

"You see?" breathed the deacon. "He has certainly been bewitched!"

"Without a doubt," whispered the captain.

The two cousins looked nervously about them. Night was falling, and Cobbie's cabin was filled with shadows. It was no place to be with a person who was bewitched. They hurried outside and mounted their horses.

"Cobbie Bean," warned the deacon, when he was safely in his saddle, "see that you make something of yourself."

"Before it's too late!" bellowed the captain. And away they trotted down the hill toward Salem.

Poor Cobbie stared after them. Was he bewitched? Nonsense! "Anyway, they're right about one thing," he told his Conscience sadly. "I'm a do-nothing, all right. I didn't even hoe down the cornfield today!" And Cobbie Bean made for the hilltop to hoe a row or two by moonlight.

" 'The gift of happiness!' Pooh!" He struck the earth such a mighty blow that the hoe caught in the roots of a hobblebush growing at the edge of the field. Like a good farmer, Cobbie seized his axe to chop it down. But its twisting branches and its snowy blossoms made so handsome a picture in the moonlight, that Cobbie grew weak with happiness. Besides, he had heard that a hobblebush holds all sorts of magic. Slowly, he lowered his axe and turned to go home.

Then it happened. Alone in the moonlight, Cobbie heard something more than the peepers in the marsh below. He heard a strange voice whisper, "Cobbie Bean . . . Cobbie Bean . . ." It was the voice of the wind or of the sea. But there was no wind at all that night. Nor could the sound of the sea be heard from Cobbie's lonely hill. Under the hobblebush there was nothing but moon-shadow. Cobbie felt the hair prickle on his neck.

The voice rose from the hobblebush tree and filled the air between earth and heaven like the pealing of bells: "Cobbie Bean . . . Cobbie Bean. . . . Stranger things will come to pass than you have ever seen. . . ."

The voice died away among the hills. For a moment the tree tossed violently as if in a windstorm. Then there was only the moonlight, flowing peacefully over hobblebush and cornfield.

Cobbie took to his heels. His axe went one way, his hoe the other. Down the hill he sprinted with his shadow close behind. He pounded across the footbridge where the mist reached after him with wet fingers. He burst into his hut and bolted the door and leaned against it, panting.

But he was not alone. There on the stool, full in the moonlight, sat a large, gray cat. She wore a black cloak and a high-crowned hat, and her eyes glittered like ice!

Cobbie Bean started at the cat and the cat glared back at Cobbie with eyes that glittered in the moonlight. Cobbie opened his mouth to say "Scat!" but he could only hiss in a jiggly sort of way. He was shaking like the hobblebush he had just fled. After all, it isn't every day that a fellow runs home from a voice in a tree to find in his house a strange cat wearing a cloak and hat!

Cobbie decided to leave. Keeping his eyes on the cat's—for, truly, he could not look away—he moved the bolt, very slowly. Very softly, he lifted the latch.

"Stop that," the Cat said calmly.

Startled, Cobbie dropped the latch with a clatter.

"Now, come over here," directed the Cat, "and stop acting like those two ninnies you have for cousins."

Cobbie swallowed, and made a wide circle around his guest.

"People!" chuckled the Cat. "Nothing but a bunch of nerves. Here, you might hang up my things before you sit down."

Cobbie Bean took the small cloak and the steeple-crowned hat as one would take up a white-hot poker. He hung them on a peg by the door and seated himself gingerly across the table from the stranger. Finally he cleared his throat. "You can talk!" he croaked.

"So can you!" said the Cat with relief. "I was beginning to wonder if you did anything but hiss. It would be dull to stay with someone who hissed all the time."

"S-stay?" stammered Cobbie. "Did you s-say 's-stay'?"

"There you go hissing again," said the Cat. "And I did say 'stay.' "

Cobbie blinked. "S-stay here?"

"Where else?" asked the Cat.

"But what will folks say?"

The Cat's laugh was like the chiming of bells. "They'd say I am a witch, naturally. And they would hang you for witchcraft, of course. So you must never tell a soul that I am anything but an ordinary cat."

Speechless, Cobbie shook his head.

"And now, Cobbie Bean, I should like my supper. It has been a long journey." The large, gray Cat gazed at Cobbie with eyes as chilly as the northeast wind.

Cobbie Bean shivered. He served the porridge with a shaky hand, placing it carefully on the hearth.

His guest sniffed. "On the table, Cobbie Bean. Do you take me for a common cat?"

Cobbie hastened to place the bowl on the table, along with a wooden spoon. The Cat ate with the grace of a queen, but when she was done she wrinkled her nose.

"Porridge. Wooden spoons. We shall have to do better than that."

"Yes, ma'am," said Cobbie humbly.

"Still, thanks to me," the Cat went on dryly, "you do have the gift of happiness, surely the greatest gift on earth."

"Yes, ma'am," said Cobbie, blushing. "Thank you, ma'am."

"Oh, I know what those cousins of yours think about happiness! They do and they get, but they will leave the world just the way they found it. You, Cobbie Bean, have a gift to share. You can make the world a happier place. People are funny. They listen only to their betters."

Cobbie nodded doubtfully.

"In short, Cobbie Bean," said the Cat brisky, "if you are to make the world happier, you must first turn into a gentleman!"

Alarmed, Cobbie bit his fingernail. "But I don't know how."

"Fingers out of your mouth!" ordered the Cat. "I'll teach you, of course. And after that, I shall bewitch you again."

Cobbie moved hastily toward the door.

"Oh, go sit down," said his guest. "I don't mean the turn-you-into-a-mouse sort of bewitching. I do that all the time." To prove it, the Cat suddenly took the shape of a mouse.

"I can do people, too," she said. And there, in place of the mouse, sat the captain, stroking his five chins. Immediately after, the captain gave way to the deacon, stiff as a ramrod and pointing a long finger straight at Cobbie. Then there sat the Cat again, not even breathing hard.

She shrugged. "Low-grade witchcraft. Nothing to it. Making you rich and famous is just as easy. I can do that overnight. But turning you into a gentleman," the Cat looked Cobbie over carefully, "will take a little longer."

And that was the way the magic began. Each day the Cat stayed with

Cobbie Bean. Each night she returned to the hobblebush. "Where do you think the magic comes from, eh, Cobbie?" she said, winking broadly.

As the warm summer days went by, the Cat taught Cobbie how to act kindly and speak gently, and how to live with love toward his fellows. "Think high," said the Cat. "That makes it easy."

And since no true gentleman lacks wisdom, she told him where the birds go in winter and what makes the wind blow, and the tide move, and people do as they do. On the golden afternoons when the corn waved high, Cobbie and the Cat lay side by side on the hilltop. They watched the captain's ships, like great, white birds on a blue wind, sail off to far corners of the earth. Then the Cat told Cobbie wonderful tales about other countries and other times, and a great friendship grew between them.

But sometimes, listening, Cobbie felt a shiver go up his spine. For the voice of the Cat seemed not to be a voice at all. At times it was the night wind blowing. At times it was the sea, hushing into a cove. The Cat must be very wise, and very, very old. Or the Cat must really be, as the cousins had said, a witch!

One day Cobbie dared to ask, "Cat, how is it that you, being—er, what you are, can talk?"

The Cat looked back at him with the gaze of an old idol. She glanced at the hobblebush. "Magic," she said. "The world's full of it."

And Cobbie was left still wondering if his friend was, after all, a witch. Yet, it seemed that he had never been without the Cat's wisdom. The days when he had put off his hoeing to whistle at the clouds seemed far away. For after Cobbie had learned to think high and act the part of a gentleman, the Cat said, "Now you must learn to work well, or all I have taught you will come to nothing." She showed Cobbie how to plan his time and use his strength so cleverly that he could farm better than before and still have time to study the world around him.

And all this time, the two cousins, through the captain's spyglass, kept an eye on Cobbie's hill. Amazed, they saw Cobbie busily hoeing and busily weeding, and they saw his corn grow like magic!

"I guess that talk of ours did him a world of good," declared the captain.

"Maybe," said the deacon. "Maybe not."

Then one day, when the corn was beginning to tassle, the Cat turned to Cobbie a little sadly. "You are ready now," she told him. "You have learned to think high and to work well. Tonight at midnight, if there is a ring around the moon, come with your cow to the hobblebush. We'll make the world a happier place, all right! And while we're about it, we'll make those cousins of yours pipe a different tune!"

"Cat," said Cobbie, touching her fur fondly, "thank you."

The Cat gazed at him with frosty eyes. "You're welcome. Only beware, Cobbie Bean. Never tell a living soul where the magic comes from!" Then, in a blinding flash of lightning that ringed her round and round, and with a thunderclap that echoed after her through the hills, she disappeared.

A low wind blew in from the sea and the hill was filled with shadows. At the end of the cornfield, the hobblebush began to whisper and toss. His scalp prickling, Cobbie sprang to his feet and sprinted down the hill as if the devil himself were after him. Across the bridge he raced and into the hut, and shot the bolt. Half-afraid, half-hopeful, Cobbie looked about him for the large, gray Cat. But the cottage was empty.

Slowly, the night drew out of the sea and lowered over Salem. A dark wind sent clouds racing down the sky. The pale moon rose, like a circle of silk. Higher and higher it climbed, until Cobbie Bean could see full and clear the great ring of light around it!

Then he left for the hilltop, pulling the cow by her halter. His hands were icy and his heart pounded as he picked his way past the boulders and the stiff forms of junipers. Had he taken a witch for his teacher? Would the devil come for him tonight, up here in the full of the moon? The wind rushed past him in a panic. Ahead crouched the hobblebush, like a giant spider. Cobbie's throat was dry, and his tongue felt too large for his mouth. Fearfully, he tied the cow to a branch of the hobblebush.

Then it happened, the thing he was waiting for. A cloud covered the moon. An icy mist rose from the hill, and the hobblebush tossed wildly. As Cobbie stared, the cow bellowed in fear and fell to the ground. Then came the voice that Cobbie remembered. First it was soft like the sea. Then it filled the air like the chant of a winter wind. "Cobbie Bean . . . Cobbie Bean . . . Never tell what you have seen. . . ."

A wailing of voices rose to fill the night. It was a witches' Sabbath! Stiff with fright and cold, Cobbie saw tall figures swirling slowly in the mist. Chanting, they moved like shadows around the hobblebush, each in turn casting something underneath its branches.

> "Blood of bat and bone of cat,
> Tongue of frog and tooth of rat,
> Hog's hair, claw of bear,
> Three times three, now follow me. . . ."

Faster and faster they whirled and louder they shrieked, until Cobbie's head reeled. Then, quite suddenly, the wind died. The mist rolled back into the earth, taking the shadowy shapes along with it. The tossing branches came to rest.

Unbelieving, Cobbie Bean stared at the ground beneath the hobblebush.

Cobbie Bean's eyes all but popped from his head. In place of his cow stood a splendid black steed; bridled and saddled and pawing the ground. Over a branch of the hobblebush hung a fine suit of clothes, and on the grass lay bags bulging with gold.

"Cat," breathed Cobbie, "wherever you are, listen to me. I don't care if you are a witch! You're a good witch, anyway." Then, never forgetting that he was to make the world happier, he changed his rags for the finery. He filled his saddlebags with gold. Then he leaped into the saddle and set off for Salem.

Like a golden ribbon, the path wound down the rocky hill to the village and the bright harbor. The rising sun touched the junipers with fire. It brought sparks out of every boulder.

"Magic," breathed Cobbie Bean, trotting a little faster.

He passed the meetinghouse where, long ago, the Cat had come to his christening. He began to smell the sea, and the wharf smells of cordage, of tar and of spices. The world was so full of magic that Cobbie joined with the birds in a jolly whistle, for he longed to tell everyone about it.

The good folk of Salem peeped out of their windows, or paused at their milking, surprised to see what a gentleman Cobbie Bean had become. All day long his wonderful tune went round in their heads and made the day merry.

Only the two cousins were too busy to listen. After working all night, the deacon was finishing up a book that would frighten the sins right out of folk and make him more famous than ever. And down on the wharf, the captain had been thundering at his men since cockcrow. Doing and getting, the two cousins had no time for tunes.

Suddenly, Cobbie's horse stopped before a splendid new house. It had many steep gables and windows of glass cut in the shape of diamonds. A servant with frosty eyes bowed low at the door. "Welcome home, Master."

Closing the door behind him, the servant turned at once into the large, gray Cat. She winked solemnly. "Quite a job of witchcraft, eh, Cobbie?" And she showed him over his house with its fine furnishings and its stores of food, its servants and gardens and coaches and horses.

Cobbie was bewildered. "Is it a dream?"

The Cat's laugh rang out like the chiming of bells. "No more a dream than the rest of life," said she. "Here your happiness will be no greater than on your hill. But you can share it better."

And Cobbie did. Wherever he went, the people of Salem were the happier for Cobbie Bean. He made the old feel young with his wonderful tales of faraway times and places. He made the sick feel well again with his secrets about how the grass grows and where the wind goes. And sometimes at night, the poor would find at their door a bag of gold or a sack of food. "Cobbie Bean," they would tell each other, blessing him in their hearts.

With the lads in town, Cobbie was a favorite. "You never worry," they told him, "about saving people's souls or getting more money than anybody else. Yet, you're happy and successful. Tell us your secret, Cobbie," they begged.

"It's easy," he laughed. "Think high. Work well. Pass your happiness along."

And so they did, laughing and singing at their tasks and working as never before. Only now and then people wondered. "Who told these marvelous things to Cobbie Bean?" they asked each other.

But Cobbie only smiled. For he knew that magic was thought evil, and that witchcraft was punished by death. He would keep his promise to the Cat never to tell where the magic came from.

Nor did Cobbie himself forget what the Cat had taught him. Thinking high and working well, he became in time as rich and famous as he was beloved.

Now his two cousins did not know what to make of all this. "Perhaps he has some secret," whispered the deacon, "about how to become rich and famous."

"After all we have done for that ne'er-do-well," blustered the captain, "he should be made to share it with us!"

So, with canes tapping on the cobbles, off they trotted to learn how Cobbie Bean had become richer and more famous than they.

Once at Cobbie's house, they roared at the servant who led them to the study. Brutally, they kicked at the large, gray Cat that came to greet them. "If I didn't know better," hissed the deacon, "I'd say that was the same beast that came to the christening!"

"Hush," said the captain, as Cobbie entered, wearing the fine garb of a gentleman.

"Well, Cobbie Bean," purred the deacon. "We see that you have come up in the world."

"That I have," smiled Cobbie, remembering his promise to the Cat.

"But, Cobbie," added the captain shrewdly, "we hardly expected this much profit from our advice. Have you some secret, perhaps, to share with us?"

"I have, Cousins," said Cobbie earnestly. "Think high. Work well. Pass your happiness along."

But the deacon squinted darkly into Cobbie's soul. "Cobbie Bean, you are not telling the whole truth. There's more to this than meets the eye!"

Cobbie shuffled his feet. Before he could think of an answer, the Cat silently walked into the room on all fours, like any common cat. She leaped into a chair and stared at the cousins with eyes like the northeast wind. They shook with cold and tried to look away. But the eyes of the Cat held them stiff and frost-bound. Finally, with teeth chattering, they left the room as fast as shaking legs could carry them.

The two looked so miserable that Cobbie followed them to the door. "Wait!" he said. Surely, as long as he kept the Cat's secret, he might tell about the hobblebush.

He whispered swiftly, "Go to the hobblebush on the hill when there's a ring around the moon."

Scarcely able to hide their delight, the two cousins took their leave.

That very night there came a pale circle around the moon that half-filled the heavens. Two figures, one as fat as a pudding, one as thin as a bone, rode stealthily up Cobbie's lonely hill. Soon they reached the hobblebush.

"This must be the place," whispered the deacon nervously.

The captain rubbed his fat hands together. "Now for the gifts that will make us as rich and famous as Cobbie Bean."

"Hark!" cried the deacon. "Is that the wind?"

Startled, the two saw the branches begin to toss. They felt a chill rushing of wind and saw a gray mist rise around the hobblebush. They heard a voice that rode the wind like the tolling of a bell. "Cobbie Bean . . . told. . . . Cobbie Bean . . . told. . . ."

Then the night was filled with the wailing of voices and the swirling of dark figures. The cousins stared like statues, as faster and dizzier whirled the shapes. Then straight toward the two on horseback they came, screaming and scratching and pounding and beating. The wretched pair threw their arms over their heads. Plunging in terror, their horses turned into squealing pigs that bore them pell-mell down the hill, beaten and battered and bleeding and tattered.

"Witchcraft!" gasped the deacon as they galloped into Salem.

Straight to the house of the magistrate they rode. Pounding on the door, they got that gentleman out of bed and told him their story.

"So Cobbie Bean can't be our cousin at all," finished the deacon. "If his cat is a witch, then he must be a witch himself!"

Horrified, the magistrate threw on his clothes. With trembling legs, the three crept down the dark street. They peered through the window into Cobbie Bean's study, where a candle still burned.

There sat Cobbie before his fire, looking handsome and scholarly in his fine clothes. Opposite him in a high-backed chair sat the great, gray Cat, still in her cap and cloak. Her strange voice filled the room with the sound of the wind and the sea.

"You broke your promise, Cobbie Bean," the Cat was saying sadly. "And now, evil will come of it."

"Witchcraft!" gasped the magistrate, with every hair on end.

"Witchcraft!" nodded the cousins.

"Cobbie Bean!" called the magistrate in a shaking voice. *"In the name of the Governor of Massachusetts Bay, I arrest you for witchcraft!"*

Poor Cobbie Bean was as damp as a mushroom. He sat on the jail floor with a chain around his leg. There was not a window in the place, but Cobbie knew by the nearby crowing of a cock that the night had run out. Now they would come and take him away to be hanged for witchcraft.

Cobbie shivered and tightened his belt. Hanging is not a pleasant thought on an empty stomach.

"Oh, Cat," moaned Cobbie for the hundredth time. "I'm sorry I told about the hobblebush. If you are really magic, help me now!"

But the Cat did not appear. All though the dark days of Cobbie's trial the Cat had not come, either by day or night. Now, as then, there was only the *drip, drip,* of water down the dungeon wall. For a long time, Cobbie thought of their golden hours together on the hilltop above the sea, where even now the gallows tree was waiting.

Suddenly, a key grated in the lock. In came his friend, the jailer, looking so miserable that Cobbie felt sorry for him. "Here, take my hanky," said Cobbie.

"I can't help it," sniffed the jailer, unlocking Cobbie's chain. "You were so good to me when I had the mumps." At the thought, he buried his face in Cobbie's hanky and sobbed.

The magistrate waited at the front door to tie Cobbie's hands behind his back. Under his eyes were circles the size of saucers. "I haven't slept a wink all night," he said, with his lip quivering. "You cheered up the town so nicely, Cobbie, I still don't see how you can be a witch. I'm all mixed up."

"So am I, sir," said Cobbie. "But you must do your duty." With that, Cobbie led the way out into the sunlight. The dew sparkled on the grass. The sparrows twittered in the trees. The bright air was filled with the smell of the tide and the bayberry growing on the beach. Cobbie sniffed deeply. It was a wonderful world, and this was his last morning in it!

There stood the militia, as colorful as a quilt. Behind them the cart waited, with a tired old horse to draw it. The deacon and the captain sat on horseback at either side. They sat rather painfully, and their horses were brand-new. Behind the cart waited the people of Salem, silent and sad. But nowhere in all that staring crowd was the familiar, furry face with the eyes of ice.

"You broke your promise, Cobbie Bean," the Cat had said that night of his arrest. "And now, evil will come of it."

Cobbie bowed his head and climbed into the cart. "Serves me right," he muttered. "After all you did for me, I had to go break my promise."

The drum started its slow, deep *beat, beat, beat.* The jailer blew his nose and pulled the old horse forward. *Clop, clop,* Cobbie bounced over the cobbles, with the people of Salem following behind. They were the old and the ill and the poor and the young, whom Cobbie had made happy. And at the very end walked the hangman, all in black. No one would speak to him, and he was feeling very sorry for himself.

Slowly, the procession wound up the hill, behind the magistrate on his white horse. At the very top rose the gallows, dark against the sky. Nearby stood the hobblebush. But the Cat was nowhere at all.

Maybe, thought poor Cobbie, it was all a wonderful dream. And this is the nightmare ending.

Up rode the magistrate, splendid in his red cloak. "Cobbie Bean!" he called. "Come forward."

Cobbie climbed down from the cart and mounted the steps to the gallows. The minister read a prayer. There was a long roll of the drums. The hangman stood waiting.

Then the crowd broke their silence. "Witches are evil!" cried one. "But Cobbie Bean is the best lad in town!"

"Witches hurt people!" cried another. "But Cobbie has helped every one of us!"

"Witches are full of woe!" called a third. "But Cobbie is the happiest lad in Salem!"

"Silence!" shouted the magistrate in a quavering voice. "I feel the same way. But Cobbie Bean will not confess, and we must do our duty. Hangman, carry on." Then the poor magistrate rode off behind the hobblebush to have a good cry.

Cobbie looked his last at the sky. A little breeze sprang up, and the hobblebush started to toss. But then the blindfold was tied on, tickling his nose. The hangman placed the rope around his neck.

The wind began to blow so cold that the people hugged themselves to keep warm. It blew so high that it sounded like the wailing of a giant cat. An icy mist rose up from the hill.

Back rode the magistrate with his scarlet cloak billowing behind. "Cobbie Bean . . . Have you anything to say before you die?"

Amazed, the townspeople looked at one another. The magistrate's voice sounded quite different. It sounded like the wind itself, or like the sea. His eyes, too, looked strange. They were frosty and cold, like eyes of ice. The people shivered and tried to peer through the mist. Some said later that it seemed not to be the magistrate at all, but rather, a large, gray cat.

Cobbie Bean took hope. "Not guilty, sir!" he cried.

At that, the magistrate threw back his head and laughed. His laugh sounded like the chiming of bells, and it filled the very heavens. "Not guilty? Why, then, there has been a mistake! Hangman, set Cobbie Bean free!"

The people cheered as the hangman hastened to obey.

"Go back to your homes, good people!" shouted the magistrate. "And let's have no more foolishness about witchcraft. Remember, the world is full of magic, and most of it is good!"

Again the people cheered.

But a loud voice rose above the wind. "I object!" It was the deacon, looking as dreadful as he knew how.

"And so do I!" thundered the captain, his five chins shaking with rage.

The magistrate turned to where the captain and the deacon sat astride their new horses. He fixed his icy eyes upon them and said in a terrible voice, *"Scat!"*

Now what happened next may not be so. It is difficult to see, with the wind in your eyes. But some said that the horses turned into pigs and ran squealing down the hill, with the deacon and the captain hanging on for dear life. As far as anybody knows, they kept on going all the way to China, for never again were the cousins seen in Salem, from that day to this.

The wind blew like a hurricane, and the townspeople ran for home. It blew so hard that the gallows tree toppled and fell onto the hobblebush, carrying it to the ground, along with Cobbie and the magistrate.

At that, the wind stopped as suddenly as it had started. The sun shone warm on the hill, and the birds sang again in the trees.

Cobbie crept out of the wreckage and helped the magistrate to his feet.

"What happened?" asked the magistrate in his usual voice and with his eyes as red as before.

"The wind blew the gallows down, sir," explained Cobbie.

"So it did," frowned the magistrate, feeling the bump on his head. "I seem to have forgotten what happened after I rode back here to—er, blow my nose."

"You came back and set me free," said Cobbie.

The magistrate brightened. "I did, did I? Good for me! That's the smartest thing I ever did in my life. Well, good day to you, Cobbie Bean."

And the magistrate rode off down the hill, rubbing his head.

Frantically, Cobbie looked through the wreckage. "Cat," he whispered, "where are you?"

There lay his Cat under a branch of the fallen hobblebush. Cobbie freed her and held her on his lap. Her eyes were open, but Cobbie could see that the frost was leaving them.

"Oh, Cat, you are dying," cried Cobbie.

"Don't be silly," said the Cat. "Magic never dies." She winked solemnly at Cobbie. But her voice was getting weaker.

"What do you think of that show we just put on, eh, Cobbie?"

"It was wonderful, Cat," said Cobbie warmly. "Thank you very much."

"Don't mention it," whispered the Cat. With the last of her voice she reminded Cobbie of something important to ordinary cats. "Fish . . ." she gasped, "for breakfast . . . cream . . . for supper. . . ." Now the frost had gone entirely. She looked at Cobbie with the hungry eyes of any ordinary cat.

"Then home we go to breakfast," said Cobbie Bean, blinking his eyes very fast. The Cat had given her magic to save him. The hobblebush was gone. Now, to the end of her days, she would be nothing but a common cat, a large, gray cat, that loved him very much.

He lifted her tenderly into the cart, where she curled up in his lap. Before they were halfway down the hill, the cat had closed her eyes and was purring splendidly.

Cobbie looked out to where the sea and the sky came together. "I won't forget you, Cat," he whispered. And he never did forget.

In a few years' time, Cobbie married a fine girl in Salem. Never did he tire of telling his children, and later on his grandchildren, the story about his wonderful Cat.

And the people of Salem have not forgotten. To this very day, whenever the moon is full and the wind howls and the sea is running high on the beach, they remember that the world is filled with magic.

"Listen!" they tell one another. "It's the wonderful Cat of Cobbie Bean, going by on the wind."

Little Orphant Annie

JAMES WHITCOMB RILEY

Little Orphant Annie

Little Orphant Annie's come to our house to stay,
An' wash the cups an' saucers up, an' brush the crumbs away,
An' shoo the chickens off the porch, an' dust the hearth, an' sweep,
An' make the fire, an' bake the bread, an' earn her board-an'-keep;
An' all us other children, when the supper things is done,
We set around the kitchen fire an' has the mostest fun
A-list'nin' to the witch-tales 'at Annie tells about,
An' the Gobble-uns 'at gits you
    Ef you
        Don't
            Watch
                Out!

    Onc't there was a little boy wouldn't say his prayers,—
    An' when he went to bed at night, away upstairs,
    His Mammy heered him holler, an' his Daddy heered him bawl,
    An' when they turn't the kivvers down, he wasn't there at all!
    An' they seeked him in the rafter-room, an' cubby-hole, an' press,
    An' seeked him up the chimbly-flue, an' ever'wheres, I guess;
    But all they ever found was thist his pants an' roundabout:—
    An' the Gobble-uns 'll git you
        Ef you
            Don't
              Watch
                Out!

An' one time a little girl 'ud allus laugh an' grin,
An' make fun of ever'one, an' all her blood an' kin;
An' onc't, when they was "company," an' ole folks was there,
She mocked 'em an' shocked 'em, an' said she didn't care!
An' thist as she kicked her heels, an' turn't to run an' hide,
They was two great Gobble Things a-standin' by her side,
An' they snatched her through the ceilin' 'fore she knowed what she's about!
An' the Gobble-uns'll git you
  Ef you
    Don't
      Watch
        Out!

    An' little Orphant Annie says, when the blaze is blue,
    An' the lamp-wick sputters, an' the wind goes *woo-oo!*
    An' you hear the crickets quit, an' the moon is gray,
    An' the lightnin'-bugs in dew is all squenched away,—
    You better mind yer parents, an' yer teachers fond an' dear,
    An' churish them 'at loves you, an' dry the orphant's tear,
    An' he'p the pore an' needy ones 'at clusters all about,
    Er the Gobble-uns'll git you
      Ef you
        Don't
          Watch
            Out!

To Starch A Spook

ANDREW BENEDICT

There were exactly 51 ghosts in the old house—including a skeleton in armor and a fire-breathing dragon . . . .

To Starch A Spook

GROWN-UPS are so strange. I mean, how can you ever understand them? For one thing, they worry so much. They worry about the stock market and the lawn and the price of building materials—Dad is an architect— and Europe and Asia and Africa and the world situation and just everything.

They even worry about ghosts! I just discovered that this week. How old-fashioned can you get? Why, worrying about ghosts is prehistoric! But I suppose it's a symptom of getting old.

The other evening I was studying my math and Mom was making a braided rug out of old nylon stockings. All of a sudden Dad rushed in, looking pale, his eyes big and his hair practically on end.

At first Mom was sure he'd been in an accident. But it wasn't that. After Dad had had a cup of strong coffee to calm him down—it wasn't really coffee, but I'm not going to tattle about Dad even to you—he was able to tell us what had happened.

"By George, Mary!" he said—Mary is Mom—"Harry Gerber has a haunted house on his hands. I just came from the place with him. It's absolutely crawling with ghosts. He's so upset, he almost wrecked us getting back to town. I don't blame him! We saw some of the spooks and—"

At that point Dad needed some more coffee. Of course, I was all ears. I'll just put down the simple details as Dad told them to us.

As I said, Dad is an architect, and Mr. Gerber, the big real estate man— he's very fat and also he owns a lot of real estate—had hired him for a job.

On the edge of town there is a grand old mansion, built to imitate an English castle. It's made of stone and timber and has about fifty rooms. It

57

was put up way back when, by a very rich man named Mr. Ferguson. After Mrs. Ferguson, who lived to be ninety-nine, lost Mr. Ferguson, she stayed right on living in the big house in spite of high taxes and the cost of help these days.

But when finally Mrs. Ferguson went, too, the old house stayed empty for a long time. Dad said it was a shame, because they don't build houses like that any more. But nobody wanted it, the taxes were so high. Then Dad had an idea. It could be remodeled into a retirement home for elderly people who liked nice surroundings.

Dad persuaded Mr. Gerber to buy Ferguson's Castle, as the house is called by just everybody, and hire him to remodel it. They were out looking the property over, lingered until after dark, and suddenly had a terrible shock when a positive parade of phantoms started appearing.

To quote Dad, he and Mr. Gerber got out of there fast. Now, and I'm quoting him again—grown-ups use such prehistoric language—the fat was in the fire. Mr. Gerber blamed Dad for ever getting him into the deal. In fact, Mr. Gerber was coming over soon to see what ideas Dad had for de-spooking Ferguson's Castle, and if Dad didn't have any, Mr. Gerber was going to get nasty.

Dad was drinking his third cup of coffee when Mr. Gerber burst in. I mean he really did. Just stormed in and threw his hat on the floor and shouted.

"Carter, you've ruined me! You got me to invest two hundred thousand dollars in a hotel for haunts, and I hold you personally responsible!"

His manners were simply terrible. But then, what can you expect of the older generation these days?

Dad gave Mr. Gerber some coffee, and by and by they were able to talk without anybody shouting.

"I've done some fast checking, Carter," Mr. Gerber said. "I've learned where those ghosts in Ferguson's Castle came from. Every single one of them is imported."

"Imported?" Mom asked. "What do you mean?"

"The Fergusons were great travelers," Mr. Gerber sighed. "And Mrs. Ferguson was psychic. She could get in touch with spirits. See them. Talk to them. Naturally, being a lady, she never made it public. I learned about this from a daughter of her former maid."

"Go on," Dad urged him. "Do I understand that Mrs. Ferguson, in her travels abroad, used to meet up with ghosts and bring them back home with her?"

"That's exactly what she did. She and her husband wanted a collection that would be unique, something no one, no matter how rich, could match. So they collected ghosts. They didn't stop until they had one for every room in the place, including the main entrance hall. That Thing that chased us out of there is an authentic Japanese dragon ghost from the Fifth century, and we were right—it *was* breathing fire at us!"

He shuddered so hard that in order not to spill his coffee he had to drink it all. Then he said in a hollow voice:

"Do you understand, Carter? Every single room in that confounded place is haunted!"

I thought it was a wonderful idea myself. Mr. and Mrs. Ferguson must have been very unusual grown-ups to think of collecting ghosts.

"You realize what this means, Carter," Mr. Gerber said. "I can never house retirement guests in that castle. One sight of one of those spooks and half a dozen might have fatal attacks. I could be sued for millions!"

"I realize that." Dad sounded very gloomy. I certainly felt bad for his sake. On top of worrying about everything grown-ups worry about, now he had to worry about a haunted house, too.

"Also," Mr. Gerber continued, "just let one word get out that the place is haunted and I can never hope to unload it—I mean resell it. I'm stuck. Just stuck!"

His little eyes in his big red face glared at Dad in a very mean way.

"Carter, I hold you responsible. You talked me into this. Now just how do you propose to get that place de-haunted?"

Dad suggested sending to England, where they have lots of haunted castles and are very familiar with the problem, to get a psychic expert. He also suggested exorcism by churchly rites and—but Mr. Gerber wouldn't even let him finish.

"Too expensive!" he barked. "Too time-consuming! Too much publicity! Don't you realize, Carter, that if we do any of those things we as much as admit we have a haunted house on our hands? The story will get into every newspaper in the country!"

Dad poured some more coffee and looked even gloomier.

"I'd give a thousand dollars to be rid of those ghosts," Mr. Gerber rumbled. "If it could be done quickly and quietly. Yes sir, a thousand dollars!"

That was when I had my inspiration.

"If you mean that, Mr. Gerber," I said, putting away my math, "I'll get rid of them for you."

Mr. Gerber stared at me. Dad stared at me. Mom stared at me. Why are grown-ups always staring at you? I mean, as if they'd never seen you before when you've been part of the family for positively years?

"This is no joking matter, young lady," Mr. Gerber said severely. "And I hope you aren't going to be telling about what you have just heard in school tomorrow."

He stuck out his jaw at me—I told you he has terrible manners. I just smiled my extra sweet smile.

"I'm not joking, Mr. Gerber, and I won't tell anyone. That is, I'll just tell one other person because I have to have a helper. But he won't tell anyone."

Dad started to say something but Mom signaled him to silence. Mom can be very understanding sometimes. Even though she is almost thirty-five.

"Very well, young lady," Mr. Gerber said. "I'm going to take you up on that. You have the job of de-ghosting Ferguson Castle. How long do you think it will take you?"

I knew he was just having fun with me, but I didn't let him know I knew.

"I can't tell until I have surveyed the job," I said, using language I had heard Dad use. I looked at the clock. It was only nine. Quite early, actually. "I'll survey the situation tonight and give you an estimate." I turned to Mom. "If I can stay out a little extra late," I said.

Dad looked bewildered and Mom looked baffled—poor things, grown-ups are bewildered or baffled so much of the time.

"I think we can trust Sue to at least try whatever she has in mind," Mom told Dad. He nodded. Mr. Gerber started to ask me what I planned but stopped. He wouldn't give me the satisfaction of taking me seriously. I told Mom I would need all the old nylon hose she had collected for making her braided rugs and, after blinking, she put them into a bag for me.

I got my sweater and a flashlight, told them all I'd be back as soon as I could, went out and got my bike, and bicycled three blocks to Bill Arnold's home. Bill was the helper I'd decided I needed.

I found Bill where I thought I would—out in his family's garage which he has turned into his own laboratory. Bill is tall and very intellectual. He also plays football.

"What's up, Sue?" he asked as I walked in. The door was open for ventilation—some of his experiments generate a lot of bad smells.

"Bill, do you believe in ghosts?"

"Sure," he said. "Why not?"

"Some people don't," I told him. "Do you know what they are?"

"The ghosts? No. But that doesn't prove anything. The world is full of things people don't understand. Take the modern transistor in the transistor radio. Thirty years ago even Einstein couldn't have understood it. Ghosts are a natural phenomenon we'll probably understand some day, even if we don't now."

You can see why I admire Bill. He has a clear, logical mind.

"Well, I want to catch some ghosts," I told him. "Will you help me?"

As he wiped his hands, he asked me how I planned to do it. I got out the nylon hose Mom had given me.

"Ghosts are very insubstantial," I told him. "They can go through keyholes and underneath doors. But I figure that there must be something they can't get through, and if there is, that something is fine nylon hose. I thought we'd take all these stockings and sew them together into a ghost-catching net."

Bill just stood there, thinking. I used the time while he was thinking to fill him in on the ghost situation at Ferguson Castle. At the end of two minutes, he nodded twice and shook his head once.

"Good idea, Sue," he said. "But it'll take too long to sew the stockings together. Mr. Henderson."

Sometimes Bill is a little enigmatic. But I knew Mr. Henderson was the biology teacher at school, and that Bill had thought of something. To tell the truth, I had been counting on Bill to think of something.

Bill has a driver's license, so he went in and got permission to use the family car. Then we drove over to Mr. Henderson's house.

When we rang, Mr. Henderson, a small man with large glasses, came to the door, blinking inquiringly.

"Good evening, Mr. Henderson," Bill said. "Could I borrow your largest specimen-collecting net, the one with the fine mesh?"

Mr. Henderson didn't seem surprised. Bill was always working on two or three scientific experiments. He just went in and came back with a big net on a long handle. It was made of nylon almost as fine as sheer hose. He also had a big jar.

"Going after some rare specimen, Bill?" he asked, handing Bill the net and me the jar. "If so you'll need a jar for it."

"Yes, sir," Bill always believes in telling the truth. "We're after a ghost."

"A ghost moth?" Mr. Henderson asked. "I didn't know they could be found around here."

But we were already halfway back to the car. Ten minutes later we were outside Ferguson's Castle.

Well, it did look as if it should be haunted, but that was just because there weren't any lights on. Bill and I had flashlights and we went up the stone steps and into the entrance hall.

It was a beautiful entrance hall, lined with fine carved chairs and tapestries. But we didn't spend much time looking at them because we'd hardly got inside before the Japanese dragon ghost Mr. Gerber had mentioned appeared.

It stood on the stairs, a real dragon at least ten feet long—a ghost of a real dragon, I ought to say—and it stared at us. We stared back at it. It had curly horns and a pug-nosed snout and little legs with big clawy toes, and a tail with a tip like the head of an arrow. It was adorable!

"Oh, Bill!" I said. "Isn't it cute!"

"No wonder Mrs. Ferguson brought it back for her collection," Bill said. "Well, here it comes, it's charging us."

After waiting for us to get scared and run, as we would have if we'd been so old we didn't know better, the dragon realized it would have to chase us. So it charged down the steps and came at us, breathing flames from its nostrils. Real flames! They were simply beautiful!

We stepped to one side and Bill swung the specimen-collecting net.

The dragon ghost's head went into it, and the rest of him followed. Apparently ghosts can be squeezed into a very small size when necessary. Anyway, the dragon ghost's charge carried him right into the net, the fine nylon stopped him from going any farther, and his speed sort of collapsed him or condensed him into a small dragon only about two feet long.

Bill quickly swirled the net so that the mouth was closed off and we'd caught our first ghost!

The poor thing was so frightened! It snorted and snarled inside the net, and breathed flames at us with all its might. Bill put his hand into the flame and reported that the flame had no heat.

"Cold flame, like the light from a firefly," he said. "That's about what I'd expect, otherwise he'd burn down every house he haunted."

"How are we ever going to get it into the specimen jar?" I asked.

But Bill was already twisting the net, making the space inside it smaller and smaller. As he twisted, the dragon ghost got smaller and smaller, too, until it was no bigger than a mouse.

Then I held the specimen jar and Bill quickly pushed the tiny little dragon spook into the specimen jar. I snapped on the lid and we had him, safe and sound. There wasn't the tiniest crack for him to ooze out of, and, of course, a ghost has to have *some* space to move in, even if it's no bigger than a keyhole.

For a while we watched him run around and around inside the jar, giving off tiny flashes of light with his breathing, like a firefly. But by and by we realized we only had one ghost and there were at least fifty more to catch.

So we went on into the library. The library's ghost was stalking back and forth, making a rattling noise. He was a beauty. He was wearing full armor, which Bill said dated back at least to the sixth century, and when he saw us, he lifted the front of his vizor—that's the part that protects his face— and let us see him.

Diary, inside that suit of ghostly armor was a ghostly skeleton! He clashed his teeth at us with the most frightening noise. Bill and I were speechless in admiration.

"Mrs. Ferguson certainly knew quality when she collected phantoms," Bill said.

He swung the collecting net at the armored spook. But this wasn't a dragon with just enough sense to charge. This one ducked. All Bill caught in the net was an armored arm. The rest of the ghost oozed away and clashed his teeth at us some more.

When Bill approached it, it retreated. Finally Bill chased it all around the room, swinging the net in vain. He caught little bits and pieces of the phantom in armor—a foot, a hand, part of his shield—but the main part of the spook always oozed from the net. Finally, the ghost in armor slipped into a crack in the woodwork and got away.

Panting a little bit, Bill and I looked at each other. Bill dumped the ghostly bits and pieces out of the net and they floated over into the woodwork to rejoin the rest of the hiding spook.

"Guess that first one was luck," Bill said. "But we'll see. Let's try the dining room next."

The dining room was a big formal room, and it had a ghost in it that we had to admire just as much as the others. This was the ghost of some medieval headsman, or executioner, complete with a black hood over his head and huge-bladed axe.

"Probably from Germany," Bill said. "Early 16th century, I'd judge."

The phantom headman glided toward us and raised his axe. Bill raised his net. The axe came down and Bill caught it in the net. It broke off in the middle of the handle, and the phantom headsman, seeming very confused, turned the broken handle over several times to look at it. While he was doing this, Bill tried to take him by surprise.

The headsman ducked. Bill's net hit him on the shoulder and Bill got one side of him into the net. But the ghostly executioner was quick. He shot free from the net, grabbing his axe while he was at it, and in no time he'd scooted up a chimney where we couldn't get at him.

"Darn!" Bill said. "They're so insubstantial. They tear apart. I get part of one and the rest just pulls loose."

"Now if only we had some way to stiffen them up a little," I said. "That would help, wouldn't it?"

Bill looked at me. Then he went into one of his silent thinking periods. Then he nodded.

"Sue," he said, "you have some darned good ideas. We'll come back tomorrow night and do it."

I didn't know I'd had an idea, but it was awfully nice of Bill to say so.

Bill drove me back to his house and put the specimen bottle with the phantom dragon on a shelf. He hung up the net and we agreed to meet there same time the next night. Then I biked on home.

Dad and Mom and Mr. Gerber were still sitting there. They looked as if they were waiting for me.

"Well, young lady?" Mr. Gerber rumbled. "Chased all my ghosts away?"

"No, sir," I said. "But I can give you an estimate. We can have Ferguson's Castle de-ghosted by the end of the week."

Mr. Gerber swallowed hard.

"Just what plan of operation do you intend to use?" he asked.

If I'd known I might have told him, just to be polite. But as I didn't know, all I could do was smile mysteriously.

"I'm sorry, Mr. Gerber," I said. "That's a professional secret."

He gave a big snort. Then he got up and jammed on his hat.

"Carter," he said to Dad, "I have to go to New York until Saturday. On Saturday night you and I will inspect Ferguson's Castle. If those ghosts are gone, we proceed. If they're not—"

He left it at that and stamped out. Dad rubbed his jaw.

"Sue," he asked, "would you care to tell me what you are up to?"

I wanted to, but as I didn't know, I couldn't.

"I'm sorry, Dad," I said. "I can't. But don't worry. Bill and I have some ideas. We've already got rid of one ghost."

Dad rubbed his jaw some more. Then he rolled his eyes and looked at Mom.

"Thank heaven for small favors," he said, a remark which I did not understand at all. "Let's go to bed."

Honestly, communication with grown-ups is so *difficult*.

The next night Dad was working late and Mom didn't object when I biked over to Bill's place. He was in his lab, just filling two plant sprayers—you know, the kind with handles you push in and out to kill bugs—with some kind of gunk.

"Hi, Sue!" he said. "We're taking the delivery truck tonight. Let's go!"

Bill's father owns a big dry cleaning establishment, and Bill had the truck there. Sometimes he drove it on week-ends. We rode over to Ferguson's Castle in it, and as we went, Bill told me what I was to do, though he didn't explain.

"If it works, you'll see the results," he said. "And if it doesn't, back to the drawing board!"

We hurried inside, into the library. The skeleton-in-armor phantom was already there, marching up and down. When he saw us, he waved his arms at us and made chattery noises with his skeleton teeth. Either he wasn't afraid of us because we didn't have the net, or he didn't remember us. I suspect that to a ghost people all look alike.

We let him get close, then Bill said, "Now!"

The minute he spoke, I started working my sprayer on the ghost's feet, and Bill started in on his head. We worked our way toward the middle.

In about one second that skeleton in armor was enveloped in a white mist. The white mist seemed to settle right on him—whatever a ghost is made of, it's substantial enough for tiny droplets to cling to—and in another second the spook was standing in front of us, one arm upraised, looking for all the world like a marble statue.

He started to topple over and Bill and I caught him. He couldn't have weighed more than four ounces altogether. But he was certainly stiff! He was stiffer than a newly starched shirt collar.

"It worked!" Bill acted pleased. "Your idea, Sue. You said we needed to stiffen up these ghosts to catch them. So I put a lot of liquid starch into the sprayers, with some goo to make the starch harden on contact with air."

"We have just starched a spook!"

I marvelled at our starched ghost. Every detail of his armor was perfect, right down to the last link on his chain-mail shirt. He was too stiff to risk moving his arms or legs, and every little draught almost blew him away. We finally laid him on the floor and put a very light rug over him to hold him in place.

Then we went into the dining room to tackle the ghostly headsman with the axe.

It was practically a repetition of our success with the skeleton in armor. Two or three puffs from the sprayers, the starch took effect, and we had a snow-white statue of a starched spook, with his axe upraised in a most fearsome manner.

We weighted him down and went on to the next rooms.

In quick succession we bagged fifteen more. I'd like to describe them to you, but it would take too long. One was a goblin ghost, small, gnarled, with a long nose, long hair and long teeth. He was just *beautifully* ugly.

After we had starched so many spooks and were a little tired of pumping on those sprayers, we had to stop. Anyway, it was getting late. I wondered what we would do with them, but Bill was all prepared. In the delivery truck he had a lot of those big, plastic bags dry cleaning companies put over your overcoat. He got them, and we slipped each starched spook into a neat plastic bag and tied the end. Then all we had to do was carry them to the truck and stow them in, being careful not to crush any of them.

They were so light, the only hard part was that they kept trying to blow out of our hands.

When we got back to Bill's place, we stored the ghosts in the old stables that still stand in his backyard. As a matter of fact, when we were smaller, Bill owned a couple of ponies. But the stable is empty now, except for some old hay up in the loft, and we laid our starched spooks out in a row up there.

Poor things. I felt rather sorry for them. All their lives they had been able to slide through keyholes and now they couldn't so much as quiver an eyelash.

When I got home, Dad was still away and Mom was working on her braided rug—I had given her back the old nylon hose.

"It's okay, Mom," I told her. "Bill and I are making just terrific progress. Dad doesn't have a thing to worry about."

Mom gave a stifled sob. Deciding for the ninetieth time you just can't understand grown-ups, I went to bed.

The next night we starched and stored twenty spooks, and last night, Friday, we finished off the rest. Ferguson's Castle was positively de-ghosted, and we had a hayloft crammed to overflowing with starched spooks which I, for one, didn't know what to do with.

I really hadn't seen Dad for three days, what with my school and his work. But Saturday I saw him as he was starting for the office.

"It's all right, Dad," I told him. "You can take Mr. Gerber out to Ferguson's Castle now and you won't find as much as a ghost mouse."

Dad gave me a weak smile.

"I'm keeping my fingers crossed," he said. "He's coming in on the eight o'clock plane, and he phoned he wants to examine the castle first thing. So I won't be home to dinner."

Poor Mom was on pins and needles all during dinner. I was calm because of course I knew Ferguson's Castle was totally de-ghosted. Sure enough, a little after nine, Dad and Mr. Gerber came in and they were both grinning.

"Well!" Mr. Gerber said, slapping Dad on the back. "Funny, isn't it, what two grown men can think they see? That place isn't haunted and never was! It was all in our imagination."

Well, how do you like that? I was highly indignant, but I kept my voice low and sweet.

"There were fifty-one ghosts in it, Mr. Gerber," I said. "Bill and I counted them carefully."

Mr. Gerber's round, red face split in a grin just like a jack-o'-lantern.

"Wonderful!" he chuckled. "Wonderful sense of humor your daughter has, Carter! Well, you can start the renovations first thing Monday morning. Now I have to get back to my house. Little poker game going on. Important people going to be there. Might mean some big contracts!"

He started to go, but I called to him.

"Mr. Gerber!" I said. "You haven't forgotten, have you? About the thousand-dollar fee for getting rid of your ghosts?"

He didn't grin now. He scowled.

"Young lady," he said. "A joke is a joke, but you youngsters must learn not to carry one too far. Just because your father and I had a slight brain lapse and thought we saw some ghosts, when, of course, there weren't any—as you no doubt realized—you mustn't overdo it by actually trying to get money out of me! I'm Gerber the builder, and I don't like such tactics!"

He slammed on his hat and marched out. Well, honestly, you see what I mean about grown-ups? Some are—I hate to say it—but they're *sneaky*.

Dad put his arm around me.

"You're my girl, Sue," he said, "and I love you. But Gerber's right. Of course, there weren't any ghosts. I'm sure you tried, though. What did you do, go out there with Bill and recite an incantation or something?"

"Something like that, Dad," I told him. I couldn't let him know I was boiling inside. After all, grown-ups have so many troubles that I hate to add to them.

"It's all right," I said. "But if Mr. Gerber wants any more ghosts got rid of, even one teeny little one, the price is doubled. May I go over and see Bill for a few minutes?"

Well, it was Saturday night, so that part was all right, and I biked over to Bill's lab. He was there, working, but this time he was working at his little printing press.

"Hi, Sue!" he said. "Look! I haven't finished yet but this will give you the idea."

He inked some type and drew off a quick proof of what he had been setting.

It said:

OFFERED FOR SALE!

Petrified Phantoms

Our petrified phantoms are of the finest imported quality, suitable for institutions or private collectors.

Only a few of the available models
are listed below. Many more in stock!

Skeleton in Armor (Fifth Century) $250.00

Goblin (Probably from Hartz Mts.) 150.00

Headsman with Axe (16th Century) 225.00

Fire-breathing Japanese Dragon 450.00

"You see," he said, "I feel sorry for those poor ghosts. After all, they were just being themselves. Any one of them would be fine to haunt a museum, and if a private collector wants an imported ghost, we have the best stock in this country. They can keep them starched, or, by adding water, restore them to their normal, phantasmal shape. By selling them we can make enough to send us both through college. And with the thousand we're getting from Mr. Gerber—"

That reminded me. I had been so overwhelmed by Bill's brilliance, I had forgotten Mr. Gerber. Now I told Bill just what Mr. Gerber had said.

Bill went into one of his thinking periods. Then he nodded.

"The trouble is, he doesn't believe any more," he said. "His faith in phantoms must be restored. You say he is playing poker at home tonight?"

I nodded.

"Okay, Sue. You go on home. I'll handle it from here."

I biked home. As I left, I could see Bill already getting the truck out.

I stayed in my room, waiting for developments. Mom and Dad were downstairs, reading. I'd been so quiet they'd forgotten about me. I certainly hoped Bill—

There! There was a lot of excitement downstairs! Mr. Gerber just arrived and he was absolutely frothing at the mouth. I mean, he was *wild*. It seems that in the middle of his card game, three ghosts from Ferguson's Castle showed up. And they were all hopping mad!

The skeleton in armor raced around the room, gnashing his teeth at the guests. The phantom headsman swung his axe and did his best to behead Senator Jones. The Senator fainted and knocked over Mr. Gerber's antique cabinet full of rare dishes and did a thousand dollars worth of damage. Assemblyman Smith had a slight fit and had to be carried out. The others simply ran for their cars and left as fast as they could.

Gerber followed them. As he left, the goblin ghost was making magic spells with his fingers and turning all the expensive food for refreshments into—yes, honestly—garbage!

Mr. Gerber begged and pleaded with me to do something. I reminded him he didn't believe in ghosts, and he said now he did, he certainly did, cross his heart. I acted very unconcerned about the whole thing, until he not only promised me two thousand dollars to de-ghost his house, but wrote out the check and handed it to Dad.

Then I agreed. Reluctantly. I do think that when grown-ups misbehave, they should be disciplined, but perhaps Mr. Gerber had been punished enough.

I saw Bill's car out in the driveway, so I slipped out to speak to him. What he had done, he told me, was just to take three of the ghosts in their plastic bags in the car to Mr. Gerber's big, expensive home. Then he took them out and sprayed water on them.

The water softened the starch, the ghosts were able to move again, and they immediately slipped into the nearest house.

Mr. Gerber's house.

Mr. Gerber left to go to a motel and I promised him we'd have his house de-ghosted by morning. Bill is waiting for me with the big sprayers full of his special solution.

So excuse me.

I have to go starch a spook.

The Open Window

SAKI

In quiet tones the little girl told the tragic story, and did not seem to see the horror that strode toward them outside. . . .

The Open Window

"MY AUNT will be down presently, Mr. Nuttel," said a very self-possessed young lady of fifteen; "in the meantime you must try and put up with me."

Framton Nuttel endeavoured to say the correct something which should duly flatter the niece of the moment without unduly discounting the aunt that was to come. Privately he doubted more than ever whether these formal visits on a succession of total strangers would do much toward helping the nerve cure which he was supposed to be undergoing.

"I know how it will be," his sister had said when he was preparing to migrate to this rural retreat; "you will bury yourself down there and not speak to a living soul, and your nerves will be worse than ever from moping. I shall just give you letters of introduction to all the people I know there. Some of them, as far as I can remember, were quite nice."

Framton wondered whether Mrs. Sappleton, the lady to whom he was presenting one of the letters of introduction, came into the nice division.

"Do you know many of the people round here?" asked the niece, when she judged that they had had sufficient silent communion.

"Hardly a soul," said Framton. "My sister was staying here, at the rectory, you know, some four years ago, and she gave me letters of introduction to some of the people here."

He made the last statement in a tone of distinct regret.

"Then you know practically nothing about my aunt?" pursued the self-possessed young lady.

"Only her name and address," admitted the caller. He was wondering whether Mrs. Sappleton was in the married or widowed state. An undefinable something about the room seemed to suggest masculine habitation.

71

"Her great tragedy happened just three years ago," said the child; "that would be since your sister's time."

"Her tragedy?" asked Framton; somehow in this restful country spot tragedies seemed out of place.

"You may wonder why we keep that window wide open on an October afternoon," said the niece, indicating a large french window that opened onto a lawn.

"It is quite warm for the time of the year," said Framton; "but has that window got anything to do with the tragedy?"

"Out through that window, three years ago to a day, her husband and her two young brothers went off for their day's shooting. They never came back. In crossing the moor to their favourite snipe-shooting ground they were all three engulfed in a treacherous piece of bog. It had been that dreadful wet summer, you know, and places that were safe in other years gave way suddenly without warning. Their bodies were never recovered. That was the dreadful part of it." Here the child's voice lost its self-possessed note and became falteringly human. "Poor aunt always thinks that they will come back some day, they and the little brown spaniel that was lost with them, and walk in at that window just as they used to do. That is why the window is kept open every evening till it is quite dusk. Poor dear aunt, she has often told me how they went out, her husband with his white waterproof coat over his arm, and Ronnie, her youngest brother, singing, 'Bertie, why do you bound?' as he always did to tease her, because she said it got on her nerves. Do you know, sometimes on still, quiet evenings like this, I almost get a creepy feeling that they will all walk in through that window—"

She broke off with a little shudder. It was a relief to Framton when the aunt bustled into the room with a whirl of apologies for being late in making her appearance.

"I hope Vera has been amusing you?" she said.

"She has been very interesting," said Framton.

"I hope you don't mind the open window," said Mrs. Sappleton briskly; "my husband and brothers will be home directly from shooting, and they always come in this way. They've been out for snipe in the marshes today, so they'll make a fine mess over my poor carpets. So like you men-folk, isn't it?"

She rattled on cheerfully about the shooting and the scarcity of birds, and the prospects for duck in the winter. To Framton it was all purely horrible. He made a desperate but only partially successful effort to turn the talk on to a less ghastly topic; he was conscious that his hostess was giving him only a fragment of her attention, and her eyes were constantly straying past him to the open window and the lawn beyond. It was certainly an unfortunate coincidence that he should have paid his visit on this tragic anniversary.

"The doctors agree in ordering me complete rest, an absence of mental excitement, and avoidance of anything in the nature of violent physical exercise," announced Framton, who laboured under the tolerably wide-spread delusion that total strangers and chance acquaintances are hungry for the least detail of one's ailments and infirmities, their cause and cure. "On the matter of diet they are not so much in agreement," he continued.

"No?" said Mrs. Sappleton, in a voice which only replaced a yawn at the last moment. Then she suddenly brightened ito alert attention—but not to what Framton was saying.

"Here they are at last!" she cried. "Just in time for tea, and don't they look as if they were muddy up to the eyes!"

Framton shivered slightly and turned toward the niece with a look intended to convey sympathetic comprehension. The child was staring out through the open window with dazed horror in her eyes. In a chill shock of nameless fear Framton swung round in his seat and looked in the same direction.

In the deepening twilight three figures were walking across the lawn toward the window; they all carried guns under their arms, and one of them was additionally burdened with a white coat hung over his shoulders. A tired brown spaniel kept close at their heels. Noiselessly they neared the house, and then a hoarse young voice chanted out of the dusk: "I said, Bertie, why do you bound?"

Framton grabbed wildly at his stick and hat; the hall-door, the gravel-drive, and the front gate were dimly noted stages in his headlong retreat. A cyclist coming along the road had to run into the hedge to avoid imminent collision.

"Here we are, my dear," said the bearer of the white mackintosh, coming in through the window; "fairly muddy, but most of it's dry. Who was that who bolted out as we came up?"

"A most extraordinary man, a Mr. Nuttel," said Mrs. Sappleton; "could only talk about his illnesses, and dashed off without a word of good-bye or apology when you arrived. One would think he had seen a ghost."

"I expect it was the spaniel," said the niece calmly; "he told me he had a horror of dogs. He was once hunted into a cemetery somewhere on the banks of the Ganges by a pack of pariah dogs, and had to spend the night in a newly dug grave with the creatures snarling and grinning and foaming just above him. Enough to make anyone lose their nerve."

Romance at short notice was her specialty.

The Moor's Legacy

WASHINGTON IRVING

Strong magic protected the hidden treasure—but Peregil the water-carrier had a mystic scroll which would unlock the enchantment. . . .

The Moor's Legacy

1.

JUST WITHIN the fortress of the Alhambra, in front of the royal palace, is the little park of the cisterns where reservoirs of water, hidden from sight, have existed from the time of the Moors. At one corner is a Moorish well, cut through the living rock to a great depth, the water of which is cold as ice and clear as crystal. It is famous throughout Granada; and water-carriers, some bearing great water-jars on their shoulders, others driving donkeys laden with earthen vessels, ascend and descend the steep woody avenues of the Alhambra from early dawn until late at night.

Among the water-carriers who once resorted to this well there was a sturdy, strong-backed, bandy-legged little fellow, named Pedro Gil, but called Peregil for shortness. He was a Gallego, or native of Gallicia. Nature seems to have formed races of men as she has species of animals for different kinds of drudgery. In France the shoe-blacks are all Savoyards, the porters of hotels all Swiss. So in Spain the carriers of water and bearers of burdens are all sturdy little natives of Gallicia. No man says, "Get me a porter," but, "Call a Gallego."

Peregil the Gallego had begun business with merely a great earthen jar, which he carried upon his shoulder; by degrees he rose in the world, and was enabled to purchase a stout shaggy-haired donkey. On each side of this, his long-eared helper, in a kind of pannier, were slung his water-jars covered with fig leaves to protect them from the sun. There was not a more industrious water-carrier in all Granada, nor one more merry withal. The streets rang with his cheerful voice as he trudged after his donkey, singing: "Who wants water—water colder than snow—who wants water from the well of the Alhambra—cold as ice and clear as crystal?"

77

When he served a customer with a sparkling glass, it was always with a pleasant word that caused a smile. Thus Peregil the Gallego was noted throughout all Granada for being one of the pleasantest, and happiest, of mortals.

Yet it is not he who sings loudest and jokes most that has the lightest heart. Under all this air of merriment, honest Peregil had his cares and troubles.

He had a large family of ragged children to support, who were hungry and clamorous as a nest of young swallows, and beset him with their outcries for food whenever he came home in the evening. He had a helpmate, too, who was anything but a help to him. She had been a village beauty before marriage, noted for her skill in dancing the bolero and rattling the castanets, and she still retained her early propensities, spending the hard earnings of honest Peregil in frippery, and laying the very donkey under requisition for junketing parties into the country on Sundays, and saints' days, and those innumerable holidays which are rather more numerous in Spain than the days of the week. With all this she was a little of a slattern, something more of a lie-a-bed, and, above all, a gossip of the first order; neglecting house, household and everything else, to loiter slip-shod in the houses of her gossipy neighbours.

Peregil bore all the heavy dispensations of wife and children with as meek a spirit as his donkey bore the water-jars; and, however he might shake his ears in private, never ventured to question the household virtues of his slatternly spouse.

He loved his children, too, even as an owl loves its owlets, seeing in them his own image multiplied and perpetuated, for they were a sturdy, long-backed, bandy-legged little brood. The great pleasure of honest Peregil was, whenever he could afford himself a scanty holiday, to take the whole litter with him, some in his arms, some tugging at his skirts, and some trudging at his heels, and to treat them to a gambol among the orchards of the Vega.

It was a late hour one summer night, and most of the water-carriers had stopped their toils. The day had been uncommonly sultry; the night was one of those delicious moonlights, which tempt the inhabitants of those southern climes to indemnify themselves for the heat and inaction of the day by lingering in the open air and enjoying its tempered sweetness until after midnight. Customers for water were therefore still abroad. Peregil, like a considerate, painstaking little father, thought of his hungry children.

"One more journey to the well," said he to himself, "to earn a good Sunday's *puchero* for the little ones."

So saying, he trudged rapidly up the steep avenue of the Alhambra, singing as he went.

Arriving at the well, he found it deserted by everyone except a solitary stranger in Moorish garb, seated on the stone bench in the moonlight.

Peregil paused at first, and regarded him with surprise, not unmixed with awe, but the Moor feebly beckoned him to approach.

"I am faint and ill," said he; "aid me to return to the city, and I will pay thee double what thou couldst gain by thy jars of water."

The honest heart of the little water-carrier was touched with compassion at the appeal of the stranger. "God forbid," said he, "that I should ask fee or reward for doing a common act of humanity."

He accordingly helped the Moor on his donkey, and set off slowly for Granada, the poor Moslem being so weak that it was necessary to hold him on the animal to keep him from falling to the earth.

When they entered the city, the water-carrier demanded whither he should conduct him. "Alas!" said the Moor, faintly, "I have neither home nor habitation. I am a stranger in the land. Suffer me to lay my head this night beneath thy roof, and thou shall be amply repaid."

Honest Peregil thus saw himself unexpectedly saddled with an infidel guest, but he was too humane to refuse a night's shelter to a fellow being in so forlorn a plight; so he conducted the Moor to his dwelling. The children, who had sallied forth, open-mouthed as usual, on hearing the tramp of the donkey, ran back with fright, when they beheld the turbaned stranger, and hid themselves behind their mother. The latter stepped forth intrepidly, like a ruffling hen before her brood, when a vagrant dog approaches.

"What infidel companion," cried she, "is this you have brought home at this late hour, to draw upon us the eyes of the Inquisition?"

"Be quiet, wife," replied the Gallego. "Here is a poor sick stranger, without friend or home; wouldst thou turn him forth to perish in the streets?"

The wife would still have remonstrated, for, though she lived in a hovel, she was a furious stickler for the credit of her house; the little water-carrier, however, for once was stiff-necked, and refused to bend beneath the yoke. He assisted the poor Moslem to alight, and spread a mat and a sheepskin for him, on the ground, in the coolest part of the house; being the only kind of bed that his poverty afforded.

In a little while the Moor was seized with violent convulsions, which defied all the ministering skill of the simple water-carrier. The eye of the poor patient acknowledged his kindness. During an interval of his fits he called him to his side, and addressed him in a low voice. "My end," said he, "I fear is at hand. If I die I bequeath you this box as a reward for your charity." So saying, he opened his cloak, and showed a small box of sandalwood, strapped round his body.

"God grant, my friend," replied the worthy little Gallego, "that you may live many years to enjoy your treasure, whatever it may be."

The Moor shook his head; he laid his hand upon the box, and would have said something more concerning it, but his convulsions returned with increased violence, and in a little while he expired.

The water-carrier's wife was now as one distracted. "This comes," said she, "of your foolish good nature, always running into scrapes to oblige others. What will become of us when this corpse is found in our house? We shall be sent to prison as murderers."

Poor Peregil was in equal tribulation, and almost repented himself of having done a good deed. At length a thought struck him. "It is not yet day," said he. "I can convey the dead body out of the city and bury it in the sands on the banks of the Xenil. No one saw the Moor enter our dwelling, and no one will know any thing of his death." So said, so done. The wife aided him; they rolled the body of the unfortunate Moslem in the mat on which he had expired, laid it across the ass, and set out with it for the banks of the river.

2.

As ill luck would have it, there lived opposite to the water-carrier a barber, named Pedrillo Pedrugo, one of the most prying, tattling, mischief-making men of his gossipy tribe. He was a weasel-faced, spider-legged varlet, supple and insinuating; the famous Barber of Seville could not surpass him for his universal knowledge of the affairs of others, and he had no more power of retention than a sieve. It was said that he slept with one eye at a time, and kept one ear uncovered, so that, even in his sleep, he might see and hear all that was going on. Certain it is, he was a sort of scandalous chronicle for the busybodies of Granada, and had more customers than all the rest of his fraternity.

This meddlesome barber heard Peregil arrive at an unusual hour of night, and the exclamation of his wife and children. His head was instantly popped out of a little window which served him as a lookout, and he saw his neighbour assist a man in a Moorish garb into his dwelling. This was so strange an occurrence that Pedrillo Pedrugo slept not a wink that night—every five minutes he was at his loop-hole, watching the lights that gleamed through the chinks of his neighbour's door, and before daylight he beheld Peregil sally forth with his donkey unusually laden.

The inquisitive barber was in a fidget; he slipped on his clothes, and, stealing forth silently, followed the water-carrier at a distance, until he saw him dig a hole in the sandy bank of the Xenil, and bury something that had the appearance of a dead body.

The barber hied himself home and fidgeted about his shop, setting everything upside down, until sunrise. He then took a basin under his arm, and sallied forth to the house of his daily customer, the Alcalde, or Mayor.

The Alcalde had just risen. Pedrillo Pedrugo seated him in a chair, threw a napkin round his neck, put a basin of hot water under his chin, and began to mollify his beard with his fingers.

"Strange doings," said Pedrugo, who played barber and newsmonger at the same time. "Strange doings! Robbery, and murder, and burial, all in one night!"

"Hey? How! What is it you say?" cried the Alcalde.

"I say," replied the barber, rubbing a piece of soap over the nose and mouth of the dignitary, for a Spanish barber disdains to employ a brush; "I say that Peregil the Gallego has robbed and murdered a Moorish Mussulman, and buried him this blessed night."

"But how do you know all this?" demanded the Alcalde.

"Be patient, Señor, and you shall hear all about it," replied Pedrillo, taking him by the nose and sliding a razor over his cheek. He then recounted all that he had seen, going through both operations at the same time, shaving his beard, washing his chin, and wiping him dry with a dirty napkin, while he related the robbing, murdering, and burying of the Moslem.

Now it so happened that this Alcalde was one of the most overbearing, and at the same time most gripping and corrupt curmudgeons in all Granada. It could not be denied, however, that he set a high value upon justice, for he sold it at its weight in gold. He presumed the case in point to be one of murder and robbery; doubtless there must be rich spoil; how was it to be secured by the legitimate hands of the law? For as to merely entrapping the delinquent—that would be feeding the gallows; but entrapping the booty—that would be enriching the judge; and such, according to his creed, was the great end of justice. So thinking, he summoned to his presence his trustiest police officer: a gaunt, hungry-looking varlet, clad, according to the custom of his order, in the ancient Spanish garb—a broad black beaver, turned up at the sides; a quaint ruff, a small black cloak dangling from his shoulders; rusty black underclothes that set off his spare wiry form; while in his hand he bore a slender white wand, the dreaded insignia of his office. Such was the legal bloodhound of the ancient Spanish breed that he put upon the traces of the unlucky water-carrier; and such was his speed and certainty that he was upon the haunches of poor Peregil before the latter had returned to his dwelling, and brought both him and his donkey before the dispenser of justice.

The Alcalde bent upon him one of his most terriffic frowns. "Hark ye, culprit," roared he in a voice that made the knees of the little Gallego smite together,—"Hark ye, culprit! there is no need of denying thy guilt: everything is known to me. A gallows is the proper reward for the crime thou hast committed, but I am merciful, and readily listen to reason. The man that has been murdered in thy house was a Moor, an infidel, the enemy of our faith. It was doubtless in a fit of religious zeal that thou hast slain him. I will be indulgent, therefore; render up the property of which thou hast robbed him, and we will hush the matter up."

The poor water-carrier called upon all the saints to witness his innocence; alas! not one of them appeared, and if there had, the Alcalde would not have believed him. The water-carrier related the whole story of the dying Moor with the straightforward simplicity of truth, but it was all in vain.

"Wilst thou persist in saying," demanded the judge, "that this Moslem had neither gold nor jewels, which were the object of thy cupidity?"

"As I hope to be saved, your worship," replied the water-carrier, "he had nothing but a small box of sandalwood, which he bequeathed to me in reward of my services."

"A box of sandalwood! A box of sandalwood!" exclaimed the Alcalde, his eyes sparkling at the idea of precious jewels. "And where is this box? Where have you concealed it?"

"An' it please your grace," replied the water-carrier, "it is in one of the panniers of my mule, and heartily at the service of your worship."

He had hardly spoken the words when the keen police officer darted off and reappeared in an instant with the mysterious box of sandalwood. The Alcalde opened it with an eager and trembling hand; all pressed forward to gaze upon the treasures it was expected to contain; when, to their disappointment, nothing appeared within but a parchment scroll, covered with Arabic characters, and an end of a waxen taper!

When there is nothing to be gained by the conviction of a prisoner, justice, even in Spain, is apt to be impartial. The Alcalde, having recovered from his disappointment and found there was really no booty in the case, now listened dispassionately to the explanation of the water-carrier, which was corroborated by the testimony of his wife. Being convinced, therefore, of his innocence, he discharged him from arrest; nay more, he permitted him to carry off the Moor's legacy, the box of sandalwood and its contents, as the well-merited reward of his humanity; but he retained his donkey in payment of cost and charges.

3.

Behold the unfortunate little Gallego reduced once more to the necessity of being his own water-carrier, and trudging up to the well of the Alhambra with a great earthen jar upon his shoulder. As he toiled up the hill in the heat of a summer noon his usual good-humour forsook him.

"Dog of an Alcalde!" would he cry, "to rob a poor man of the means of his subsistence—of the best friend he had in the world!" And then, at the remembrance of the beloved companion of his labours, all the kindness of his nature would break forth. "Ah, donkey of my heart!" would he exclaim, resting his burden on a stone, and wiping the sweat from his brow, "Ah, donkey of my heart! I warrant me thou thinkest of thy old master! I warrant me thou missest the water-jars—poor beast!"

To add to his afflictions his wife received him, on his return home, with whimperings and repinings; she had clearly the upper-hand, having warned him not to commit the act of hospitality that had brought on him all these misfortunes, and like a knowing woman, she took every occasion to remind him of it. If ever her children lacked food, or needed a new garment, she would answer with a sneer, "Go to your father; he's heir to King Chico of Alhambra. Ask him to help you out of the Moor's strongbox."

At length one evening, when, after a hot day's toil, she taunted him in the usual manner, he lost all patience. He did not venture to retort, but his eye rested upon the box of sandalwood, which lay on a shelf with lid half open, as if laughing in mockery of his vexation. Seizing it up he dashed it with indignation on the floor.

"Unlucky was the day that I ever set eyes on thee," he cried, "or sheltered thy master beneath my roof."

As the box struck the floor the lid flew wide open, and the parchment scroll rolled forth. Peregil sat regarding the scroll for some time in moody silence. At length rallying his ideas, "Who knows," thought he, "but this writing may be of some importance, as the Moor seems to have guarded it with such care." Picking it up, therefore, he put it in his bosom, and the next morning, as he was crying water through the streets, he stopped at the shop of a Moor, a native of Tangiers, who sold trinkets and perfumery, and asked him to explain the contents.

The Moor read the scroll attentively, then stroked his beard and smiled. "This manuscript," said he, "is a form of incantation for the recovery of hidden treasure, that is under the power of enchantment. It is said to have such virtue that the strongest bolts and bars, nay rock itself will yield before it."

"Bah!" cried the little Gallego. "What is all that to me? I am no enchanter, and know nothing of buried treasure." So saying he shouldered his water-jar, left the scroll in the hands of the Moor, and trudged forward on his daily rounds.

That evening, however, as he rested himself at the well of the Alhambra, he found a number of gossips assembled at the place, and their conversation, as is not unusual at that shadowy hour, turned upon old tales and traditions of a supernatural nature. Being all poor as rats, they dwelt with peculiar fondness upon the popular theme of enchanted riches left by the Moors in various parts of the Alhambra. Above all, they concurred in the belief that there were great treasures buried deep in the earth under the tower of the Seven Floors.

These stories made an unusual impression on the mind of honest Peregil, and they sank deeper and deeper into his thoughts as he returned alone down the darkling avenues. "What if, after all, there should be treasure hid beneath that tower—and if the scroll I left with the Moor should enable me to get at it!"

That night he tumbled and tossed, and could scarcely get a wink of sleep for the thoughts that were bewildering his brain. In the morning, bright and early, he went to the shop of the Moor, and told him all that was passing in his mind.

"You can read Arabic," said he. "Suppose we go together to the tower and try the effect of the charm; if it fails we are no worse off than before, but if it succeeds we will share equally all the treasure we may discover."

"Hold," replied the Moslem, "this writing is not sufficient of itself; it must be read at midnight, by the light of a taper singularly compounded and prepared, the ingredients of which are not within my reach. Without such a taper the scroll is of no use."

"Say no more!" cried the little Gallego. "I have such a taper at hand and will bring it here in a moment." So saying he hastened home, and soon returned with the end of a yellow wax taper that he had found in the box of sandalwood. The Moor felt it, and smelt to it. "Here are rare and costly perfumes," said he, "combined with this yellow wax. This is the kind of taper specified in the scroll. While this burns, the strongest walls and most secret caverns will remain open; woe to him, however, who lingers within until it be extinguished. He will remain enchanted with the treasure."

It was now agreed between them to try the charm that very night. At a late hour, therefore, when nothing was stirring but bats and owls, they ascended the woody hill of the Alhambra, and approached that awful tower, shrouded by trees and rendered formidable by so many traditionary tales.

By the light of a lantern, they groped their way through bushes, and over fallen stones, to the door of a vault beneath the tower. With fear and trembling they descended a flight of steps cut into the rock. It led to an empty chamber, damp and drear, from which another flight of steps led to a deeper vault. In this way they descended four flights, leading into as many vaults, one below the other, but the floor of the fourth was solid, and though, according to tradition, there remained three vaults still below, it was said to be impossible to penetrate farther.

The air of this vault was damp and chilly, and had an earthy smell, and the light scarce cast forth any rays. They paused here for a time in breathless suspense, until they faintly heard the clock of the watchtower strike midnight; upon this they lit the waxen taper, which diffused an odour of myrrh, and frankincense, and storax.

The Moor began to read in a hurried voice. He had scarce finished, when there was a noise as of subterraneous thunder. The earth shook, and the floor yawning open disclosed a flight of steps. Trembling with awe they descended, and by the light of the lantern found themselves in another vault, covered with Arabic inscriptions. In the centre stood a great chest, secured with seven bands of steel, at each end of which sat an enchanted Moor in armor, but motionless as a statue, being controlled by the power of the incantation. Before the chest were several jars filled with gold and silver and precious stones. In the largest of these they thrust their arms up to the elbow, and at every dip hauled forth hands full of broad yellow pieces of Moorish gold, or bracelets and ornaments of the same precious metal, while occasionally a necklace of oriental pearl would stick to their fingers. Still they trembled and breathed short while cramming their pockets with the spoils; and cast many a fearful glance at the two enchanted Moors, who sat grim and motionless, glaring upon them with unwinking eyes. At length, struck with a sudden fear of some fancied noise, they both rushed up the staircase, tumbled over one another into the upper apartment, overturned and extinguished the waxen taper, and the pavement again closed with a thundering sound.

Filled with dismay, they did not pause until they had groped their way out of the tower, and beheld the stars shining through the trees. Then seating themselves upon the grass, they divided the spoil, determining to content themselves for the present with this mere skimming of the jars, but to return on some future night and drain them to the bottom. To make sure of each other's good faith, also, they divided the talismans between them, one retaining the scroll and the other the taper; this done, they set off with light hearts and well-lined pockets for Granada.

As they wended their way down the hill, the shrewd Moor whispered a word of counsel in the ear of the simple little water-carrier.

"Friend Peregil," said he, "all this affair must be kept a profound secret until we have secured the treasure and conveyed it out of harm's way. If a whisper of it gets to the ear of the Alcalde we are undone!"

"Certainly!" replied the Gallego; "nothing can be more true."

"Friend Peregil," said the Moor, "you are a discreet man, and I have no doubt you can keep a secret; but—you have a wife—"

"She shall not know a word of it!" replied the little water-carrier sturdily.

"Enough," said the Moor. "I depend upon thy discretion and thy promise."

4.

Never was promise more positive and sincere; but alas! what man can keep a secret from his wife? Certainly not such a one as Peregil the water-carrier, who was one of the most loving and tractable of husbands. On his return home he found his wife moping in a corner.

"Mighty well!" cried she, as he entered; "you've come at last; after rambling about until this hour of the night. I wonder you have not brought home another Moor as a housemate." Then bursting into tears she began to wring her hands and smite her breast. "Unhappy women that I am!" exclaimed she; "what will become of me! My house stripped and plundered by lawyers and police; my husband a do-no-good who no longer brings home bread for his family, but goes rambling about, day and night, with infidel Moors. Oh, my children! my children! what will become of us; we shall all have to beg in the streets!"

Honest Peregil was so moved by the distress of his spouse, that he could not help whimpering also. His heart was as full as his pocket, and not to be restrained. Thrusting his hand into the latter he hauled forth three or four broad gold pieces. The poor woman stared with astonishment, and could not understanding the meaning of this golden shower. Before she could recover her surprise, the little Gallego drew forth a chain of gold and dangled it before her.

"Holy Virgin protect us!" exclaimed the wife. "What hast thou been doing, Peregil? Surely thou hast not been committing murder and robbery!"

The idea scarce entered the brain of the poor woman than it became a certainty with her. She saw a prison and a gallows in the distance, and a little bandy-legged Gallego dangling pendant from it; and, overcome by the horrors conjured up by her imagination, fell into violent hysterics.

What could the poor man do? He had no other means of pacifying his wife and dispelling the phantoms of her fancy, than by relating the whole story of his good fortune. This, however, he did not do until he had exacted from her the most solemn promise to keep it a profound secret from every living being.

To describe her joy would be impossible. She flung her arms round the neck of her husband, and almost strangled him with her caresses.

"Now, wife!" exclaimed the little man with honest exultation; "what say you now to the Moor's legacy? Henceforth never abuse me for helping a fellow creature in distress."

The honest Gallego retired to his sheepskin mat, and slept as soundly as if on a bed of down. Not so his wife. She emptied the whole contents of his pockets upon the mat, and sat all night counting gold pieces of Arabic coin, trying on necklaces and ear-rings, and fancying the figure she should one day make when permitted to enjoy her riches.

On the following morning the honest Gallego took a broad golden coin to a jeweller's shop to offer it for sale; pretending to have found it among the ruins of the Alhambra. The jeweller saw that it had an Arabic inscription and was of the purest gold; he offered, however, but a third of its value, with which the water-carrier was perfectly content. Peregil now bought new clothes for his little flock, and all kinds of toys, together with ample provisions for a hearty meal, and returning to his dwelling set all his children dancing around him, while he capered in their midst, the happiest of fathers.

The wife of the water-carrier kept her promise of secrecy with surprising strictness. For a whole day and a half she went about with a look of mystery and a heart swelling almost to bursting, yet she held her peace, though surrounded by her gossips. It is true she could not help giving herself a few airs, apologized for her ragged dress, and talked of ordering a new one all trimmed with gold lace, and a new lace mantilla. She threw out hints of her husband's intention of leaving his trade of water-carrying, as it did not altogether agree with his health. In fact she thought they should all retire to the country for the summer so that the children might have the benefit of the mountain air, for there was no living in the city in this sultry season.

The neighbours stared at each other, and thought the poor woman had lost her wits, and her airs and graces and elegant pretensions were the theme of universal scoffing and merriment among her friends, the moment her back was turned.

If she restrained herself abroad, however, she indemnified herself at home, and, putting a string of rich oriental pearls round her neck, Moorish bracelets on her arms, an aigrette of diamonds on her head, sailed backwards and forwards in her slatternly rags about the room, now and then stopping to admire herself in a piece of broken mirror. Nay, in the impulse of her simple vanity, she could not resist on one occasion showing herself at the window, to enjoy the effect of her finery on the passers-by.

As the fates would have it, Pedrillo Pedrugo, the meddlesome barber, was at this moment sitting idly in his shop on the opposite side of the street, when his ever-watchful eye caught the sparkle of a diamond. In an instant he was at his loop-hole, reconnoitring the slattern spouse of the water-carrier, decorated with the splendor of an Eastern bride. No sooner had he taken an accurate inventory of her ornaments than he posted off with all speed to the Alcalde. In a little while the hungry policeman was again on the scent, and before the day was over, the unfortunate Peregil was again dragged into the presence of the judge.

5.

"How is this, villain!" cried the Alcalde in a furious voice. "You told me that the infidel who died in your house left nothing behind but an empty coffer, and now I hear of your wife flaunting in her rags decked out with pearls and diamonds. Wretch, that thou art! prepare to render up the spoils of thy miserable victim, and to swing on the gallows that is already tired of waiting for thee."

The terrified water-carrier fell on his knees, and made a full relation of the marvellous manner in which he had gained his wealth. The Alcalde, the policeman, and the inquisitive barber listened with greedy ears to this Arabian tale of enchanted treasure. The policeman was dispatched to bring the Moor who had assisted in the incantation. The Moslem entered half frightened out of his wits at finding himself in the hands of the harpies of the law. When he beheld the water-carrier standing with sheepish look and downcast countenance, he comprehended the whole matter. "Miserable animal," said he, as he passed near him, "did I not warn thee against babbling to thy wife?"

The story of the Moor coincided exactly with that of his colleague; but the Alcalde affected to be slow of belief, and threw out menaces of imprisonment and rigorous investigation.

"Softly, good Señor Alcalde," said the Mussulman, who by this time had recovered his usual shrewdness and self-possession. "Let us not mar fortune's favours in the scramble for them. Nobody knows anything of this matter but ourselves; let us keep the secret. There is wealth enough in the cave to enrich us all. Promise a fair division, and all shall be produced; refuse, and the cave shall remain forever closed."

The Alcalde consulted apart with his officer. The latter was an old fox in his profession.

"Promise anything," said he, "until you get possession of the treasure. You may then seize upon the whole, and if he and his accomplice dare to murmur, threaten them with the faggot and the stake as infidels and sorcerers."

The Alcalde relished the advice. Smoothing his brow and turning to the Moor, "This is a strange story," said he, "and may be true, but I must have proof of it. This very night you must repeat the incantation in my presence. If there be really such treasure, we will share it amicably between us, and say nothing further of the matter; if you have deceived me, expect no mercy at my hands. In the meantime you must remain in custody."

The Moor and the water-carrier cheerfully agreed to these conditions, satisfied that the event would prove the truth of their words.

Toward midnight the Alcalde sallied forth secretly, attended by his officer and the meddlesome barber, all strongly armed. They conducted the Moor and the water-carrier as prisoners, and were provided with the stout donkey of the latter, to bear off the expected treasure. They arrived at the tower without being observed, and tying the donkey to a fig-tree, descended into the fourth vault of the tower.

The scroll was produced, the yellow waxen taper lighted, and the Moor read the form of incantation. The earth trembled as before, and the pavement opened with a thundering sound, disclosing the narrow flight of steps. The Alcalde, the policeman, and the barber were struck aghast, and could not summon courage to descend. The Moor and the water-carrier entered the lower vault and found the two Moors seated as before, silent and motionless. They removed two of the great jars, filled with golden coin and precious stones. The water-carrier bore them up one by one upon his shoulders, but though a strong-backed little man, and accustomed to carry burdens, he staggered beneath their weight, and found, when slung on each side of his donkey, they were as much as the animal could bear.

"Let us be content for the present," said the Moor. "Here is as much treasure as we can carry off without being perceived, and enough to make us all wealthy to our heart's desire."

"Is there more treasure remaining behind?" demanded the Alcalde.

"The greatest prize of all," said the Moor; "a huge coffer, bound with bands of steel, and filled with pearls and precious stones."

"Let us have up the coffer by all means," cried the grasping Alcalde.

"I will descend for no more," said the Moor, doggedly. "Enough is enough for a reasonable man; more is superfluous."

"And I," said the water-carrier, "will bring up no further burthen to break the back of my poor donkey."

Finding commands, threats, and entreaties equally vain, the Alcalde turned to his two adherents. "Aid me," said he, "to bring up the coffer, and its contents shall be divided between us." So saying he descended the steps, followed, with trembling reluctance, by the policeman and the barber.

No sooner did the Moor behold them fairly earthed than he extinguished the yellow taper: the pavement closed with its usual crash, and the three worthies remained buried inside.

He then hastened up the different flights of steps, nor stopped until in the open air. The little water-carrier followed him as fast as his short legs would permit.

"What have you done?" cried Peregil, as soon as he could recover his breath. "The Alcalde and the other two are shut up in the vault!"

"It is the will of Allah!" said the Moor, devoutly.

"And will you not release them?" demanded the Gallego.

"Allah forbid!" replied the Moor, smoothing his beard. "It is written in the book of fate that they shall remain enchanted until some future adventurer shall come to break the charm. The will of god be done!" So saying he hurled the end of the waxen taper far among the gloomy thickets of the glen.

There was now no remedy; so the Moor and the water-carrier proceeded with the richly laden donkey toward the city; nor could honest Peregil refrain from hugging and kissing his long-eared fellow-labourer, thus restored to him from the clutches of the law; and, in fact, it is doubtful which gave the simple-hearted little man most joy at the moment, the gaining of the treasure or the recovery of the donkey.

The two partners in good luck divided their spoil amicably and fairly, except that the Moor, who had a little taste for trinketry, made out to get into his heap most of the pearls and precious stones, and other baubles, but then he always gave the water-carrier in lieu magnificent jewels of massy gold four times the size, with which the latter was heartily content. They took care not to linger within reach of accidents, but made off to enjoy their wealth undisturbed in other countries. The Moor returned into Africa, to his native city of Tetuan, and the Gallego, with his wife, his children, and his donkey, made their way to Portugal. Here, under the admonition and tuition of his wife, he became a personage of some consequence, for she made the little man array his long body and short legs in doublet and hose, with a feather in his hat and a sword by his side; and, laying aside the familiar appellation of Peregil, assume the more sonorous title of Don Pedro Gil. His progeny grew up a thriving and merry-hearted, though short and bandy-legged generation; while the Senora Gil, be-fringed, be-laced, and be-tasselled from her head to her heels, with glittering rings on every finger, became a model of slatternly fashion and finery.

As to the Alcalde, and his adjuncts, they remained shut up under the great tower of the Seven Floors, and there they remain spell-bound to the present day.

Nine Little Goblins

JAMES WHITCOMB RILEY

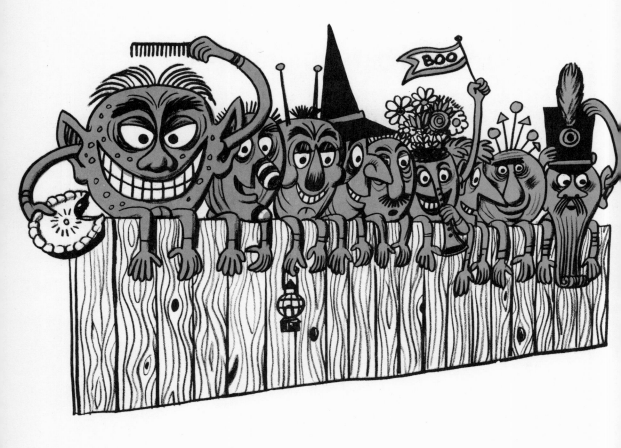

Nine Little Goblins

They all climbed up on a high board fence—
   Nine little goblins, with green-glass eyes—
Nine little goblins that had no sense,
    And couldn't tell coppers from cold mince pies;
      And they all climbed up on the fence, and sat—
      And I asked them what they were staring at.

    And the first one said, as he scratched his head
      With a queer little arm that reached out of his ear
    And rasped its claws in his hair so red—
      "This is what this little arm is fer!"
        And he scratched and stared, and the next one said,
        "How on earth do *you* scratch your head?"

      And he laughed like the screech of a rusty hinge—
        Laughed and laughed till his face grew black;
      And when he choked, with a final twinge
        Of his stifling laughter, he thumped his back
          With a fist that grew on the end of his tail
          Till the breath came back to his lips so pale.

And the third little goblin leered round at me—
  And there were no lids on his eyes at all—
And he clucked one eye, and he says, says he,
    "What is the style of your socks this fall?"
      And he clapped his heels—and I sighed to see
      That he had hands where his feet should be.

    Then a bald-faced goblin, gray and grim,
      Bowed his head, and I saw him slip
  His eyebrows off, as I looked at him,
    And paste them over his upper lip;
      And then he moaned in remorseful pain—
      "Would—Ah, would I'd me brows again!"

      And then the whole of the goblin band
        Rocked on the fence-top to and fro,
    And clung, in a long row, hand in hand,
      Singing the songs that they used to know—
        Singing the songs that their grandsires sung
        In the goo-goo days of the goblin-tongue.

      And ever they kept their green-glass eyes
        Fixed on me with a stony stare—
    Till my own grew glazed with a dread surmise,
      And my hat whooped up on my lifted hair,
        And I felt the heart in my breast snap to,
        As you've heard the lid of a snuff-box do.

        And they sang "You're asleep! There is no board fence,
          And never a goblin with green-glass eyes!—
      'Tis only a vision the mind invents
        After a supper of cold mince pies.—
          And you're doomed to dream this way," they said,—
          "And you sha'nt wake up till you're clean plum dead!"

The Ghost Ship

RICHARD MIDDLETON

It blew into the village from the sea one stormy night—a ghostly ship, with a ghostly crew and ghostly ways. . . .

The Ghost Ship

FAIRFIELD IS a little village lying near the Portsmouth Road about halfway between London and the sea. Strangers who find it by accident now and then call it a pretty, old-fashioned place; we who live in it and call it home don't find anything very pretty about it, but we should be sorry to live anywhere else. Our minds have taken the shape of the inn and the church and the green, I suppose. At all events, we never feel comfortable out of Fairfield.

Of course, the Cockneys, with their vasty houses and noise-ridden streets, can call us rustics if they choose, but for all that Fairfield is a better place to live in than London. Doctor says that when he goes to London his mind is bruised with the weight of the houses, and he was a Cockney born. He had to live there himself when he was a little chap, but he knows better now. You gentlemen may laugh—perhaps some of you come from London way —but it seems to me that a witness like that is worth a gallon of arguments.

Dull? Well, you might find it dull, but I assure you that I've listened to all the London yarns you have spun tonight, and they're absolutely nothing to the things that happen at Fairfield. It's because of our way of thinking and minding our own business. If one of your Londoners were set down on the green of a Saturday night when the ghosts of the lads who died in the war keep tryst with the lasses who lie in the churchyard, he couldn't help being curious and interfering, and then the ghosts would go somewhere where it was quieter. But we just let them come and go and don't make any fuss, and in consequence Fairfield is the ghostliest place in all England. Why, I've seen a headless man sitting on the edge of the well in broad daylight, and the children playing about his feet as if he were their father. Take my word for it, spirits know when they are well off as much as human beings.

97

Still, I must admit that the thing I'm going to tell you about was queer even for our part of the world, where three packs of ghosthounds hunt regularly during the season, and blacksmith's great-grandfather is busy all night shoeing the dead gentlemen's horses. Now that's a thing that wouldn't happen in London, because of their interfering ways, but blacksmith he lies up aloft and sleeps as quiet as a lamb. Once when he had a bad head he shouted down to them not to make so much noise, and in the morning he found an old guinea left on the anvil as an apology. He wears it on his watch chain now. But I must get on with my story; if I start telling you about the queer happenings at Fairfield I'll never stop.

It all came of the great storm in the spring of '97, the year that we had two great storms. This was the first one, and I remember it very well, because I found in the morning that it had lifted the thatch of my pigsty into the widow's garden as clean as a boy's kite. When I looked over the hedge, widow—Tom Lamport's widow that was—was prodding for her nasturtiums with a daisy-grubber. After I had watched her for a little I went down to the "Fox and Grapes" to tell landlord what she had said to me. Landlord he laughed, being a married man and at ease with the sex. "Come to that," he said, "the tempest has blowed something into my field. A kind of a ship I think it would be."

I was surprised at that until he explained that it was only a ghost ship and would do no hurt to the turnips. We argued that it had been blown up from the sea at Portsmouth, and then we talked of something else. There were two slates down at the parsonage and a big tree in Lumley's meadow. It was a rare storm.

I reckon the wind had blown our ghosts all over England. They were coming back for days afterwards with foundered horses and as footsore as possible, and they were so glad to get back to Fairfield that some of them walked up the street crying like little children. Squire said that his great-grandfather's great-grandfather hadn't looked so dead-beat since the Battle of Naseby, and he's an educated man.

What with one thing and another, I should think it was a week before we got straight again, and then one afternoon I met the landlord on the green and he had a worried face. "I wish you'd come and have a look at that ship in my field," he said to me; "it seems to me it's leaning real hard on the turnips. I can't bear thinking what the missus will say when she see it."

I walked down the lane with him, and sure enough there was a ship in the middle of his field, but such a ship as no man had seen on the water for three hundred years, let alone in the middle of a turnip field. It was all painted black and covered with carvings, and there was a great bay window in the stern for all the world like the Squire's drawing-room. There was a crowd of little black cannon on deck and looking out of her portholes, and she was anchored at each end to the hard ground. I have seen the wonders of the world on picture-postcards, but I have never seen anything to equal that.

"She seems very solid for a ghost ship," I said, seeing the landlord was bothered.

"I should say it's a betwixt and between," he answered, puzzling it over, "but it's going to spoil a matter of fifty turnips, and missus she'll want it moved." We went up to her and touched the side, and it was as hard as a real ship. "Now there's folks in England would call that very curious," he said.

Now I don't know much about ships, but I should think that that ghost ship weighed a solid two hundred tons, and it seemed to me that she had come to stay, so that I felt sorry for the landlord, who was a married man. "All the horses in Fairfield won't move her out of my turnips," he said, frowning at her.

Just then we heard a noise on her deck, and we looked up and saw that a man had come out of her front cabin and was looking down at us very peaceably. He was dressed in a black uniform set out with rusty gold lace, and he had a great cutlass by his side in a brass sheath. "I'm Captain Bartholomew Roberts," he said, in a gentleman's voice, "put in for recruits. I seem to have brought her rather far up the harbour."

"Harbour!" cried landlord; "why; you're fifty miles from the sea."

Captain Roberts didn't turn a hair. "So much as that, is it?" he said coolly. "Well, it's of no consequence."

Landlord was a bit upset at this. "I don't want to be unneighbourly," he said, "but I wish you hadn't brought your ship into my field. You see, my wife sets great store on these turnips."

The Captain took a pinch of snuff out of a fine gold box that he pulled out of his pocket, and dusted his fingers with a silk handkerchief in a very genteel fashion. "I'm only here for a few months," he said; "but if a testimony of my esteem would pacify your good lady I should be content," and with the words he loosed a great gold brooch from the neck of his coat and tossed it down to landlord.

Landlord blushed as red as a strawberry. "I'm not denying she's fond of jewellery," he said, "but it's too much for half a sackful of turnips." And indeed it was a handsome brooch.

The Captain laughed. "Tut, man," he said, "it's a forced sale, and you deserve a good price. Say no more about it." And nodding good-day to us, he turned on his heel and went into the cabin. Landlord walked back up the lane like a man with a weight off his mind. "That tempest has blowed me a bit of luck," he said. "The missus will be main pleased with that brooch. It's better than blacksmith's guinea, any day."

Ninety-seven was Jubilee year, the year of the second Jubilee, you remember, and we had great doings at Fairfield, so that we hadn't much time to bother about the ghost ship, though anyhow it isn't our way to meddle in things that don't concern us. Landlord, he saw his tenant once or twice when he was hoeing his turnips and passed the time of day, and landlord's wife wore her new brooch to church every Sunday. But we didn't mix much with the ghosts at any time, all except an idiot lad there was in the village, and he didn't know the difference between a man and a ghost, poor innocent! On Jubilee Day, however, somebody told Captain Roberts why the church bells were ringing, and he hoisted a flag and fired off his guns like a loyal Englishman. 'Tis true the guns were shotted, and one of the round shot knocked a hole in Farmer Johnstone's barn, but nobody thought much of that in such a season of rejoicing.

It wasn't till our celebrations were over that we noticed that anything was wrong in Fairfield. 'Twas shoemaker who told me first about it one morning at the "Fox and Grapes." "You know my great-great-uncle?" he said to me.

"You mean Joshua, the quiet lad," I answered, knowing him well.

"Quiet!" said shoemaker indignantly. "Quiet you call him, coming home at three o'clock every morning as drunk as a magistrate and waking up the whole house with his noise."

"Why, it can't be Joshua!" I said, for I knew him for one of the most respectable young ghosts in the village.

"Joshua it is," said shoemaker; "and one of these nights he'll find himself out in the street if he isn't careful."

This kind of talk shocked me, I can tell you, for I don't like to hear a man abusing his own family, and I could hardly believe that a steady youngster like Joshua had taken to drink. But just then in came Butcher Aylwin in such a temper that he could hardly drink his beer. "The young puppy! The young puppy!" he kept on saying; and it was some time before shoemaker and I found out that he was talking about his ancestor that fell at Senlac.

"Drink?" said shoemaker hopefully, for we all like company in our misfortunes, and butcher nodded grimly.

"The young noodle," he said, emptying his tankard.

Well, after that I kept my ears open, and it was the same story all over the village. There was hardly a young man among all the ghosts of Fairfield who didn't roll home in the small hours of the morning the worse for liquor. I used to wake up in the night and hear them stumble past my house, singing outrageous songs. The worst of it was that we couldn't keep the scandal to ourselves, and the folk at Greenhill began to talk of "sodden Fairfield," and taught their children to sing a song about us:

> *"Sodden Fairfield, sodden Fairfield, has no use for bread-and-butter;*
> *Rum for breakfast, rum for dinner, rum for tea, and rum for supper!"*

We are easy-going in our village, but we didn't like that.

Of course, we soon found out where the young fellows went to get the drink, and landlord was terribly cut up that his tenant should have turned out so badly, but his wife wouldn't hear of parting with the brooch, so that he couldn't give the Captain notice to quit. But as time went on, things grew from bad to worse, and at all hours of the day you would see those young reprobates sleeping it off on the village green. Nearly every afternoon a ghost wagon used to jolt down to the ship with a lading of rum, and though the older ghosts seemed inclined to give the Captain's hospitality the go-by, the youngsters were neither to hold nor to bind.

So one afternoon when I was taking my nap I heard a knock at the door, and there was parson looking very serious, like a man with a job before him that he didn't altogether relish. "I'm going down to talk to the Captain about all this drunkenness in the village, and I want you to come with me," he said straight out.

I can't say that I fancied the visit much myself, and I tried to hint to parson that as, after all, they were only a lot of ghosts, it didn't very much matter.

"Dead or alive, I'm responsible for their good conduct," he said, "and I'm going to do my duty and put a stop to this continued disorder. And you are coming with me, John Simmons." So I went, parson being a persuasive kind of man.

We went down to the ship, and as we approached her I could see the Captain tasting the air on deck. When he saw parson he took off his hat very politely, and I can tell you that I was relieved to find that he had a preper respect for the cloth. Parson acknowledged his salute and spoke out stoutly enough. "Sir, I should be glad to have a word with you."

"Come on board, sir; come on board," said the Captain, and I could tell by his voice that he knew why we were there. Parson and I climbed up an uneasy kind of ladder, and the Captain took us into the great cabin at the back of the ship, where the bay window was. It was the most wonderful place you ever saw in your life, all full of gold and silver plate, swords with jewelled scabbards, carved oak chairs, and great chests that looked as though they were bursting with guineas. Even parson was surprised, and he did not shake his head very hard when the Captain took down some silver cups and poured us out a drink of rum. I tasted mine, and I don't mind saying that it changed my view of things entirely. There was nothing betwixt and between about that rum, and I felt that it was ridiculous to blame the lads for drinking too much of stuff like that. It seemed to fill my veins with honey and fire.

Parson put the case squarely to the Captain, but I didn't listen much to what he said; I was busy sipping my drink and looking through the window at the fishes swimming to and fro over landlord's turnips. Just then it seemed the most natural thing in the world that they should be there, though afterwards, of course, I could see that that proved it was a ghost ship.

But even then I thought it was queer when I saw a drowned sailor float by in the thin air with his hair and beard all full of bubbles. It was the first time I had seen anything quite like that at Fairfield.

All the time I was regarding the wonders of the deep, parson was telling Captain Roberts how there was no peace or rest in the village owing to the curse of drunkenness, and what a bad example the youngsters were setting to the older ghosts. The Captain listened very attentively, and only put in a word now and then about boys being boys and young men sowing their wild oats. But when parson had finished his speech he filled up our silver cups and said to parson, with a flourish, "I should be sorry to cause trouble anywhere where I have been made welcome, and you will be glad to hear that I put to sea tomorrow night. And now you must drink me a prosperous voyage." So we all stood up and drank the toast with honour, and that noble rum was like hot oil in my veins.

After that Captain showed us some of the curiosities he had brought back from foreign parts, and we were greatly amazed, though afterwards I couldn't clearly remember what they were. And then I found myself walking across the turnips with parson, and I was telling him of the glories of the deep that I had seen through the window of the ship. He turned on me severely. "If I were you, John Simmons," he said, "I should go straight home to bed." He has a way of putting things that wouldn't occur to an ordinary man, has parson, and I did as he told me.

Well, next day it came on to blow, and it blew harder and harder, till about eight o'clock at night I heard a noise and looked out into the garden. I dare say you won't believe me, it seems a bit tall even to me, but the wind had lifted the thatch of my pigsty into the widow's garden a second time. I thought I wouldn't wait to hear what widow had to say about it, so I went across the green to the "Fox and Grapes," and the wind was so strong that I danced along on tiptoe like a girl at the fair. When I got to the inn landlord had to help me shut the door; it seemed as though a dozen goats were pushing against it to come in out of the storm.

"It's a powerful tempest," he said, drawing the beer. "I hear there's a chimney down at Dickory End."

"It's a funny thing how these sailors know about the weather," I answered. "When Captain said he was going tonight, I was thinking it would take a capful of wind to carry the ship back to sea, but now here's more than a capful."

"Ah, yes," said landlord, "it's tonight he goes true enough, and, mind you, though he treated me handsome over the rent, I'm not sure it's a loss to the village. I don't hold with gentrice who fetch their drink from London instead of helping local traders to get their living."

"But you haven't got any rum like his," I said, to draw him out.

His neck grew red above his collar, and I was afraid I'd gone too far; but after a while he got his breath with a grunt.

"John Simmons," he said, "if you've come down here this windy night to talk a lot of fool's talk, you've wasted a journey."

Well, of course, then I had to smooth him down with praising his rum, and Heaven forgive me for swearing it was better than Captain's. For the like of that rum no living lips have tasted save mine and parson's. But somehow or other I brought landlord round, and presently we must have a glass of his best to prove its quality.

"Beat that if you can!" he cried, and we both raised our glasses to our mouths, only to stop halfway and look at each other in amaze. For the wind that had been howling outside like an outrageous dog had all of a sudden turned as melodious as the carol-boys of a Christmas Eve.

"Surely that's not my Martha," whispered landlord, Martha being his great-aunt that lived in the loft overhead.

We went to the door, and the wind burst it open so that the handle was driven clean into the plaster of the wall. But we didn't think about that at the time; for over our heads, sailing very comfortably through the windy stars, was the ship that had passed the summer in landlord's field. Her portholes and her bay window were blazing with lights, and there was a noise of singing and fiddling on her decks. "He's gone," shouted landlord above the storm, "and he's taken half the village with him!" I could only nod in answer, not having lungs like bellows of leather.

In the morning we were able to measure the strength of the storm, and over and above my pigsty there was damage enough wrought in the village to keep us busy. True it is that the children had to break down no branches for the firing that autumn, since the wind had strewn the woods with more than they could carry away. Many of our ghosts were scattered abroad, but this time very few came back, all the young men having sailed with Captain; and not only ghosts, for a poor half-witted lad was missing, and we reckoned that he had stowed himself away or perhaps shipped as cabin-boy, not knowing any better.

What with the lamentations of the ghost-girls and the grumblings of families who had lost an ancestor, the village was upset for a while, and the funny thing was that it was the folk who had complained most of the carryings-on of the youngsters, who made most noise now that they were gone. I hadn't any sympathy with shoemaker or butcher, who ran about saying how much they missed their lads, but it made me grieve to hear the poor bereaved girls calling their lovers by name on the village green at nightfall. It didn't seem fair to me that they should have lost their men a second time, after giving up life in order to join them, as like as not. Still, not even a spirit can be sorry forever, and after a few months we made up our mind that the folk who had sailed in the ship were never coming back, and we didn't talk about it any more.

And then one day, I dare say it would be a couple of years after, when the whole business was quite forgotten, who should come trapesing along the road from Portsmouth but the daft lad who had gone away with the ship, without waiting till he was dead to become a ghost. You never saw such a boy as that in all your life. He had a great rusty cutlass hanging to a string at his waist, and he was tattooed all over in fine colours, so that even his face looked like a girl's sampler. He had a handkerchief in his hand full of foreign shells and old-fashioned pieces of small money, very curious, and he walked up to the well outside his mother's house and drew himself a drink as if he had been nowhere in particular.

The worst of it was that he had come back as soft-headed as he went, and try as we might we couldn't get anything reasonable out of him. He talked a lot of gibberish about keel-hauling and walking the plank and crimson murders—things which a decent sailor should know nothing about, so that it seemed to me that for all his manners Captain had been more of a pirate than a gentleman mariner. But to draw sense out of that boy was as hard as picking cherries off a crabtree. One silly tale he had that he kept on drifting back to, and to hear him you would have thought that it was the only thing that happened to him in his life. "We was at anchor," he would say, "off an island called the Basket of Flowers, and the sailors had caught a lot of parrots and we were teaching them to swear. Up and down the decks, up and down the decks, and the language they used was dreadful. Then we looked up and saw the masts of the Spanish ship outside the harbour. Outside the harbour they were, so we threw the parrots into the sea and sailed out to fight. And all the parrots were drownded in the sea and the language they used was dreadful." That's the sort of boy he was, nothing but silly talk of parrots when we asked him about the fighting. And we never had a chance of teaching him better, for two days after he ran away again, and hasn't been seen since.

That's my story, and I assure you that things like that are happening at Fairfield all the time. The ship has never come back, but somehow as people grow older they seem to think that one of these windy nights she'll come sailing in over the hedges with all the lost ghosts on board. Well, when she comes, she'll be welcome. There's one ghost-lass that has never grown tired of waiting for her lad to return. Every night you'll see her out on the green, straining her poor eyes with looking for the mast-lights among the stars. A faithful lass you'd call her, and I'm thinking you'd be right.

Landlord's field wasn't a penny the worse for the visit, but they do say that since then the turnips that have been grown in it have tasted of rum.

The Boy
Who Drew Cats

LAFCADIO HEARN

*In the pitch darkness of the old temple,
danger threatened—and to protect
him there were only the cats he had
drawn. . . .*

The Boy
Who Drew Cats

A LONG, long time ago, in a small country village in Japan, there lived a poor farmer and his wife, who were very good people. They had a number of children, and found it hard to feed them all. The elder son was strong enough when only fourteen years old to help his father; and the little girls learned to help their mother almost as soon as they could walk.

But the youngest child, a little boy, did not seem to be fit for hard work. He was very clever—cleverer than all his brothers and sisters; but he was quite weak and small, and people said he could never grow very big. So his parents thought it would be better for him to become a priest than to become a farmer. They took him with them to the village temple one day, and asked the good old priest who lived there if he would have their little boy for his pupil, and teach him all that a priest ought to know.

The old man spoke kindly to the lad, and asked him some hard questions. So clever were the answers that the priest agreed to take the little fellow into the temple as an acolyte, and to educate him for the priesthood.

The boy learned quickly what the old priest taught him, and was very obedient in most things. But he had one fault. He liked to draw cats during study-hours, and to draw cats when cats ought not to have been drawn at all.

Whenever he found himself alone, he drew cats. He drew them on the margins of the priest's books, and on all the screens of the temple, on the walls, and on the pillars. Several times the priest told him this was not right; but he did not stop drawing cats. He drew them because he could not really help it. He had what is called "the genius of an artist," and just for that reason he was not quite fit to be an acolyte; a good acolyte should study books.

107

One day after he had drawn some very clever pictures of cats upon a paper screen, the old priest said to him severely, "My boy, you must go away from this temple at once. You will never make a good priest, but perhaps you will become a great artist. Now let me give you a last piece of advice, and be sure you never forget it. *Avoid large places at night; keep to small!"*

The boy did not know what the priest meant by saying, *"Avoid large places; keep to small!"* He thought and thought, while he was tying up his little bundle of clothes to go away; but he could not understand those words, and he was afraid to speak to the priest any more, except to say good-bye.

He left the temple very sorrowfully, and began to wonder what he should do. If he went straight home he felt his father would punish him for having been disobedient to the priest: so he was afraid to go home. All at once he remembered that at the next village, twelve miles away, there was a very big temple. He had heard there were several priests at that temple; and he made up his mind to go to them and ask them to take him for their acolyte.

Now that big temple was closed up but the boy did not know this fact. The reason it had been closed up was that a goblin had frightened the priests away, and had taken possession of the place. Some brave warriors had afterwards gone to the temple at night to kill the goblin; but they had never been seen alive again. Nobody had ever told these things to the boy; so he walked all the way to the village hoping to be kindly treated by the priests.

When he got to the village it was already dark, and all the people were in bed; but he saw the big temple on a hill on the other end of the principal street, and he saw there was a light in the temple. People who tell the story say the goblin used to make that light, in order to tempt lonely travellers to ask for shelter. The boy went at once to the temple, and knocked. There was no sound inside. He knocked and knocked again; but still nobody came. At last he pushed gently at the door, and was glad to find that it had not been fastened. So he went in and saw a lamp burning—but no priest.

He thought that some priest would be sure to come very soon, and he sat down and waited. Then he noticed that everything in the temple was gray with dust, and thickly spun over with cobwebs. So he thought to himself that the priests would certainly like to have an acolyte, to keep the place clean. He wondered why they had allowed the place to get so dusty. What most pleased him, however, were some big white screens, good to paint cats upon. Though he was tired, he looked at once for a writing-box, and found one, and ground some ink, and began to paint cats.

He painted a great many cats upon the screens; and then he began to feel very, very sleepy. He was just on the point of lying down to sleep beside one of the screens, when he suddenly remembered the words: *"Avoid large places—keep to small!"*

The temple was very large; he was alone; and as he thought of these words—though he could not quite understand them—he began to feel for the first time a little afraid; and he resolved to look for a small place in which to sleep. He found a little cabinet, with a sliding door, and went into it and shut himself up. Then he lay down and fell fast asleep.

Very late in the night he was awakened by a most terrible noise—a noise of fighting and screaming. It was so dreadful that he was afraid even to look through a chink of the little cabinet; he lay very still, holding his breath for fright.

The light that had been in the temple went out; but the awful sounds continued, and became more awful, and all the temple shook. After a long time silence came; but the boy was still afraid to move. He did not move until the light of the morning sun shone into the cabinet through the chinks of the little door.

Then he got out of his hiding-place very cautiously, and looked about. The first thing he saw was that all the floor of the temple was covered with blood. And then he saw, lying dead in the middle of it, an enormous monstrous rat—a goblin-rat—bigger than a cow!

But who or what could have killed it? There was no man or other creature to be seen. Suddenly the boy observed that the mouths of all the cats he had drawn the night before were red and wet with blood. Then he knew that the goblin had been killed by the cats which he had drawn. And then also, for the first time, he understood why the wise old priest had said to him:—"*Avoid large places at night; keep to small.*". . .

Afterwards that boy became a very famous artist. Some of the cats which he drew are still shown to travellers in Japan.

The Haunted Trailer

ROBERT ARTHUR

The newest thing in haunted houses—
a mobile home for footloose ghosts!

The Haunted Trailer

IT WAS inevitable, of course. Bound to happen some day. But why did it have to happen to me? What did *I do* to deserve the grief? And I was going to be married, too. I sank my last thousand into that trailer, almost. In it Monica and I were going on a honeymoon tour of the United States. We were going to see the country. I was going to write, and we were going to be happy as two turtledoves.

Ha!

Ha ha!

If you detect bitterness in that laughter, I'll tell you why I'm bitter.

Because it had to be me, Mel—for Melvin—Mason who became the first person in the world to own a haunted trailer!

Now, a haunted castle is one thing. Even an ordinary haunted house can be livable. In a castle, or a house, if there's a ghost around, you can lock yourself in the bedroom and get a little sleep. A nuisance, yes. But nothing a man couldn't put up with.

In a trailer, though! What are you going to do when you're sharing a trailer, even a super-de-luxe model with four built-in bunks, a breakfast nook, a complete bathroom, a radio, electric range, and easy chair, with a ghost? Where can you go to get away from it?

Ha!

Ha ha!

I've heard so much ghostly laughter the last week that I'm laughing that way now myself.

There I was. I had the trailer. I had the car to pull it, naturally. I was on my way to meet Monica in Hollywood, where she was living with an

113

aunt from Iowa. And twelve miles west of Albany, the first night out, my brand-new, spic-and-span trailer picks up a hitch-hiking haunt!

But maybe I'd better start at the beginning. It happened this way. I bought the trailer in New England—a Custom Clipper, with chrome and tan outside trim—for $2998. I hitched it on behind my sedan and headed westward, happier than a lark when the dew's on the thorn. I'd been saving up for this day for two years, and I felt wonderful.

I took it easy, getting the feel of the trailer, and so I didn't make very good time. I crossed the Hudson just after dark, trundled through Albany in a rainstorm, and half an hour later pulled off the road into an old cow-path between two big rocks to spend the night.

The thunder was rolling back and forth overhead, and the lightning was having target practice with the trees. But I'd picked out a nice secluded spot and I made myself comfortable. I cooked up a tasty plate of beans, some coffee, and some home fries. When I had eaten I took off my shoes, slumped down in the easy chair, lit a cigarette, and leaned back.

"Ah!" I said aloud. "Solid comfort. If only Monica were here, how happy we would be."

But she wasn't, so I picked up a book.

It wasn't a very good book. I must have dozed off. Maybe I napped a couple of hours. Maybe three. Anyway, I woke with a start, the echo of a buster of a thunderbolt still rattling the willow-ware set in the china closet. My hair was standing on end from the electricity in the air.

Then the door banged open, a swirl of rain swept in, and the wind—anyway, I thought it was the wind—slammed the door to. I heard a sound like a ghost—there's no other way to describe it—of a sigh.

"Now this," said a voice, "is something like!"

I had jumped up to shut the door, and I stood there with my unread book in my hand, gaping. The wind had blown a wisp of mist into my trailer and the mist, instead of evaporating, remained there, seeming to turn slowly and to settle into shape. It got more and more solid until—

Well, you know. It was a spectre. A haunt. A homeless ghost.

The creature remained there, regarding me in a decidedly cool manner.

"Sit down, chum," it said, "and don't look so pop-eyed. You make me nervous. This is my first night indoors in fifteen years, and I wanta enjoy it."

"Who—" I stammered—"who—"

"I'm not," the spectre retorted, "a brother owl, so don't who-who at me. What do I look like?"

"You look like a ghost," I told him.

"Now you're getting smart, chum. I *am* a ghost. What *kind* of a ghost do I look like?"

I inspected it more closely. Now that the air inside my trailer had stopped eddying, it was reasonably firm of outline. It was a squat, heavy-set ghost, attired in ghostly garments that certainly never had come to it new. It wore the battered ghost of a felt hat, and a stubble of ghostly beard showed on its jowls.

"You look like a tramp ghost," I answered with distaste, and my uninvited visitor nodded.

"Just what I am, chum," he told me. "Call me Spike Higgins. Spike for short. That was my name before it happened."

"Before what happened?" I demanded. The ghost wafted across the trailer to settle down on a bunk, where he lay down and crossed his legs, hoisting one foot encased in a battered ghost of a shoe into the air.

"Before I was amachoor enough to fall asleep riding on top of a truck, and fall off right here fifteen years ago," he told me. "Ever since I been forced to haunt this place. I wasn't no Boy Scout, so I got punished by bein' made to stay here in one spot. Me, who never stayed in one spot two nights running before!

"I been gettin' kind of tired of it the last couple of years. They wouldn't even lemme haunt a house. No, I hadda do all my haunting out in th' open, where th' wind an' rain could get at me, and every dog that went by could bark at me. Chum, you don't know what it means to me to have you pick this place to stop."

"Listen," I said firmly, "you've got to get out of here!"

The apparition yawned.

"Chum," he said, "you're the one that's trespassin', not me. This is my happy haunting ground. Did I ask you to stop here?"

'You mean," I asked between clenched teeth, "that you won't go? You're going to stay here all night?"

"Right, chum," the ghost grunted. "Gimme a call for six A.M." He closed his eyes, and began snoring in an artificial and highly insulting manner.

Then I got sore. I threw the book at him, and it bounced off the bunk without bothering him in the least. Spike Higgins opened an eye and leered at me.

"Went right through me," he chortled. "Instead of me goin' through it. Ha ha! Ha ha ha! Joke."

"You—" I yelled, in a rage. "You—stuff!"

And I slammed him with the chair cushion, which likewise went through him without doing any damage. Spike Higgins opened both eyes and stuck out his tongue at me.

Obviously I couldn't hurt him, so I got control of myself.

"Listen," I said craftily. "You say you are doomed to haunt this spot forever? You can't leave?"

"Forbidden to leave," Spike answered. "Why?"

"Never mind," I grinned. "You'll find out."

I snatched up my slicker and hat and scrambled out into the storm. If that ghost was doomed to remain in that spot forever, I wasn't. I got in the car, got the motor going, and backed out of there. It took a lot of maneuvering in the rain, with mud underwheel, but I made it. I got straightened out on the concrete and headed westward.

I didn't stop until I'd covered twenty miles. Then, beginning to grin as I thought of the shock the ghost of Spike Higgins must have felt when I yanked the trailer right out from under him, I parked on a stretch of old, unused road and then crawled back into the trailer again.

Inside, I slammed the door and—

Ha!

Ha ha!

Ha ha ha!

Yes, more bitter laughter. Spike Higgins was still there, sound asleep and snoring.

I muttered something under my breath. Spike Higgins opened his eyes sleepily.

"Hello," he yawned. "Been having fun?"

"Listen," I finally got it out. "I—thought—you—were—doomed—to—stay—back—there—where—I—found—you—forever!"

The apparition yawned again.

"Your mistake, chum. I didn't say I was doomed to stay. I said I was forbidden to leave. I didn't leave. You hauled me away. It's all your responsibility and I'm a free agent now."

"You're a what?"

"I'm a free agent. I can ramble as far as I please. I can take up hoboing again. You've freed me. Thanks, chum. I won't forget."

"Then—then—" I sputtered. Spike Higgins nodded.

"That's right. I've adopted you. I'm going to stick with you. We'll travel together."

"But you can't!" I cried out, aghast. "Ghosts don't travel around! They haunt houses—or cemeteries—or maybe woods. But—"

"What do you know about ghosts?" Spike Higgins' voice held sarcasm. "There's all kinds of ghosts, chum. Includin' hobo ghosts, tramp ghosts, ghosts with itchin' feet who can't stay put in one spot. Let me tell you, chum, a 'bo ghost like me ain't never had no easy time of it.

"Suppose they do give him a house to haunt? All right, he's got a roof over his head, but there he is, stuck. Houses don't move around. They don't go places. They stay in one spot till they rot.

"But things are different now. You've helped bring in a new age for the brotherhood of spooks. Now a fellow can haunt a house and be on the move at the same time. He can work at his job and still see the country. These trailers are the answer to a problem that's been bafflin' the best minds in th' spirit world for thousands of years. It's the newest thing, the latest and best. Haunted trailers. I tell you, we'll probably erect a monument to you at our next meeting. The ghost of a monument, anyway."

Spike Higgins had raised up on an elbow to make his speech. Now, grimacing, he lay back.

"That's enough, chum," he muttered. "Talking uses up my essence. I'm going to merge for a while. See you in the morning."

"Merge with what?" I asked. Spike Higgins was already so dim I could hardly see him.

"Merge with the otherwhere," a faint, distant voice told me, and Spike Higgins was gone.

I waited a minute to make sure. Then I breathed a big sigh of relief. I looked at my slicker, at my wet feet, at the book on the floor, and knew it had all been a dream. I'd been walking in my sleep. Driving in it, too. Having a nightmare.

I hung up the slicker, slid out of my clothes, and got into a bunk.

I woke up late, and for a moment felt panic. Then I breathed easily again. The other bunk was untenanted. Whistling, I jumped up, showered, dressed, ate, and got under way.

It was a swell day. Blue sky, wind, sunshine, birds singing. Thinking of Monica, I almost sang with them as I rolled down the road. In a week I'd be pulling up in front of Monica's aunt's place in Hollywood and tooting the horn—

That was the moment when a cold draught of air sighed along the back of my neck, and the short hairs rose.

I turned, almost smacking into a hay wagon. Beside me was a misty figure.

"I got tired of riding back there alone," Spike Higgins told me. "I'm gonna ride up front a while an' look at th' scenery."

"You—you—" I shook with rage so that we nearly ran off the road. Spike Higgins reached out, grabbed the wheel in tenuous fingers, and jerked us back onto our course again.

"Take it easy, chum," he said. "There's enough competition in this world I'm in, without you hornin' into th' racket."

I didn't say anything, but my thoughts must have been written on my face. I'd thought he was just a nightmare. But he was real. A ghost had moved in on me, and I hadn't the faintest idea how to move him out.

Spike Higgins grinned with a trace of malice.

"Sure, chum," he said. "It's perfectly logical. There's haunted castles, haunted palaces, and haunted houses. Why not a haunted trailer?"

"Why not haunted ferryboats?" I demanded with bitterness. "Why not haunted Pullmans? Why not haunted boxcars?"

"You think there ain't?" Spike Higgins' misty countenance registered surprise at my ignorance. "Could I tell you tales! There's a haunted ferryboat makes the crossing at Poughkeepsie every stormy night at midnight. There's a haunted private car on the Atchison, Santa Fé. Pal of mine haunts it. He always rode the rods, but he was a square dealer, and they gave him the private car for a reward.

"Then there's a boxcar on the New York Central that never gets where it's going. Never has yet. No matter where it starts out for, it winds up some place else. Bunch of my buddies haunt it. And another boxcar on the Southern Pacific that never has a train to pull it. Runs by itself. It's driven I dunno how many dispatchers crazy, when they saw it go past right ahead of a limited. I could tell you—"

"Don't!" I ordered. "I forbid you to. I don't want to hear."

"Why, sure, chum," Spike Higgins agreed. "But you'll get used to it. You'll be seein' a lot of me. Because where thou ghost, I ghost. Pun." He gave a ghostly chuckle and relapsed into silence. I drove along, my mind churning. I had to get rid of him. *Had* to. Before we reached California, at the very latest. But I didn't have the faintest idea in the world how I was going to.

Then, abruptly, Spike Higgins' ghost sat up straight.

"Stop!" he ordered. "Stop, I say!"

We were on a lonely stretch of road, bordered by old cypresses, with weed-grown marshland beyond. I didn't see any reason for stopping. But Spike Higgins reached out and switched off the ignition key. Then he slammed on the emergency brake. We came squealing to a stop, and just missed going into a ditch.

"What did you do that for?" I yelled. "You almost ditched us! Confound you, you ectoplasmic, hitch-hiking nuisance! If I ever find a way to lay hands on you—"

"Quiet, chum!" the apparition told me rudely. "I just seen an old pal of mine. Slippery Samuels. I ain't seen him since he dropped a bottle of nitro just as he was gonna break into a bank in Mobile sixteen years ago. We're gonna give him a ride."

"We certainly are not!" I cried. "This is my car, and I'm not picking up any more—"

"It may be your car," Spike Higgins sneered, "but I'm the resident haunt, and I got full powers to extend hospitality to any buddy ghosts I want, see? Rule 11, subdivision c. Look it up. Hey, Slippery, climb in!"

A finger of fog pushed through the partly open window of the car at his hail, enlarged, and there was was a second apparition in the front seat with me.

The newcomer was long and lean, just as shabbily dressed as Spike Higgins, with a ghostly countenance as mournful as a Sunday School picnic on a rainy day.

"Spike, you old son of a gun," the second spook murmured, in hollow tones that would have brought gooseflesh to a statue. "How've you been? What're you doing here? Who's he?"—nodding at me.

"Never mind him," Spike said disdainfully. "I'm haunting his trailer. Listen, whatever became of the old gang?"

"Still 'boing it," the long, lean apparition sighed. "Nitro Nelson is somewhere around. Pacific Pete and Buffalo Benny are lying over in a haunted jungle some place near Toledo. I had a date to join 'em, but a storm blew me back to Wheeling a couple days ago."

"Mmm," Spike Higgins' ghost muttered. "Maybe we'll run into 'em. Let's go back in my trailer and do a little chinning. As for you, chum, make camp any time you want. Ta ta."

The two apparitions oozed through the back of the coupé and were gone. I was boiling inside, but there was nothing I could do.

I drove on for another hour, went through Toledo, then stopped at a wayside camp. I paid my dollar, picked out a spot, and parked.

But when I entered the trailer, the ghosts of Spike Higgins and Slippery Samuels, the bank robber, weren't there. Nor had they shown up by the time I finished dinner. In fact I ate, washed, and got into bed with no sign of them.

Breathing a prayer that maybe Higgins had abandoned me to go back to 'boing it in the spirit world, I fell asleep. And began to dream. About Monica—

When I woke, there was a sickly smell in the air, and the heavy staleness of old tobacco smoke.

I opened my eyes. Luckily, I opened them prepared for the worst. Even so, I wasn't prepared well enough.

Spike Higgins was back. Ha! Ha ha! Ha ha ha! I'll say he was back. He lay on the opposite bunk, his eyes shut, his mouth open, snoring. Just the ghost of a snore, but quite loud enough. On the bunk above him lay his bank-robber companion. In the easy chair was slumped a third apparition, short and stout, with a round, whiskered face. A tramp spirit, too.

So was the ghost stretched out on the floor, gaunt and cadaverous. So was the small, mournful spook in the bunk above me, his ectoplasmic hand swinging over the side, almost in my face. Tramps, all of them. Hobo spooks. Five hobo phantoms asleep in my trailer!

And there were cigarette butts in all the ash trays, and burns on my built-in writing desk. The cigarettes apparently had just been lit and let burn. The air was choking with stale smoke, and I had a headache I could have sold for a fire alarm, it was ringing so loudly in my skull.

I knew what had happened. During the night Spike Higgins and his pal had rounded up some more of their ex-hobo companions. Brought them back. To *my* trailer. Now—I was so angry I saw all five of them through a red haze that gave their ectoplasm a ruby tinge. Then I got hold of myself.

I couldn't throw them out. I couldn't harm them. I couldn't touch them.

No, there was only one thing I could do. Admit I was beaten. Take my loss and quit while I could. It was a bitter pill to swallow. But if I wanted to reach Monica, if I wanted to enjoy the honeymoon we'd planned, I'd have to give up the fight.

I got into my clothes. Quietly I sneaked out, locking the trailer behind me. Then I hunted up the owner of the trailer camp, a lanky man, hard-eyed, but well-dressed. I figured he must have money.

"Had sort of a party last night, hey?" he asked me, with a leering wink. "I seen lights, an' heard singing, long after midnight. Not loud, though, so I didn't bother you. But it looked like somebody was havin' a high old time."

I gritted my teeth.

"That was me," I said, "I couldn't sleep. I got up and turned on the radio. Truth is, I haven't slept a single night in that trailer. I guess I wasn't built for trailer life. That job cost me $2998 new, just three days ago. I've got the bill-of-sale. How'd you like to buy it for fifteen hundred, and make a few hundred easy profit on it?"

He gnawed his lip, but knew the trailer was a bargain. We settled for thirteen-fifty. I gave him the bill-of-sale, took the money, uncoupled, got into the coupé, and left there.

As I turned the bend in the road, heading westward, there was no sign that Spike Higgins' ghost was aware of what had happened.

I even managed to grin as I thought of his rage when he woke up to find I had abandoned him. It was almost worth the money I'd lost to think of it.

Beginning to feel better, I stepped on the throttle, piling up miles between me and that trailer. At least I was through with Spike Higgins and his friends.

Ha!

Ha ha!

Ha ha ha!

That's what I thought.

Along toward the middle of the afternoon I was well into Illinois. It was open country, and monotonous, so I turned on my radio. And the first thing I got was a police broadcast.

"All police, Indiana and Illinois! Be on the watch for a tan-and-chrome trailer, stolen about noon from a camp near Toledo. The thieves are believed heading west in it. That is all."

I gulped. It couldn't be! But—It sounded like my trailer, all right. I looked in my rear-vision mirror, apprehensively. The road behind was empty. I breathed a small sigh of relief. I breathed it too soon. For at that moment, around a curve half a mile behind me, something swung into sight and came racing down the road after me.

The trailer.

Ha!

Ha ha!

There it came, a tan streak that zipped around the curve and came streaking after me, zigzagging wildly from side to side of the road, making at least sixty—without any car pulling it!

My flesh crawled, and my hair stood on end. I stepped on the throttle. Hard. And I picked up speed in a hurry. In a half-minute I was doing seventy, and the trailer was still gaining. Then I hit eighty—and passed a motorcycle cop parked beside the road.

I had just a glimpse of his pop-eyed astonishment as I whizzed past, with the trailer chasing me fifty yards behind. Then, kicking on his starter, he slammed after us.

Meanwhile, in spite of everything the car would do, the trailer pulled up behind me and I heard the coupling clank as it was hitched on. At once my speed dropped. The trailer was swerving dangerously, and I had to slow. Behind me the cop was coming, siren open wide, but I didn't have to worry about him because Spike Higgins was materializing beside me.

"Whew!" he said, grinning at me. "My essence feels all used up. Thought you could give Spike Higgins and his pals the slip, huh? You'll learn, chum, you'll learn. That trooper looks like a tough baby. You'll have fun trying to talk yourself out of this."

"Yes, but see what it'll get *you,* you ectoplasmic excrescence!" I raged at him. "The trailer will be stored away in some county garage for months, as evidence while I'm being held for trial on the charge of stealing it. And how'll you like haunting a garage?"

Higgins' face changed.

"Say, that's right," he muttered. "My first trip in fifteen years, too."

He put his fingers to his lips, and blew the shrill ghost of a whistle. In a moment the coupé was filled with cold, clammy draughts as Slippery Samuels and the other three apparitions appeared in the seat beside Higgins.

Twisting and turning and seeming to intermingle a lot, they peered out at the cop, who was beside the car now, one hand on his gun butt, trying to crowd me over to the shoulder.

"All right, boys!" Higgins finished explaining. "You know what we gotta do. Me an' Slippery'll take the car. You guys take the trailer."

They slipped through the open windows like smoke. Then I saw Slippery Samuels holding to the left front fender, and Spike Higgins holding to the right, their ectoplasm streaming out horizontal to the road, stretched and thinned by the air rush. And an instant later we began to move with a speed I had never dreamed of reaching.

We zipped ahead of the astonished cop, and the speedometer needle began to climb again. It took the trooper an instant to believe his eyes. Then with a yell he yanked out his gun and fired. A bullet bumbled past; then he was too busy trying to overtake us again to shoot.

The speedometer said ninety now, and was still climbing. It touched a hundred and stuck there. I was trying to pray when down the road a mile I saw a sharp curve, a bridge, and a deep river. I froze. I couldn't even yell.

We came up to the curve so fast that I was still trying to move my lips when we hit it. I didn't make any effort to take it. Instead I slammed on the brakes and prepared to plow straight ahead into a fence, a stand of young poplars, and the river.

But just as I braked, I heard Spike Higgins' ghostly scream, "Allay-OOP!"

And before we reached the ditch, car and trailer swooped up in the air. An instant later at a height of a hundred and fifty feet, we hurtled straight westward over the river and the town beyond.

I'd like to have seen the expression on the face of the motorcycle cop then. As far as that goes, I'd like to have seen my own.

Then the river was behind us, and the town, and we were swooping down toward a dank, gloomy-looking patch of woods through which ran an abandoned railway spur. A moment later we struck earth with a jouncing shock and came to rest.

Spike Higgins and Slippery Samuels let go the fenders and straightened themselves up. Spike Higgins dusted ghostly dust off his palms and leered at me.

"How was that, chum?" he asked. "Neat, hey?"

"How—" I stuttered—"how—"

"Simple," Spike Higgins answered. "Anybody that can tip tables can do it. Just levitation, 'at's all. Hey, meet the boys. You ain't been introduced yet. This is Buffalo Benny, this one is Toledo Ike, this one Pacific Pete."

The fat spook, the cadaverous one, and the melancholy little one appeared from behind the car, and smirked as Higgins introduced them. Then Higgins waved a hand impatiently.

"C'mon, chum," he said. "There's a road there that takes us out of these woods. Let's get going. It's almost dark, and we don't wanna spend the night here. This used to be in Dan Bracer's territory."

"Who's Dan Bracer?" I demanded, getting the motor going, because I was as anxious to get away from there as Spike Higgins' spook seemed to be.

"Just a railroad dick," Spike Higgins said, with a distinctly uneasy grin. "Toughest bull that ever kicked a poor 'bo off a freight."

"So mean he always drunk black coffee," Slippery Samuels put in, in a mournful voice. "Cream turned sour when he picked up the pitcher."

"Not that we was afraid of him—" Buffalo Benny, the fat apparition, squeaked. "But—"

"We just never liked him," Toledo Ike croaked, a sickly look on his ghostly features. "O' course, he ain't active now. He was retired a couple years back, an' jes' lately I got a rumor he was sick."

"Dyin'," Pacific Pete murmured hollowly.

"Dyin'." They all sighed the word, looking apprehensive. Then Spike Higgins' ghost scowled truculently at me.

"Never mind about Dan Bracer," he snapped. "Let's just get goin' out of here. And don't give that cop no more thought. You think a cop is gonna turn in a report that a car and trailer he was chasin' suddenly sailed up in the air an' flew away like a airplane? Not on your sweet life. He ain't gonna say nothing to nobody about it."

Apparently he was right, because after I had gotten out of the woods, with some difficulty, and onto a secondary highway, there was no further sign of pursuit. I headed westward again, and Spike Higgins and his pals moved back to the trailer, where they lolled about, letting my cigarettes burn and threatening to call the attention of the police to me when I complained.

I grew steadily more morose and desperate as the Pacific Coast, and Monica, came nearer. I was behind schedule, due to Spike Higgins' insistence on my taking a roundabout route so they could see the Grand Canyon, and no way to rid myself of the obnoxious haunts appeared. I couldn't even abandon the trailer. Spike Higgins had been definite on that point. It was better to haul a haunted trailer around than to have one chasing you, he pointed out, and shuddering at the thought of being pursued by a trailer full of ghosts wherever I went, I agreed.

But if I couldn't get rid of them, it meant no Monica, no marriage, no honeymoon. And I was determined that nothing as insubstantial as a spirit was going to interfere with my life's happiness.

Just the same, by the time I had gotten over the mountains and into California, I was almost on the point of doing something desperate. Apparently sensing this, Spike Higgins and the others had been on their good behavior. But I could still see no way to get rid of them.

It was early afternoon when I finally rolled into Hollywood, haggard and unshaven, and found a trailer camp, where I parked. Heavy-hearted, I bathed and shaved and put on clean clothes. I didn't know what I was going to say to Monica, but I was already several days behind schedule, and I couldn't put off calling her.

There was a pay phone in the camp office. I looked up Ida Bracer—her aunt's name—in the book, then put through the call.

Monica herself answered. Her voice sounded distraught.

"Oh, Mel," she exclaimed, as soon as I announced myself, "where have you been? I've been expecting you for just days."

"I was delayed," I told her, bitterly. "Spirits. I'll explain later."

"Spirits?" Her tone seemed cold. "Well, anyway, now that you're here at last, I must see you at once. Mel, Uncle Dan is dying."

"Uncle Dan?" I echoed.

"Yes, Aunt Ida's brother. He used to live in Iowa, but a few months ago he was taken ill, and he came out to be with Aunt and me. Now he's dying. The doctor says it's only a matter of hours."

"Dying?" I repeated again. "Your Uncle Dan, from Iowa, dying?"

Then it came to me. I began to laugh. Exultantly.

"I'll be right over!" I said, and hung up.

Still chuckling, I hurried out and unhitched my car. Spike Higgins stared at me suspiciously.

"Just got an errand to do," I said airily. "Be back soon."

"You better be," Spike Higgins' ghost said. "We wanta drive around and see these movie stars' houses later on."

Ten minutes later Monica herself, trim and lovely, was opening the door for me. In high spirits, I grabbed her around the waist, and kissed her. She turned her cheek to me, then, releasing herself, looked at me strangely.

"Mel," she frowned, "what in the world is wrong with you?"

"Nothing," I caroled. "Monica darling, I've got to talk to your uncle."

"But he's too sick to see anyone. He's sinking fast, the doctor says."

"All the more reason why I must see him," I told her, and pushed into the house. "Where is he, upstairs?"

I hurried up, and into the sickroom. Monica's uncle, a big man with a rugged face and a chin like the prow of a battleship, was in bed, breathing heavily.

"Mr. Bracer!" I said, breathless, and his eyes opened slowly.

"Who're you?" a voice as raspy as a shovel scraping a concrete floor growled.

"I'm going to marry Monica," I told him. "Mr. Bracer, have you ever heard of Spike Higgins? Or Slippery Samuels? Or Buffalo Benny, Pacific Pete, Toledo Ike?"

"Heard of 'em?" A bright glow came into the sick man's eyes. "Ha! I'll say I have. And laid hands on 'em, too, more'n once. But they're dead now."

"I know they are," I told him. "But they're still around. Mr. Bracer, how'd you like to meet up with them again?"

"Would I!" Dan Bracer murmured, and his hands clenched in unconscious anticipation. "Ha!"

"Then," I said, "if you'll wait for me in the cemetery the first night after—after—well, anyway, wait for me, and I'll put you in touch with them."

The ex-railroad detective nodded. He grinned broadly, like a tiger viewing its prey, and eager to be after it. Then he lay back, his eyes closed, and Monica, running in, gave a little gasp.

"He's gone!" she said.

"Ha ha!" I chuckled. "Ha ha ha! What a surprise this is going to be to certain parties."

The funeral was held in the afternoon, two days later. I didn't see Monica much in the interim. In the first place, though she hadn't known her uncle well, and wasn't particularly grieved, there were a lot of details to be attended to. In the second place, Spike Higgins and his pals kept me on the jump. I had to drive around Hollywood, to all the stars' houses, to Malibu Beach, Santa Monica, Laurel Canyon, and the various studios, so they could rubberneck.

Then too, Monica rather seemed to be avoiding me, when I did have time free. But I was too inwardly gleeful at the prospect of getting rid of the ghosts of Higgins and his pals to notice.

I managed to slip away from Higgins to attend the funeral of Dan Bracer, but could not help grinning broadly, and even at times chuckling, as I thought of his happy anticipation of meeting Spike Higgins and the others again. Monica eyed me oddly, but I could explain later. It wasn't quite the right moment to go into details.

After the funeral, Monica said she had a headache, so I promised to come around later in the evening. I returned to the trailer to find Spike Higgins and the others sprawled out, smoking my cigarettes again. Higgins looked at me with dark suspicion.

"Chum," he said, "we wanta be hitting the road again. We leave tomorrow, get me?"

"Tonight, Spike," I said cheerfully. "Why wait? Right after sundown you'll be on your way. To distant parts. Tra la, tra le, tum tum te tum."

He scowled, but could think of no objection. I waited impatiently for sundown. As soon as it was thoroughly dark, I hitched up and drove out of the trailer camp, heading for the cemetery where Dan Bracer had been buried that afternoon.

Spike Higgins was still surly, but unsuspicious until I drew up and parked by the low stone wall at the nearest point to Monica's uncle's grave. Then, gazing out at the darkness-shadowed cemetery, he looked uneasy.

"Say," he snarled, "whatcha stoppin' here for? Come on, let's be movin'."

"In a minute, Spike," I said. "I have some business here."

I slid out and hopped over the low wall.

"Mr. Bracer!" I called. "Mr. Bracer!"

I listened, but a long freight rumbling by half a block distant, where the Union Pacific lines entered the city, drowned out any sound. For a moment I could see nothing. Then a misty figure came into view among the headstones.

"Mr. Bracer!" I called as it approached. "This way!"

The figure headed toward me. Behind me Spike Higgins, Slippery Samuels, and the rest of the ghostly crew were pressed against the wall, staring apprehensively into the darkness. And they were able to recognize the dim figure approaching before I could be sure of it.

"Dan Bracer!" Spike Higgins choked, in a high, ghostly squeal.

"It's him!" Slippery Samuels groaned.

"In the spirit!" Pacific Pete wailed. "Oh oh oh oh OH!"

They tumbled backwards, with shrill squeaks of dismay. Dan Bracer's spirit came forward faster. Paying no attention to me, he took out after the retreating five.

Higgins turned and fled, wildly, with the others at his heels. They were headed toward the railroad tracks, over which the freight was still rumbling, and Dan Bracer was now at their heels. Crowding each other, Higgins and Slippery Samuels and Buffalo Benny swung onto a passing car, with Pacific Pete and Toledo Ike catching wildly at the rungs of the next.

They drew themselves up to the top of the boxcars, and stared back. Dan Bracer's ghost seemed, for an instant, about to be left behind. But one long ectoplasmic arm shot out. A ghostly hand caught the rail of the caboose, and Dan Bracer swung aboard. A moment later, he was running forward along the tops of the boxcars, and up ahead of him, Spike Higgins and his pals were racing toward the engine.

That was the last I saw of them—five phantom figures fleeing, the sixth pursuing in happy anticipation. Then they were gone out of my life, headed east.

Still laughing to myself at the manner in which I had rid myself of Spike Higgins' ghost, and so made it possible for Monica and me to be married and enjoy our honeymoon trailer trip after all, I drove to Monica's aunt's house.

"Melvin!" Monica said sharply, as she answered my ring. "What are you laughing about now?"

"Your uncle," I chuckled. "He—"

"My uncle!" Monica gasped. "You—you fiend! You laughed when he died! You laughed all during his funeral! Now you're laughing because he's dead!"

"No, Monica!" I said. "Let me explain. About the spirits, and how I—"

Her voice broke.

"Forcing your way into the house—laughing at my poor Uncle Dan—laughing at his funeral—"

"But Monica!" I cried. "It isn't that way at all. I've just been to the cemetery, and—"

"And came back laughing," Monica retorted. "I never want to see you again. Our engagement is broken. And worst of all is the *way* you laugh. It's so—so ghostly! So spooky. Blood-chilling. Even if you hadn't done the other things, I could never marry a man who laughs like that. So here's your ring. And good-bye."

Leaving me staring at the ring in my hand, she slammed the door. And that was that. Monica is very strong-minded, and what she says, she means. I couldn't even try to explain. About Spike Higgins. And how I'd unconsciously come to laugh that way through associating with five phantoms. After all, I'd just rid myself of them for good. And the only way Monica would ever have believed my story would have been from my showing her Spike Higgins' ghost himself.

Ha!

Ha ha!

Ha ha ha!

If you know anyone who wants to buy a practically unused trailer, cheap, have them get in touch with me.

The Superstitious Ghost

ARTHUR GUITERMAN

The Superstitious Ghost

I'm such a quiet little ghost,
   Demure and inoffensive,
The other spirits say I'm most
   Absurdly apprehensive.

     Through all the merry hours of night
       I'm uniformly cheerful;
     I love the dark; but in the light,
       I own I'm rather fearful.

         Each dawn I cower down in bed,
           In every brightness seeing,
         That weird uncanny form of dread—
           An awful Human Being!

            Of course I'm told they can't exist,
              That Nature would not let them;
            But Willy Spook, the Humanist,
              Declares that he has met them!

He says they do not glide like us,
　　But walk in eerie paces;
They're solid, not diaphanous,
　　With arms! and legs!! and faces!!!

　　And some are beggars, some are kings,
　　　　Some have and some are wanting,
　　They squander time in doing things,
　　　　Instead of simply haunting.

　　　　They talk of "art," the horrid crew,
　　　　　　And things they call "ambitions."
　　　　Oh, yes, I know as well as you
　　　　　　They're only superstitions.

　　　　　　But should the dreadful day arrive
　　　　　　　　When, starting up, I see one,
　　　　　　I'm sure 'twill scare me quite alive;
　　　　　　　　And then—Oh, then I'll be one!

O Ugly Bird!

MANLY WADE WELLMAN

Mr. Onselm and his ugly bird had the whole region completely terrified. Then along came John and his guitar with the silver strings. . . .

O Ugly Bird!

I SWEAR I'm licked before I start, trying to tell you all what Mr. Onselm looked like. Words give out sometimes. The way you're purely frozen to death for fit words to tell the favor of the girl you love. And Mr. Onselm and I pure poison-hated each other from the start. That's a way that love and hate are alike.

He's what folks in the country call a low man, meaning he's short and small. But a low man is low other ways than in inches, sometimes. Mr. Onselm's shoulders didn't wide out as far as his big ears, and they sank and sagged. His thin legs bowed in at the knee and out at the shank, like two sickles put point to point. His neck was as thin as a carrot, and on it his head looked like a swollen-up pale gourd. Thin hair, gray as tree moss. Loose mouth, a little bit open to show long, straight teeth. Not much chin. The right eye squinted, mean and dark, while the hike of his brow stretched the left one wide open. His good clothes fitted his mean body as if they were cut to its measure. Those good clothes of his were almost as much out of match to the rest of him as his long, soft, pink hands, the hands of a man who'd never had to work a tap's worth.

You see now what I mean? I can't say just how he looked, only that he looked hateful.

I first met him when I was coming down from that high mountain's comb, along an animal trail—maybe a deer made it. I was making to go on across the valley and through a pass, on to Hank Mountain where I'd heard tell was the Bottomless Pool. No special reason, just I had the notion to go there. The valley had trees in it, and through and among the trees I saw, here and there down the slope, patchy places and cabins and yards.

135

I hoped to myself I might could get fed at one of the cabins, for I'd run clear out of eating some spell back. I didn't have any money, nary coin of it; just only my hickory shirt and blue-jeans pants and torn old army shoes, and my guitar on its sling cord. But I knew the mountain folks. If they've got anything to eat, a decent-spoken stranger can get the half part of it. Town folks ain't always the same way about that.

Down the slope I picked my way, favoring the guitar just in case I slipped and fell down, and in an hour I'd made it to the first patch. The cabin was two rooms, dog-trotted and open through the middle. Beyond it was a shed and a pigpen. In the yard was the man of the house, talking to who I found out later was Mr. Onselm.

"You don't have any meat at all?" Mr. Onselm inquired him, and Mr. Onselm's voice was the last you'd expect his sort of man to have, it was full of broad low music, like an organ in a big town church. But I decided not to ask him to sing when I'd taken another closer glimpse of him— sickle-legged and gourd-headed, and pale and puny in his fine-fitting clothes. For, small as he was, he looked mad and dangerous; and the man of the place, though he was a big, strong-seeming old gentleman with a square jaw, looked scared.

"I been right short this year, Mr. Onselm," he said, and it was a half-begging way he said it. "The last bit of meat I done fished out of the brine on Tuesday. And I'd sure enough rather not to kill the pig till December."

Mr. Onselm tramped over to the pen and looked in. The pig was a friendly-acting one; it reared up with its front feet against the boards and grunted up, the way you'd know he hoped for something nice to eat. Mr. Onselm spit into the pen.

"All right," he said, granting a favor. "But I want some meal."

He sickle-legged back toward the cabin. A brown barrel stood out in the dog-trot. Mr. Onselm flung off the cover and pinched up some meal between the tips of his pink fingers. "Get me a sack," he told the man.

The man went quick indoors, and quick out he came, with the sack. Mr. Onselm held it open while the man scooped out enough meal to fill it up. Then Mr. Onselm twisted the neck tight shut and the man lashed the neck with twine. Finally Mr. Onselm looked up and saw me standing there with my guitar under my arm.

"Who are you?" he asked, sort of crooning.

"My name's John," I said.

"John what?" Then he never waited for me to tell him John what. "Where did you steal that guitar?"

"This was given to me," I replied him. "I strung it with the silver wires myself."

"Silver," said Mr. Onselm, and he opened his squint eye by a trifle bit.

"Yes, sir." With my left hand I clamped a chord. With my right thumb I picked the silver strings to a whisper. I began to make up a song:

> *"Mister Onselm,*
> *They do what you tell 'em—"*

"That will do," said Mr. Onselm, not so singingly, and I stopped with the half-made-up song. He relaxed and let his eye go back to a squint again.

"They do what I tell 'em," he said, halfway to himself. "Not bad."

We studied each other, he and I, for a few ticks of time. Then he turned away and went tramping out of the yard and off among the trees. When he was gone from sight, the man of the house asked me, right friendly enough, what he could do for me.

"I'm just a-walking through," I said. I didn't want to ask him right off for some dinner.

"I heard you name yourself John," he said. "Just so happens my name's John, too. John Bristow."

"Nice place you got here, Mr. Bristow," I said, looking around. "You cropping or you renting?"

"I own the house and the land," he told me, and I was surprised; for Mr. Onselm had treated him the way a mean-minded boss treats a cropper.

"Oh," I said, "then that Mr. Onselm was just a visitor."

"Visitor?" Mr. Bristow snorted out the word. "He visits ary living soul here around. Lets them know what thing he wants, and they pass it to him. I kindly thought you knew him, you sang about him so ready."

"Oh, I just got that up." I touched the silver strings again. "Many a new song comes to me, and I just sing it. That's my nature."

"I love the old songs better," said Mr. Bristow, and smiled; so I sang one:

> *"I had been in Georgia*
> *Not a many more weeks than three*
> *When I fell in love with a pretty fair girl*
> *And she fell in love with me.*
>
> *"Her lips were red as red could be,*
> *Her eyes were brown as brown,*
> *Her hair was like the thundercloud*
> *Before the rain comes down."*

Gentlemen, you'd ought to been there, to see Mr. Bristow's face shine. He said: "John, you sure enough can sing it and play it. It's a pure pleasure to hark at you."

"I do my possible best," I said. "But Mr. Onselm doesn't like it." I thought for a moment, then I inquired him: "What's the way he can get ary thing he wants in this valley?"

"Shoo, can't tell you what way. Just done it for years, he has."

"Doesn't anybody refuse him?"

"Well, it's happened. Once, they say, Old Jim Desbro refused him a chicken. And Mr. Onselm pointed his finger at Old Jim's mules, they was a-plowing at the time. Them mules couldn't move nary hoof, not till Mr. Onselm had the chicken from Old Jim. Another time there was, Miss Tilly Parmer hid a cake she'd just baked when she seen Mr. Onselm a-coming. He pointed a finger and he dumbed her. She never spoke one mumbling word from that day on to the day she laid down and died. Could hear and know what was said to her, but when she tried to talk she could only just gibble."

"Then he's a hoodoo man," I said. "And that means, the law can't do a thing to him."

"No sir, not even if the law worried itself up about anything going on this far from the county seat." He looked at the meal sack, still standing in the dog-trot. "Near about time for the Ugly Bird to come fetch Mr. Onselm's meal."

"What's the Ugly Bird?" I asked, but Mr. Bristow didn't have to tell me that.

It must have been a-hanging up there over us, high and quiet, and now it dropped down into the yard, like a fish hawk into a pond.

First out I could see it was dark, heavy-winged, bigger by right much than a buzzard. Then I made out the shiny gray-black of the body, like wet slate, and how the body looked to be naked, how it seemed there were feathers only on the wide wings. Then I saw the long thin snaky neck and the bulgy head and the long crane beak. And I saw the two eyes set in the front of the head—set man-fashion in the front, not bird-fashion one on each side.

The feet grabbed for the sack and taloned onto it, and they showed pink and smooth, with five grabby toes on each one. Then the wings snapped, like a tablecloth in a high wind, and it went churning up again, and away over the tops of the trees, taking the sack of meal with it.

"That's the Ugly Bird," said Mr. Bristow to me, so low I could just about hear him. "Mr. Onselm's been companioning with it ever since I could recollect."

"Such a sort of bird I never before saw," I said. "Must be a right scarced-out one. Do you know what struck me while I was a-watching it?"

"Most likely I do know, John. It's got feet look like Mr. Onselm's hands."

"Could it maybe be," I asked, "that a hoodoo man like Mr. Onselm knows what way to shape himself into a bird thing?"

But Mr. Bristow shook his gray head. "It's known that when he's at one place, the Ugly Bird's been sighted at another." He tried to change the subject. "Silver strings on your guitar; I never heard tell of aught but steel strings."

"In the olden days," I told him, "silver was used a many times for strings. It gives a more singy sound."

In my mind I had it made sure that the subject wasn't going to be changed. I tried a chord on my guitar, and began to sing:

> *"You all have heard of the Ugly Bird*
> *So curious and so queer,*
> *It flies its flight by day and night*
> *And fills folks' hearts with fear."*

"John—" Mr. Bristow began to butt in. But I sang on:

> *"I never came here to hide from fear,*
> *And I give you my promised word*
> *That I soon expect to twist the neck*
> *Of the ugly Ugly Bird."*

Mr. Bristow looked sick at me. His hand trembled as it felt in his pocket.

"I wish I could bid you stop and eat with me," he said, "but—here, maybe you better buy you something."

What he gave me was a quarter and a dime. I near about gave them back, but I saw he wanted me to have them. So I thanked him kindly and walked off down the same trail through the trees Mr. Onselm had gone. Mr. Bristow watched me go, looking shrunk up.

Why had my song scared him? I kept singing it:

> *"O Ugly Bird! O Ugly Bird!*
> *You spy and sneak and thieve!*
> *This place can't be for you and me,*
> *And one of us got to leave."*

Singing, I tried to recollect all I'd heard or read or guessed that might help toward studying out what the Ugly Bird was.

Didn't witch folks have partner animals? I'd read, and I'd heard tell, about the animals called familiars. Mostly they were cats or black dogs or such matter as that, but sometimes they were birds.

That might could be the secret, or a right much of it. For the Ugly Bird wasn't Mr. Onselm, changed by witching so he could fly. Mr. Bristow had said the two of them were seen different places at one and the same time. So Mr. Onselm could no way turn himself into the Ugly Bird. They were close partners, no more. Brothers. With the Ugly Bird's feet looking like Mr. Onselm's pink hands.

I was ware of something up in the sky, the big black V of something that flew. It quartered over me, half as high as the highest scrap of woolly white cloud. Once or twice it made a turn, seemingly like wanting to stoop for me like a hawk for a rabbit; but it didn't do any such. Looking up at it and letting my feet find the trail their own way, I rounded a bunch of mountain laurel and there, on a rotten log in the middle of a clearing, sat Mr. Onselm.

His gourd head was sunk down on his thin neck. His elbows set on his crooked knees, and the soft, pink, long hands hid his face, as if he felt miserable. The look of him made me feel disgusted. I came walking close to him.

"You don't feel so brash, do you?" I asked him.

"Go away," he sort of gulped, soft and tired and sick.

"What for?" I wanted to know. "I like it here." Sitting on the log next to him, I pulled my guitar across me. "I feel like singing, Mr. Onselm."

I made it up again, word by word as I sang it:

> *"His father got hung for hog stealing,*
> *His mother got burnt for a witch,*
> *And his only friend is the Ugly Bird. . . ."*

Something hit me like a shooting star, a-slamming down from overhead.

It hit my back and shoulder, and it knocked me floundering forward on one hand and one knee. It was only the mercy of God I didn't fall on my guitar and smash it. I crawled forward a few quick scrambles and made to get up again, shaky and dizzy, to see what had happened.

I saw. The Ugly Bird had flown down and dropped the sack of meal on me. Now it skimmed across the clearing, at the height of the low branches. Its eyes glinted at me, and its mouth came open like a pair of scissors. I saw teeth, sharp and mean, like the teeth of a garfish. Then the Ugly Bird swooped for me, and the wind of its wings was colder than a winter tempest storm.

Without thinking or stopping to think, I flung up my both hands to box it off from me, and it gave back, it flew back from me like the biggest, devilishest hummingbird you'd ever see in a nightmare. I was too dizzy and scared to wonder why it pulled off like that; I had barely the wit to be glad it did.

"Get out of here," moaned Mr. Onselm, not stirring from where he sat.

I take shame to say, I got. I kept my hands up and backed across the clearing and to the trail on the far side. Then I halfway thought I knew where my luck had come from. My hands had lifted my guitar up as the Ugly Bird flung itself at me, and some way it hadn't liked the guitar.

Reaching the trail again, I looked back. The Ugly Bird was perching on the log where I'd been sitting. It slaunched along close to Mr. Onselm, sort of nuzzling up to him. Horrible to see, I'll be sworn. They were sure enough close together. I turned and stumbled off away, along the trail down the valley and off toward the pass beyond the valley.

I found a stream, with stones making steps across it. I followed it down to where it made a wide pool. There I got on my knee and washed my face—it looked pale as clabber in the water image—and sat down with my back to a tree and hugged my guitar and had a rest.

I was shaking all over. I must have felt near about as bad for a while as Mr. Onselm had looked to feel, sitting on that rotten log to wait for his Ugly Bird and—what else?

Had he been hungry near to death? Sick? Or maybe had his own evil set back on him? I couldn't rightly say which.

But after a while I felt some better. I got up and walked back to the trail and along it again, till I came to what must have been the only store thereabouts.

It faced one way on a rough gravelly road that could carry wagon traffic, car traffic, too, if you didn't mind your car getting a good shakeup, and the trail joined on there, right across from the doorway. The building wasn't big but it was good, made of sawed planks, and there was paint on it, well painted on. Its bottom rested on big rocks instead of posts, and it had a roofed open front like a porch, with a bench in there where folks could sit.

Opening the door, I went in. You'll find a many such stores in back country places through the land, where folks haven't built their towns up too close. Two-three counters. Shelves of cans and packages. Smoked meat hung up in one corner, a glass-fronted icebox for fresh meat in another. Barrels here and there, for beans or meal or potatoes. At the end of one counter, a sign says U. S. POST OFFICE, and there's a set of maybe half a dozen pigeonholes to put letters in, and a couple of cigar boxes for stamps and money order blanks. That's the kind of place it was.

The proprietor wasn't in just then. Only a girl, scared and shaky back of the counter, and Mr. Onselm, there ahead of me, a-telling her what it was he wanted.

"I don't care a shuck if Sam Heaver did leave you in charge here," he said with the music in his voice. "He won't stop my taking you with me."

Then he heard me come in, and he swung round and fixed his squint eye and his wide-open eye on me, like two mismated gun muzzles. "You again," he said.

He looked right hale and hearty again. I strayed my hands over the guitar's silver strings, just enough to hear, and he twisted up his face as if it colicked him.

"Winnie," he told the girl, "wait on this stranger and get him out of here."

Her round eyes were scared in her scared face. I thought inside myself that seldom I'd seen as sweet a face as hers, or as scared a one. Her hair was dark and thick. It was like the thundercloud before the rain comes down. It made her paleness look paler. She was small and slim, and she cowered there, for fear of Mr. Onselm and what he'd been saying to her.

"Yes, sir?" she said to me, hushed and shaky.

"A box of crackers, please, ma'am," I decided, pointing to where they were on the shelf behind her. "And a can of those little sardine fish."

She put them on the counter for me. I dug out the quarter Mr. Bristow had given me up the trail, and slapped it down on the counter top between the scared girl and Mr. Onselm.

"Get away!" he squeaked, shrill and sharp and mean as a bat. When I looked at him, he'd jumped back, almost halfway across the floor from the counter. And for just once, his both eyes were big and wide.

"Why, Mr. Onselm, what's the matter?" I wondered him, and I purely was wondering. "This is a good quarter."

I picked it up and held it out for him to take and study.

But he flung himself around, and he ran out of that store like a rabbit. A rabbit with dogs running it down.

The girl he'd called Winnie just leaned against the wall as if she was bone tired. I asked her: "Why did he light out like that?"

I gave her the quarter, and she took it. "That money isn't a scary thing, is it?" I asked.

"It doesn't much scare me," she said, and rang it up on the old cash register. "All that scares me is—Mr. Onselm."

I picked up the box of crackers and the sardines. "Is he courting you?"

She shivered, although it was warm in the store. "I'd sooner be in a hole with a snake than be courted by Mr. Onselm."

"Then why not just tell him to leave you be?"

"He wouldn't hark at that," she said. "He always just does what pleasures him. Nobody dares to stop him."

"So I've heard tell," I nodded. "About the mules he stopped where they stood, and the poor old lady he struck dumb." I returned to the other thing we'd been talking. "But what made him squinch away from that money piece? I'd reckon he loved money."

She shook her head, and the thundercloud hair stirred. "Mr. Onselm never needs any money. He takes what he wants, without paying for it."

"Including you?" I asked.

"Not including me yet." She shuddered again. "He reckons to do that later on."

I put down my dime I had left from what Mr. Bristow had gifted me. "Let's have a coke drink together, you and me."

She rang up the dime, too. There was a sort of dried-out chuckle at the door, like a stone flung rattling down a deep dark well. I looked quick, and I saw two long, dark wings flop away outside. The Ugly Bird had come to spy what we were doing.

But the girl Winnie hadn't seen, and she smiled over her coke drink. I asked her permission to open my fish and crackers on the bench outside. She said I could. Out there, I worried open the can with that little key that comes with it, and had my meal. When I'd finished I put the empty can and cracker box in a garbage barrel and tuned my guitar.

Hearing that, Winnie came out. She told me how to make my way to the pass and on beyond to Hark Mountain. Of the Bottomless Pool she'd heard some talk, though she'd never been to it. Then she harked while I picked the music and sang the song about the girl whose hair was like the thundercloud before the rain comes down. Harking, Winnie blushed till she was pale no more.

Then we talked about Mr. Onselm and the Ugly Bird, and how they had been seen in two different places at once. "But," said Winnie, "nobody's ever seen the two of them together."

"I have," I told her. "And not an hour back."

And I related about how Mr. Onselm had sat, all sick and miserable, on that rotten log, and how the Ugly Bird had lighted beside him and crowded up to him.

She was quiet to hear all about it, with her eyes staring off, the way she might be looking for something far away. When I was done, she said: "John, you tell me it crowded right up to him."

"It did that thing," I said again. "You'd think it was studying how to crawl right inside him."

"Inside him!"

"That's the true fact."

She kept staring off, and thinking.

"Makes me recollect something I heard somebody say once about hoodoo folks," she said after a time. "How there's hoodoo folks can sometimes put a sort of stuff out, mostly in a dark room. And the stuff is part of them, but it can take the shape and mind of some other person—and once in a while, the shape and mind of an animal."

"Shoo," I said, "now you mention it, I've heard some talk of the same thing. And somebody reckoned it might could explain those Louisiana stories about the werewolves."

"The shape and mind of an animal," she repeated herself. "Maybe the shape and mind of a bird. And that stuff, they call it echo—no, ecto— ecto—"

"Ectoplasm," I remembered the word. "That's it. I've even seen a book with pictures in it, they say were taken of such stuff. And it seems to be alive. It'll yell if you grab it or hit it or stab at it or like that."

"Couldn't maybe—" Winnie began, but a musical voice interrupted.

"I say he's been around here long enough," Mr. Onselm was telling somebody.

Back he came. Behind him were three men. Mr. Bristow was one, and there was likewise a tall, gawky man with wide shoulders and a black-stubbly chin, and behind him a soft, smooth-grizzled old man with an old fancy vest over his white shirt.

Mr. Onselm was like the leader of a posse. "Sam Heaver," he crooned at the soft grizzled one, "do you favor having tramps come and loaf around your store?"

The soft old storekeeper looked at me, dead and gloomy. "You better get going, son," he said, as if he'd memorized it.

I laid my guitar on the bench beside me, very careful of it. "You men ail my stomach," I said, looking at them, from one to the next to the next. "You come at the whistle of this half-born, half-bred witch-man. You let him sic you on me like dogs, when I'm hurting nobody and nothing."

"Better go," said the old storekeeper again.

I stood up and faced Mr. Onselm, ready to fight him. He just laughed at me, like a sweetly played horn.

"You," he said, "without a dime in your pocket! What are you a-feathering up about? You can't do anything to anybody."

Without a dime. . . .

But I'd had a dime. I'd spent it for the coke drinks for Winnie and me. And the Ugly Bird had spied in to see me spend it, my silver money, the silver money that scared and ailed Mr. Onselm. . . .

"Take his guitar, Hobe," Mr. Onselm said an order, and the gawky man moved, clumsy but quick and grabbed my guitar off the bench and backed away to the inner door.

"There," said Mr. Onselm, soft of purring, "that takes care of him."

He fairly jumped, too, and grabbed Winnie by her wrist. He pulled her along out of the porch toward the trial, and I heard her whimper.

"Stop him!" I yelled out, but the three of them stood and looked, scared to move or say a word. Mr. Onselm, still holding Winnie with one hand, faced me. He lifted his other hand and stuck out the pink forefinger at me, like the barrel of a pistol.

Just the look his two eyes, squint and wide, gave me made me weary and dizzy to my bones. He was going to witch me, as he'd done the mules, as he'd done the woman who'd tried to hide her cake from him. I turned away from his gaze, sick and—sure, I was afraid. And I heard him giggle, think-ing he'd won already. I took a step, and I was next to that gawky fellow named Hobe, who held my guitar.

I made a quick long jump and started to wrestle it away from him.

"Hang onto that thing, Hobe!" I heard Mr. Onselm sort of choke out, and, from Mr. Bristow:

"Take care, there's the Ugly Bird!"

Its big dark wings flapped like a storm in the air just behind me. But I'd shoved my elbow into Hobe's belly-pit and I'd torn my guitar from his hands, and I turned on my heel to face what was being brought upon me.

A little way off in the open, Mr. Onselm stood stiff and straight as a stone figure in front of an old court house. He still held Winnie by the wrist. Right betwixt them came a-swooping the Ugly Bird at me, the ugliest ugly of all, its long sharp beak pointing for me like a sticky knife.

I dug in my toes and smashed the guitar at it. I swung the way a player swings a ball bat at a pitched ball. Full-slam I struck its bulgy head, right above that sharp beak and across its two eyes, and I heard the loud noise as the polished wood of my music-maker crashed to splinters.

Oh, gentlemen, and down went that Ugly Bird!

Down it went, falling just short of the porch.

Quiet it lay.

Its great big feathered wings stretched out either side, without ary flutter to them. Its beak was driven into the ground like a nail. It didn't kick or flop or stir once.

But Mr. Onselm, where he stood holding Winnie, screamed out the way he might scream if something had clawed out all his insides with one single tearing dig and grab.

He didn't move. I don't even know if his mouth came rightly open to make that scream. Winnie gave a pull with all the strength she had, and tottered back, loose from him. Then, as if only his hold on her had kept him standing, Mr. Onselm slapped right over and dropped down on his face, his arms flung out like the Ugly Bird's wings, his face in the dirt like the Ugly Bird's face.

Still holding on to my broken guitar by the neck, like a club, I walked quick over to him and stooped. "Get up," I bade him, and took hold of what hair he had and lifted up his face to look at it.

One look was a-plenty. From the war, I know a dead man when I see one. I let go Mr. Onselm's hair, and his face went back into the dirt the way you'd know it belonged there.

The other men moved at last, slow and tottery like old men. And they didn't act like my enemies now, for Mr. Onselm who'd made them act thataway was down and dead.

Then Hobe gave a short of shaky scared shout, and we looked where he was looking.

The Ugly Bird looked all of a sudden rotten and mushy, and while we saw that, it was soaking into the ground. To me, anyhow, its body had seemed to turn shadowy and misty, and I could see through it, to pebbles on the ground beneath. I moved close, though I didn't relish moving. The Ugly Bird was melting away, like dirty snow on top of a hot stove; only no wetness left behind.

It was gone, while we watched and wondered and felt bad all over, and at the same time glad to see it go. Nothing left but the hole punched in the dirt by its beak. I stepped closer yet, and with my shoe I stamped the hole shut.

Then Mr. Bristow kneeled on his knee and turned Mr. Onselm over. On the dead face ran lines across, thin and purple, as though he'd been struck down by a blow from a toaster or a gridiron.

"Why," said Mr. Bristow. "Why, John, them's the mark of your guitar strings." He looked up at me. "Your silver guitar strings."

"Silver?" said the storekeeper. "Is them strings silver? Why, friends, silver finishes a hoodoo man."

That was it. All of us remembered that at once.

"Sure enough," put in Hobe. "Ain't it a silver bullet that it takes to kill a witch, or hanging or burning? And a silver knife to kill a witch's cat?"

"And a silver key locks out ghosts, doesn't it?" said Mr. Bristow, getting up to stand among us again.

I looked at my broken guitar and the dangling strings of silver.

"What was the word you said?" Winnie whispered to me.

"Ectoplasm," I replied her. "Like his soul coming out of him—and getting itself struck dead outside his body."

Then there was talk, more important, about what to do now. The men did the deciding. They allowed to report to the county seat that Mr. Onselm's heart had stopped on him, which was what it had done, after all. They went over the tale three-four times, to make sure they'd all tell it the same. They cheered up while they talked it. You couldn't ever call for a bunch of gladder folks to get shed of a neighbor.

Then they tried to say their thanks to me.

"John," said Mr. Bristow, "we'd all of us sure enough be proud and happy if you'd stay here. You took his curse off us, and we can't never thank you enough."

"Don't thank me," I said. "I was fighting for my life."

Hobe said he wanted me to come live on his farm and help him work it on half shares. Sam Heaver offered me all the money he had in his old cash register. I thanked them. To each I said, no, sir, thank you kindly, I'd better not. If they wanted their tale to sound true to the sheriff and the coroner, they'd better help it along by forgetting that I'd ever been around when Mr. Onselm's heart stopped. Anyhow, I meant to go look at that Bottomless Pool. All I was truly sorry about was my guitar had got broken.

But while I was saying all that, Mr. Bristow had gone running off. Now he came back, with a guitar he'd had at his place, and he said he'd be honored if I'd take it instead of mine. It was a good guitar, had a fine tone. So I put my silver strings on it and tightened and tuned them, and tried a chord or two.

Winnie swore by all that was pure and holy she'd pray for me by name each night of her life, and I told her that that would sure enough see me safe from any assault of the devil.

"Assault of the devil, John!" she said, almost shrill in the voice, she meant it so truly. "It's been you who drove the devil from out this valley."

And the others all said they agreed her on that.

"It was foretold about you in the Bible," said Winnie, her voice soft again. " 'There was a man sent from God, whose name was John—' "

But that was far too much for her to say, and she dropped her sweet dark head down, and I saw her mouth tremble and two tears sneak down her cheeks. And I was that abashed, I said good-bye all around in a hurry.

Off I walked toward where the pass would be, strumming my new guitar as I walked. Back into my mind I got an old, old song. I've heard tell that the song's written down in an old-timey book called *Percy's Frolics,* or *Relics,* or some such name:

> *"Lady, I never loved witchcraft,*
> *Never dealt in privy wile,*
> *But evermore held the high way*
> *Of love and honor, free from guile. . . ."*

And though I couldn't bring myself to look back yonder to the place I was leaving forever, I knew that Winnie was a-watching me, and that she listened, listened, till she had to strain her ears to catch the last, faintest end of my song.

The Canterville Ghost

OSCAR WILDE

*For generations his haunting had
spread terror through the castle—and
then an American family arrived to
live there. . . .*

The Canterville Ghost

1

WHEN MR. Hiram B. Otis, the American Minister, bought Canterville Chase, everyone told him he was doing a very foolish thing, as there was no doubt at all that the place was haunted. Indeed, Lord Canterville himself, who was a man of the most punctilious honour, had felt it his duty to mention the fact to Mr. Otis when they came to discuss terms.

"We have not cared to live in the place ourselves," said Lord Canterville, "since my grand-aunt, the Dowager Duchess of Bolton, was frightened into a fit, from which she never really recovered, by two skeleton hands being placed on her shoulders as she was dressing for dinner, and I feel bound to tell you, Mr. Otis, that the ghost has been seen by several living members of my family, as well as by the rector of the parish, the Rev. Augustus Dampier, who is a Fellow of King's College, Cambridge. After the unfortunate accident to the Duchess, none of our younger servants would stay with us, and Lady Canterville often got very little sleep at night, in consequence of the mysterious noises that came from the corridor and the library."

"My lord," answered the Minister, "I will take the furniture and the ghost at a valuation. I come from a modern country, where we have everything that money can buy; and with all our spry young fellows painting the Old World red, and carrying off your best actresses and prima donnas, I reckon that if there were such a thing as a ghost in Europe, we'd have it at home in a very short time in one of our public museums, or on the road as a show."

"I fear that the ghost exists," said Lord Canterville, smiling, "though it may have resisted the overtures of your enterprising impresarios. It has been well-known for three centuries, since 1584 in fact, and always makes its appearance before the death of any member of our family."

"Well, so does the family doctor for that matter, Lord Canterville. But there is no such thing, sir, as a ghost, and I guess the laws of Nature are not going to be suspended for the British aristocracy."

"You are certainly very natural in America," answered Lord Canterville, who did not quite understand Mr. Otis's last observation, "and if you don't mind a ghost in the house, it is all right. Only you must remember I warned you."

A few weeks after this, the purchase was completed, and at the close of the season the Minister and his family went down to Canterville Chase. Mrs. Otis, who, as Miss Lucretia R. Tappan, of West 53d Street, had been a celebrated New York belle, was now a very handsome, middle-aged woman, with fine eyes, and a superb profile. Many American ladies on leaving their native land adopt an appearance of chronic ill-health, under the impression that it is a form of European refinement, but Mrs. Otis had never fallen into this error. She had a magnificent constitution, and a really wonderful amount of animal spirits. Indeed, in many respects, she was quite English, and was an excellent example of the fact that we have really everything in common with America nowadays, except, of course, language. Her eldest son, christened Washington by his parents in a moment of patriotism, which he never ceased to regret, was a fair-haired, rather good-looking young man, who had qualified himself for American diplomacy by leading the cotillion at the Newport Casino for three successive seasons, and even in London was well-known as an excellent dancer. Gardenias and the peerage were his only weaknesses. Otherwise he was extremely sensible. Miss Virginia E. Otis was a little girl of fifteen, lithe and lovely as a fawn, and with a fine freedom in her large blue eyes. She was a wonderful amazon, and had once raced old Lord Bilton on her pony twice round the park, winning by a length and a half, just in front of the Achilles statue, to the huge delight of the young Duke of Cheshire, who proposed to her on the spot, and was sent back to Eton that very night by his guardians, in floods of tears. After Virginia came the twins, who were usually called "The Stars and Stripes," as they were always getting swished. They were delightful boys, and with the exception of the worthy Minister the only true republicans of the family.

As Canterville Chase is seven miles from Ascot, the nearest railway station, Mr. Otis had telegraphed for a waggonette to meet them, and they started on their drive in high spirits. It was a lovely July evening, and the air was delicate with the scent of the pinewoods. Now and then they heard a wood pigeon brooding over its own sweet voice, or saw, deep in the rustling fern, the burnished breast of the pheasant. Little squirrels peered at them from the beech-trees as they went by, and the rabbits scudded away through the brushwood and over the mossy knolls, with their white tails in the air. As they entered the avenue of Canterville Chase, however, the sky became suddenly overcast with clouds, a curious stillness seemed to hold the atmosphere, a great flight of rooks passed silently over their heads, and, before they reached the house, some big drops of rain had fallen.

Standing on the steps to receive them was an old woman, neatly dressed in black silk, with a white cap and apron. This was Mrs. Umney, the housekeeper, whom Mrs. Otis, at Lady Canterville's earnest request, had consented to keep on in her former position. She made them each a low curtsey as they alighted, and said in a quaint, old-fashioned manner, "I bid you welcome to Canterville Chase." Following her, they passed through the fine Tudor hall into the library, a long, low room, panelled in black oak, at the end of which was a large stained-glass window. Here they found tea laid out for them, and, after taking off their wraps, they sat down and began to look round, while Mrs. Umney waited on them.

Suddenly Mrs. Otis caught sight of a dull red stain on the floor just by the fireplace and, quite unconscious of what it really signified, said to Mrs. Umney, "I am afraid something has been spilt there."

'Yes, madam," replied the old housekeeper in a low voice, "blood has been spilt on that spot."

"How horrid," cried Mrs. Otis; "I don't at all care for blood-stains in a sitting-room. It must be removed at once."

The old woman smiled, and answered in the same low, mysterious voice, "It is the blood of Lady Eleanore de Canterville, who was murdered on that very spot by her own husband, Sir Simon de Canterville, in 1575. Sir Simon survived her nine years, and disappeared suddenly under very mysterious circumstances. His body has never been discovered, but his guilty spirit still haunts the Chase. The blood-stain has been much admired by tourists and others, and cannot be removed."

"That is all nonsense," cried Washington Otis; "Pinkerton's Champion Stain Remover and Paragon Detergent will clean it up in no time," and before the terrified housekeeper could interfere he had fallen upon his knees, and was rapidly scouring the floor with a small stick of what looked like a black cosmetic. In a few moments no trace of the blood-stain could be seen.

"I knew Pinkerton would do it," he exclaimed triumphantly, as he looked round at his admiring family; but no sooner had he said these words than a terrible flash of lightning lit up the sombre room, a fearful peal of thunder made them all start to their feet, and Mrs. Umney fainted.

"What a monstrous climate!" said the American Minister calmly, as he lit a long cheroot. "I guess the old country is so over-populated that they have not enough decent weather for everybody. I have always been of opinion that emigration is the only thing for England."

"My dear Hiram," cried Mrs. Otis, "what can we do with a woman who faints?"

"Charge it to her like breakages," answered the Minister; "she won't faint after that"; and in a few moments Mrs. Umney certainly came to. There was no doubt, however, that she was extremely upset, and she sternly warned Mr. Otis to beware of some trouble coming to the house.

"I have seen things with my own eyes, sir," she said, "that would make any Christian's hair stand on end, and many and many a night I have not closed my eyes in sleep for the awful things that are done here." Mr. Otis, however, and his wife warmly assured the honest soul that they were not afraid of ghosts, and, after invoking the blessings of Providence on her new master and making arrangements for an increase of salary, the old housekeeper tottered off to her own room.

2

The storm raged fiercely all that night, but nothing of particular note occurred. The next morning, however, when they came down to breakfast, they found the terrible stain of blood once again on the floor. "I don't think it can be the fault of the Paragon Detergent," said Washington, "for I have tried it with everything. It must be the ghost." He accordingly rubbed out the stain a second time, but the second morning it appeared again. The third morning also it was there, though the library had been locked up at night by Mr. Otis himself, and the key carried upstairs. The whole family were now quite interested; Mr. Otis began to suspect that he had been too dogmatic in his denial of the existence of ghosts, Mrs. Otis expressed her intention of joining the Psychical Society, and Washington prepared a long letter to Messrs. Myers and Podmore on the subject of the Permanence of Sanguineous Stains when connected with Crime. That night all doubts about the objective existence of phantasmata were removed for ever.

The day had been warm and sunny; and, in the cool of the evening, the whole family went out for a drive. They did not return home till nine o'clock, when they had a light supper. The conversation in no way turned upon ghosts, so there were not even those primary conditions of receptive expectation which so often precede the presentation of psychical phenomena. The subjects discussed, as I have since learned from Mr. Otis, were merely such as form the ordinary conversation of cultured Americans of the better class, such as the immense superiority of Miss Fanny Davenport over Sarah Bernhardt as an actress; the difficulty of obtaining green corn, buckwheat cakes, and hominy, even in the best English houses; the importance of Boston in the development of the world-soul; the advantages of the baggage check system in railway travelling; and the sweetness of the New York accent as compared to the London drawl. No mention at all was made of the supernatural, nor was Sir Simon de Canterville alluded to in any way. At eleven o'clock the family retired, and by half-past all the lights were out. Some time after, Mr. Otis was awakened by a curious noise in the corridor, outside his room. It sounded like the clank of metal, and seemed to be coming nearer every moment. He got up at once, and struck a match, and looked at the time. It was exactly one o'clock. He was quite calm, and felt his pulse, which was not at all feverish. The strange noise still continued, and with it he heard distinctly the sound of footsteps. He put on his slippers, took a small oblong phial out of his dressing-case, and opened the door. Right in front of him he saw, in the wan moonlight, an old man of terrible aspect. His eyes were as red burning coals; long grey hair fell over his shoulders in matted coils; his garments, which were of antique cut, were soiled and ragged, and from his wrists and ankles hung heavy manacles and rusty gyves.

"My dear sir," said Mr. Otis, "I really must insist on your oiling those chains, and have brought you for that purpose a small bottle of the Tammany Rising Sun Lubricator. It is said to be completely efficacious upon one application, and there are several testimonials to that effect on the wrapper from some of our most eminent native divines. I shall leave it here for you by the bedroom candles, and will be happy to supply you with more should you require it." With these words the United States Minister laid the bottle down on a marble table, and, closing his door, retired to rest.

For a moment the Canterville ghost stood quite motionless in natural indignation; then, dashing the bottle violently upon the polished floor, he fled down the corridor, uttering hollow groans, and emitting a ghastly green light. Just, however, as he reached the top of the great oak staircase, a door was flung open, two little white-robed figures appeared, and a large pillow whizzed past his head! There was evidently no time to be lost, so hastily adopting the Fourth Dimension of Space as a means of escape, he vanished through the wainscoting, and the house became quite quiet.

On reaching a small secret chamber in the left wing, he leaned up against a moonbeam to recover his breath, and began to try and realise his position. Never, in a brilliant and uninterrupted career of three hundred years, had he been so grossly insulted. He thought of the Dowager Duchess, whom he had frightened into a fit as she stood before the glass in her lace and diamonds; of the four housemaids, who had gone off into hysterics when he merely grinned at them through the curtains of one of the spare bedrooms; of the rector of the parish, whose candle he had blown out as he was coming late one night from the library, and who had been under the care of Sir William Gull ever since, a perfect martyr to nervous disorders; and of old Madame de Tremouillac, who, having wakened up one morning early and seen a skeleton seated in an armchair by the fire reading her diary, had been confined to her bed for six weeks with an attack of brain fever, and, on her recovery, had become reconciled to the Church, and broken off her connection with that notorious sceptic Monsieur de Voltaire. He remembered the terrible night when the wicked Lord Canterville was found choking in his dressing-room, with the knave of diamonds halfway down his throat, and confessed, just before he died, that he had cheated Charles James Fox out of £50,000 at Crockford's by means of that very card, and swore that the ghost had made him swallow it. All his great achievements came back to him again, from the butler who had shot himself in the pantry because he had seen a green hand tapping at the windowpane, to the beautiful Lady Stutfield, who was always obliged to wear a black velvet band round her throat to hide the mark of five fingers burnt upon her white skin, and who drowned herself at last in the carp-pond at the end of the King's Walk. With the enthusiastic egotism of the true artist he went over his most celebrated performances, and smiled bitterly to himself as he recalled to mind his last appearance as "Red Ruben, or the Strangled Babe," his début as "Gaunt Gibeon, the Blood-sucker of Bexley Moor," and the furore he had excited one lovely June evening by merely playing nine-pins with his own bones upon the lawn-tennis ground. And after all this, some wretched modern Americans were to come and offer him the Rising Sun Lubricator, and throw pillows at his head! It was quite unbearable. Besides, no ghosts in history had ever been treated in this manner. Accordingly, he determined to have vengeance, and remained till daylight in an attitude of deep thought.

3

The next morning when the Otis family met at breakfast, they discussed the ghost at some length. The United States Minister was naturally a little annoyed to find that his present had not been accepted. "I have no wish," he said, "to do the ghost any personal injury, and I must say that, considering the length of time he has been in the house, I don't think it is at all polite to throw pillows at him"—a very just remark, at which, I am sorry to say, the twins burst into shouts of laughter. "Upon the other hand," he continued, "if he really declines to use the Rising Sun Lubricator, we shall have to take his chains from him. It would be quite impossible to sleep, with such a noise going on outside the bedrooms."

For the rest of the week, however, they were undisturbed, the only thing that excited any attention being the continual renewal of the blood-stain on the library floor. This certainly was very strange, as the door was always locked at night by Mr. Otis, and the windows kept closely barred. The chameleon-like colour, also, of the stain excited a good deal of comment. Some mornings it was a dull (almost Indian) red, then it would be vermilion, then a rich purple, and once when they came down for family prayers, according to the simple rites of the Free American Reformed Episcopalian Church, they found it a bright emerald-green. These kaleidoscopic changes naturally amused the party very much, and bets on the subject were freely made every evening. The only person who did not enter the joke was little Virginia, who, for some unexplained reason, was always a good deal distressed at the sight of the blood-stain, and very nearly cried the morning it was emerald-green.

The second appearance of the ghost was on Sunday night. Shortly after they had gone to bed they were suddenly alarmed by a fearful crash in the hall. Rushing downstairs, they found that a large suit of old armor had become detached from its stand, and had fallen on the floor, while, seated in a high-backed chair, was the Canterville ghost, rubbing his knees with an expression of acute agony on his face. The twins, having brought their pea-shooters with them, at once discharged two pellets on him, with that accuracy of aim which can only be attained by long and careful practice on a writing-master, while the United States Minister covered him with his revolver, and called upon him, in accordance with Californian etiquette, to hold up his hands! The ghost started up with a wild shriek of rage, and swept through them like a mist, extinguishing Washington Otis' candle as he passed, and so leaving them all in total darkness. On reaching the top of the staircase he recovered himself, and determined to give his celebrated peal of demoniac laughter. This he had on more than one occasion found extremely useful. It was said to have turned Lord Raker's wig gray in a single night, and had certainly made three of Lady Canterville's French governesses give warning before their month was up. He accordingly laughed his most horrible laugh, till the old vaulted roof rang and rang again, but hardly had the fearful echo died away when a door opened, and Mrs. Otis came out in a light blue dressing-gown. "I am afraid you are far from well," she said, "and have brought you a bottle of Dr. Dobell's Tincture." If it is indigestion, you will find it a most excellent remedy." The ghost glared at her in fury, and began at once to make preparations for turning himself into a large black log, an accomplishment for which he was justly renowned, and to which the family doctor always attributed the permanent idiocy of Lord Canterville's uncle, the Hon. Thomas Horton. The sound of approaching footsteps, however, made him hesitate in his fell purpose, so he contented himself with becoming faintly phosphorescent, and vanished with a deep churchyard groan, just as the twins had come up to him.

On reaching his room he entirely broke down, and became a prey to the most violent agitation. The vulgarity of the twins, and the gross materialism of Mrs. Otis, were naturally extremely annoying, but what really distressed him most was, that he had been unable to wear the suit of mail. He had hoped that even modern Americans would be thrilled by the sight of a Spectre in Armor, if for no more sensible reason, at least out of respect for their national poet Longfellow, over whose graceful and attractive poetry he himself had whiled away many a weary hour when the Cantervilles were up in town. Besides, it was his own suit. He had worn it with great success at the Kenilworth tournament, and been highly complimented on it by no less a person than the Virgin Queen herself. Yet when he had put it on, he had been completely overpowered by the weight of the huge breastplate and steel casque, and had fallen heavily on the stone pavement, barking both his knees severely, and bruising the knuckles of his right hand.

For some days after this he was extremely ill, and hardly stirred out of his room at all, except to keep the blood-stain in proper repair. However, by taking great care of himself, he recovered, and resolved to make a third attempt to frighten the United States Minister and his family. He selected Friday, the 17th of August, for his appearance, and spent most of that day in looking over his wardrobe, ultimately deciding in favour of a large slouched hat with a red feather, a winding-sheet frilled at the wrists and neck, and a rusty dagger. Toward evening a violent storm of rain came on, and the wind was so high that all the windows and doors in the old house shook and rattled. In fact, it was just such weather as he loved. His plan of action was this. He was to make his way quietly to Washington Otis' room, gibber at him from the foot of the bed, and stab himself three times in the throat to the sound of slow music. He bore Washington a special grudge, being quite aware that it was he who was in the habit of removing the famous Canterville blood-stain, by means of Pinkerton's Paragon Detergent. Having reduced the reckless and foolhardy youth to a condition of abject terror, he was then to proceed to the room occupied by the United States Minister and his wife, and there to place a clammy hand on Mrs. Otis's forehead, while he hissed into her trembling husband's ear the awful secrets of the charnel-house. With regard to little Virginia, he had not quite made up his mind. She had never insulted him in any way, and was pretty and gentle. A few hollow groans from the wardrobe, he thought, would be more than sufficient, or, if that failed to wake her, he might grabble at the counterpane with palsy-twitching fingers. As for the twins, he was quite determined to teach them a lesson. The first thing to be done was, of course, to sit upon their chests, so as to produce the stifling sensation of nightmare. Then, as their beds were quite close to each other, to stand between them in the form of a green, icy-cold corpse, till they became paralysed with fear, and finally, to throw off the winding-sheet, and crawl round the room, with white bleached bones and one rolling eyeball, in the character of "Dumb Daniel, or the Suicide's Skeleton," a role in which he had on more than one occasion produced a great effect, and which he considered quite equal to his famous part of "Martin the Maniac, or the Masked Mystery."

At half-past ten he heard the family going to bed. For some time he was disturbed by wild shrieks of laughter from the twins, who, with the lighthearted gaiety of schoolboys, were evidently amusing themselves before they retired to rest, but at a quarter past eleven all was still, and, as midnight sounded, he sallied forth. The owl beat against the windowpanes, the raven croaked from the old yew-tree, and the wind wandered moaning round the house like a lost soul; but the Otis family slept unconscious of their doom, and high above the rain and storm he could hear the steady snoring of the Minister for the United States. He stepped stealthily out of the wainscoting, with an evil smile on his cruel, wrinkled mouth, and the moon hid her face in a cloud as he stole past the great oriel window, where his own arms and those of his murdered wife were blazoned in azure and gold. On and on he glided, like an evil shadow, the very darkness seeming to loathe him as he passed. Once he thought he heard something call, and stopped; but it was only the baying of a dog from the Red Farm, and he went on, muttering strange 16th century curses, and ever and anon brandishing the rusty dagger in the midnight air. Finally he reached the corner of the passage that led to luckless Washington's room. For a moment he paused there, the wind blowing his long gray locks about his head, and twisting into grotesque and fantastic folds the nameless horror of the dead man's shroud. Then the clock struck the quarter, and he felt the time was come. He chuckled to himself, and turned the corner; but no sooner had he done so, than, with a piteous wail of terror, he fell back, and hid his blanched face in his long, bony hands. Right in front of him was standing a horrible spectre, motion-less as a carven image, and monstrous as a madman's dream! Its head was bald and burnished; its face round, and fat, and white; and hideous laughter seemed to have writhed its features into an eternal grin. From the eyes streamed rays of scarlet light, the mouth was a wide well of fire, and a hideous garment, like to his own, swathed with its silent snows the Titan form. On its breast was a placard with strange writing in antique characters, some scroll of shame it seemed, some record of wild sins, some awful cal-endar of crime, and, with its right hand, it bore aloft a falchion of gleaming steel.

Never having seen a ghost before, he naturally was terribly frightened, and, after a second hasty glance at the awful phantom, he fled back to his room, tripping up in his long winding-sheet as he sped down the corridor, and finally dropping the rusty dagger into the Minister's jack-boots, where it was found in the morning by the butler. Once in the privacy of his own apartment, he flung himself down on a small pallet-bed, and hid his face under the clothes. After a time, however, the brave old Canterville spirit asserted itself, and he determined to go and speak to the other ghost as soon as it was daylight. Accordingly, just as the dawn was touching the hills with silver, he returned towards the spot where he had first laid eyes on the grisly phantom, feeling that, after all, two ghosts were better than one, and that, by the aid of his new friend, he might safely grapple with the twins. On reaching the spot, however, a terrible sight met his gaze. Something had evidently happened to the spectre, for the light had entirely faded from its hollow eyes, the gleaming falchion had fallen from its hand, and it was leaning up against the wall in a strained and uncomfortable attitude. He rushed forward and seized it in his arms, when, to his horror, the head slipped off and rolled on the floor, the body assumed a recumbent posture, and he found himself clasping a white dimity bed-curtain, with a sweeping-brush, a kitchen cleaver, and a hollow turnip lying at his feet! Unable to understand this curious transformation, he clutched the placard with feverish haste, and there, in the grey morning light, he read these fearful words:—

Ye Otis Ghoste.

Ye Onlie True and Original Spook.

Beware of Ye Imitationes.

All others are Counterfeite.

The whole thing flashed across him. He had been tricked, foiled, and outwitted! The old Canterville look came into his eyes; he ground his toothless gums together; and, raising his withered hands high above his head, swore, according to the picturesque phraseology of the antique school, that when Chanticleer had sounded twice his merry horn, deeds of blood would be wrought, and Murder walk abroad with silent feet.

Hardly had he finished this awful oath when, from the red-tiled roof of a distant homestead, a cock crew. He laughed a long, low, bitter laugh, and waited. Hour after hour he waited, but the cock, for some strange reason, did not crow again. Finally, at half-past seven, the arrival of the housemaids made him give up his fearful vigil, and he stalked back to his room, thinking of his vain hope and baffled purpose. There he consulted several books of ancient chivalry, of which he was exceedingly fond, and found that, on every occasion on which his oath had been used, Chanticleer had always crowed a second time. "Perdition seize the naughty fowl," he muttered, "I have seen the day when, with my stout spear, I would have run him through the gorge, and made him crow for me an 'twere in death!" He then retired to a comfortable lead coffin, and stayed there till evening.

4

The next day the ghost was very weak and tired. The terrible excitement of the last four weeks was beginning to have its effect. His nerves were completely shattered, and he started at the slightest noise. For five days he kept his room, and at last made up his mind to give up the point of the blood-stain on the library floor. If the Otis family did not want it, they clearly did not deserve it. They were evidently people on a low, material plane of exist-ence, and quite incapable of appreciating the symbolic value of sensuous phenomena. The question of phantasmic apparitions, and the development of astral bodies, was, of course, quite a different matter, and really not under his control. It was his solemn duty to appear in the corridor once a week, and to gibber from the large oriel window on the first and third Wednesday in every month, and he did not see how he could honourably escape from his obligations. It is quite true that his life had been very evil, but, upon the other hand, he was most conscientious in all things connected with the su-pernatural. For the next three Saturdays, accordingly, he traversed the corridor as usual between midnight and three o'clock, taking every possible precaution against being either heard or seen. He removed his boots, trod as lightly as possible on the old worm-eaten boards, wore a large black vel-vet cloak, and was careful to use the Rising Sun Lubricator for oiling his chains. I am bound to acknowledge that it was with a good deal of difficulty that he brought himself to adopt this last mode of protection. However, one night, while the family were at dinner, he slipped into Mr. Otis' bedroom and carried off the bottle. He felt a little humiliated at first, but afterwards was sensible enough to see that there was a great deal to be said for the invention, and, to a certain degree, it served his purpose. Still, in spite of everything, he was not left unmolested. Strings were continually being stretched across the corridor, over which he tripped in the dark, and on one occasion, while dressed for the part of "Black Isaac, or the Huntsman of Hogley Woods," he met with a severe fall, through treading on a butter-slide, which the twins had constructed from the entrance of the Tapestry Chamber to the top of the oak staircase. This last insult so enraged him, that he resolved to make one final effort to assert his dignity and social position, and determined to visit the insolent young Etonians the next night in his celebrated character of "Reckless Rupert, or the Headless Earl."

He had not appeared in this disguise for more than seventy years; in fact, not since he had so frightened pretty Lady Barbara Modish by means of it, that she suddenly broke off her engagement with the present Lord Canter-ville's grandfather, and ran away to Gretna Green with handsome Jack Castleton, declaring that nothing in the world would induce her to marry into a family that allowed such a horrible phantom to walk up and down the terrace at twilight. Poor Jack was afterwards shot in a duel by Lord Canterville on Wandsworth Common, and Lady Barbara died of a broken heart at Tunbridge Wells before the year was out, so, in every way, it had been a great success. It was, however, an extremely difficult "make-up," if I may use such a theatrical expression in connection with one of the greatest mysteries of the supernatural, or, to employ a more scientific term, the higher-natural world, and it took him fully three hours to make his preparations. At last everything was ready, and he was very pleased with his appearance. The big leather riding-boots that went with the dress were just a little too large for him, and he could only find one of the two horse-pistols, but, on the whole, he was quite satisfied, and at a quarter past one he glided out of the wainscoting and crept down the corridor. On reaching the room occupied by the twins, which I should mention was called the Blue Bed Chamber, on account of the colour of its hangings, he found the door just ajar. Wishing to make an effective entrance, he flung it wide open, when a heavy jug of water fell right down on him, wetting him to the skin, and just missing his left shoulder by a couple of inches. At the same moment he heard stifled shrieks of laughter proceeding from the four-post bed. The shock to his nervous system was so great that he fled back to his room as hard as he could go, and the next day he was laid up with a severe cold. The only thing that at all consoled him in the whole affair was the fact that he had not brought his head with him, for, had he done so, the consequences might have been very serious.

He now gave up all hope of ever frightening this rude American family, and contented himself, as a rule, with creeping about the passages in list slippers, with a thick red muffler round his throat for fear of draughts, and a small arquebuse, in case he should be attacked by the twins. The final blow he received occurred on the 19th of September. He had gone downstairs to the great entrance-hall, feeling sure that there, at any rate, he would be quite unmolested, and was amusing himself by making satirical remarks on the large Saroni photographs of the United States Minister and his wife, which had now taken the place of the Centerville family pictures. He was simply but neatly clad in a long shroud, spotted with churchyard mould, had tied up his jaw with a strip of yellow linen, and carried a small lantern and a sexton's spade. In fact, he was dressed for the character of "Jonas the Graveless, or the Corpse-Snatcher of Chertsey Barn," one of his most remarkable impersonations, and one which the Cantervilles had every reason to remember, as it was the real origin of their quarrel with their neighbour, Lord Rufford. It was about a quarter past two o'clock in the morning, and, as far as he could ascertain, no one was stirring. As he was strolling towards the library, however, to see if there were any traces left of the blood-stain, suddenly there leaped out on him from a dark corner two figures, who waved their arms wildly above their heads, and shrieked out "BOO!" in his ear.

Seized with a panic, which, under the circumstances, was only natural, he rushed for the staircase, but found Washington Otis waiting for him there with the big garden-syringe; and being thus hemmed in by his enemies on every side, and driven almost to bay, he vanished into the great iron stove, which, fortunately for him, was not lit, and had to make his way home through the flues and chimneys, arriving at his own room in a terrible state of dirt, disorder, and despair.

After this he was not seen again on any nocturnal expedition. The twins lay in wait for him on several occasions, and strewed the passages with nut-shells every night to the great annoyance of their parents and the servants, but it was of no avail. It was quite evident that his feelings were so wounded that he would not appear. Mr. Otis consequently resumed his great work on the history of the Democratic Party, on which he had been engaged for some years; Mrs. Otis organised a wonderful clambake, which amazed the whole county; the boys took to lacrosse, euchre, poker, and other American national games; and Virginia rode about the lanes on her pony, accompanied by the young Duke of Cheshire, who had come to spend the last week of his holidays at Canterville Chase. It was generally assumed that the ghost had gone away, and, in fact, Mr. Otis wrote a letter to that effect to Lord Canterville, who, in reply, expressed his great pleasure at the news, and sent his best congratulations to the Minister's worthy wife.

The Otises, however, were deceived, for the ghost was still in the house, and though now almost an invalid, was by no means ready to let matters rest, particularly as he heard that among the guests was the young Duke of Cheshire, whose grand-uncle, Lord Francis Stilton, had once bet a hundred guineas with Colonel Carbury that he would play dice with the Canterville ghost, and was found the next morning lying on the floor of the cardroom in such a helpless paralytic state, that though he lived on to a great age, he was never able to say anything again but "Double Sixes." The story was well known at the time, though, of course, out of respect to the feelings of the two noble families, every attempt was made to hush it up; and a full account of all the circumstances connected with it will be found in the third volume of Lord Tattle's *Recollections of the Prince Regent and his Friends.* The ghost, then, was naturally very anxious to show that he had not lost his influence over the Stiltons, with whom, indeed, he was distantly connected, his own first cousin having been married *en secondes noces* to the Sieur de Bulkeley, from whom, as everyone knows, the Dukes of Cheshire are lineally descended. Accordingly, he made arrangements for appearing to Virginia's little lover in his celebrated impersonation of "The Vampire Monk, or, the Bloodless Benedictine," a performance so horrible that when old Lady Startup saw it, which she did on one fatal New Year's Eve, in the year 1764, she went off into the most piercing shrieks, which culminated in violent apoplexy, and died in three days, after disinheriting the Cantervilles, who were her nearest relations, and leaving all her money to her London apothecary. At the last moment, however, his terror of the twins prevented his leaving his room, and the little Duke slept in peace under the great feathered canopy in the Royal Bedchamber, and dreamed of Virginia.

5

A few days after this, Virginia and her curly-haired cavalier went out riding on Brockley meadows, where she tore her habit so badly in getting through a hedge, that, on their return home, she made up her mind to go up by the back staircase so as not to be seen. As she was running past the Tapestry Chamber, the door of which happened to be open, she fancied she saw someone inside, and thinking it was her mother's maid, who sometimes used to bring her work there, looked in to ask her to mend her habit. To her immense surprise, however, it was the Canterville ghost himself! He was sitting by the window, watching the ruined gold of the yellowing trees fly through the air, and the red leaves dancing madly down the long avenue. His head was leaning on his hand, and his whole attitude was one of extreme depression. Indeed, so forlorn, and so much out of repair did he look, that little Virginia, whose first idea had been to run away and lock herself in her room, was filled with pity, and determined to try and comfort him. So light was her footfall, and so deep his melancholy, that he was not aware of her presence till she spoke to him.

"I am so sorry for you," she said, "but my brothers are going back to Eton tomorrow and then, if you behave yourself, no one will annoy you."

"It is absurd asking me to behave myself," he answered, looking round in astonishment at the pretty little girl who had ventured to address him, "quite absurd. I must rattle my chains, and groan through keyholes, and walk about at night, if that is what you mean. It is my only reason for existing."

"It is no reason at all for existing, and you know you have been very wicked. Mrs. Umney told us, the first day we arrived here, that you had killed your wife."

"Well, I quite admit it," said the ghost petulantly, "but it was a purely family matter, and concerned no one else."

"It is very wrong to kill anyone," said Virginia, who at times had a sweet Puritan gravity, caught from some old New England ancestor.

"Oh, I hate the cheap severity of abstract ethics! My wife was very plain, never had my ruffs properly starched, and knew nothing about cookery. Why, there was a buck I had shot in Hogley Woods, a magnificent pricket, and do you know how she had it sent up to table? However, it is no matter now, for it is all over, and I don't think it was very nice of her brothers to starve me to death, though I did kill her."

"Starve you to death? Oh, Mr. Ghost, I mean Mr. Simon, are you hungry? I have a sandwich in my case. Would you like it?"

"No, thank you, I never eat anything now; but it is very kind of you, all the same, and you are much nicer than the rest of your horrid, rude, vulgar, dishonest family."

"Stop!" cried Virginia, stamping her foot, "it is you who are rude, and horrid, and vulgar, and as for dishonesty, you know you stole the paints out of my box to try and furbish up that ridiculous blood-stain in the library. First you took all my reds, including the vermilion, and I couldn't do any more sunsets, then you took the emerald-green and the chrome-yellow, and finally I had nothing left but indigo and Chinese white, and could only do moonlight scenes, which are always depressing to look at, and not at all easy to paint. I never told on you, though I was very much annoyed, and it was most ridiculous, the whole thing; for who ever heard of emerald-green blood?"

"Well, really," said the ghost, rather meekly, "what was I to do? It is a very difficult thing to get real blood nowadays, and, as your brother began it all with his Paragon Detergent, I certainly saw no reason why I should not have your paints. As for colour, that is always a matter of taste: the Cantervilles have blue blood, for instance, the very bluest in England; but I know you Americans don't care for things of this kind."

"You know nothing about it, and the best thing you can do is to emigrate and improve your mind. My father will be only too happy to give you a free passage, and though there is a heavy duty on spirits of every kind, there will be no difficulty about the Custom House as the officers are all Democrats. Once in New York, you are sure to be a great success. I know lots of people there who would give a hundred thousand dollars to have a grandfather, and much more than that to have a family ghost."

"I don't think I should like America."

"I suppose because we have no ruins and no curiosities," said Virginia satirically.

"No ruins! no curiosities!" answered the ghost; "you have your Navy and your manners."

"Good evening; I will go and ask papa to get the twins an extra week's holiday."

"Please don't go, Miss Virginia," he cried; "I am so lonely and so unhappy, and I really don't know what to do. I want to go to sleep and I cannot."

"That's quite absurd! You have merely to go to bed and blow out the candle. It is very difficult sometimes to keep awake, especially at church, but there is no difficulty at all about sleeping. Why, even babies know how to do that, and they are not very clever."

"I have not slept for three hundred years," he said sadly, and Virginia's beautiful blue eyes opened in wonder; "for three hundred years I have not slept, and I am so tired."

Virginia grew quite grave, and her little lips trembled like rose-leaves.

She came towards him, and kneeling down at his side, looked up into his old withered face.

"Poor, poor ghost," she murmured; "have you no place where you can sleep?"

"Far away beyond the pine-woods," he answered, in a low dreamy voice, "there is a little garden. There the grass grows long and deep, there are the great white stars of the hemlock flower, there the nightingale sings all night long. All night long he sings, and the cold, crystal moon looks down, and the yew-tree spreads out its giant arms over the sleepers."

Virginia's eyes grew dim with tears, and she hid her face in her hands.

"You mean the Garden of Death," she whispered.

"Yes, Death. Death must be so beautiful. To lie in the soft brown earth, with the grasses waving above one's head, and listen to silence. To have no yesterday, and tomorrow. To forget time, to forgive life, to be at peace. You can help me. You can open for me the portals of Death's house, for Love is always with you, and Love is stronger than Death is."

Virginia trembled, a cold shudder ran through her, and for a few moments there was silence. She felt as if she was in a terrible dream.

Then the ghost spoke again, and his voice sounded like the sighing of the wind.

"Have you ever read the old prophecy on the library window?"

"Oh, often," cried the little girl, looking up; "I know it quite well. It is painted in curious black letters, and it is difficult to read. There are only six lines:

> " 'When a golden girl can win
> Prayer from out the lips of sin,
> When the barren almond bears,
> And a little child gives away its tears,
> Then shall all the house be still
> And peace come to Canterville.'

"But I don't know what they mean."

"They mean," he said sadly, "that you must weep with me for my sins, because I have no tears, and pray with me for my soul, because I have no faith, and then, if you have always been sweet, and good, and gentle, the Angel of Death will have mercy on me. You will see fearful shapes in darkness, and wicked voices will whisper in your ear, but they will not harm you, for against the purity of a little child the powers of hell cannot prevail."

Virginia made no answer, and the ghost wrung his hands in wild despair as he looked down at her bowed golden head. Suddenly she stood up, very pale, and with a strange light in her eyes. "I am not afraid," she said firmly, "and I will ask the Angel to have mercy on you."

He arose from his seat with a faint cry of joy, and taking her hand bent over it with old-fashioned grace and kissed it. His fingers were as cold as ice, and his lips burned like fire, but Virginia did not falter, as he led her across the dusky room. On the faded green tapestry were broidered little huntsmen. They blew their tasselled horns and with their tiny hands waved to her to go back. "Go back! little Virginia," they cried, "go back!" but the ghost clutched her hand more tightly, and she shut her eyes against them. Horrible animals with lizard tails, and goggle eyes, blinked at her from the carven chimney-piece, and murmured "Beware! little Virginia, beware! we may never see you again," but the ghost glided on more swiftly, and Virginia did not listen. When they reached the end of the room he stopped, and muttered some words she could not understand. She opened her eyes, and saw the wall slowly fading away like a mist, and a great black cavern in front of her. A bitter cold wind swept round them, and she felt something pulling at her dress. "Quick, quick," cried the ghost, "or it will be too late," and, in a moment, the wainscoting had closed behind them, and the Tapestry Chamber was empty.

6

About ten minutes later, the bell rang for tea, and, as Virginia did not come down, Mrs. Otis sent up one of the footmen to tell her. After a little time he returned and said that he could not find Miss Virginia anywhere. As she was in the habit of going out to the garden every evening to get flowers for the dinner-table, Mrs. Otis was not at all alarmed at first, but when six o'clock struck, and Virginia did not appear, she became really agitated, and sent the boys out to look for her, while she herself and Mr. Otis searched every room in the house. At half-past six the boys came back and said that they could find no trace of their sister anywhere. They were all now in the greatest state of excitement, and did not know what to do, when Mr. Otis suddenly remembered that, some few days before, he had given a band of gypsies permission to camp in the park. He accordingly at once set off for Blackfell Hollow, where he knew they were, accompanied by his eldest son and two of the farm-servants. The little Duke of Cheshire, who was perfectly frantic with anxiety, begged hard to be allowed to go too, but Mr. Otis would not allow him, as he was afraid there might be a scuffle. On arriving at the spot, however, he found that the gypsies had gone, and it was evident that their departure had been rather sudden, as the fire was still burning, and some plates were lying on the grass. Having sent off Washington and the two men to scour the district, he ran home, and dispatched telegrams to all the police inspectors in the county, telling them to look out for a little girl who had been kidnapped by tramps or gypsies.

He then ordered his horse to be brought round, and, after insisting on his wife and the three boys sitting down to dinner, rode off down the Ascot Road with a groom. He had hardly, however, gone a couple of miles when he heard somebody galloping after him, and, looking round, saw the little Duke coming up on his pony, with his face very flushed and no hat. "I'm awfully sorry, Mr. Otis," gasped out the boy, "but I can't eat any dinner as long as Virginia is lost. Please, don't be angry with me; if you had let us be engaged last year, there would never have been all this trouble. You won't send me back, will you? I can't go! I won't go!"

The Minister could not help smiling at the handsome young scapegrace, and was a good deal touched at his devotion to Virginia, so leaning down from his horse, he patted him kindly on the shoulders, and said, "Well, Cecil, if you won't go back I suppose you must come with me, but I must get you a hat at. Ascot."

"Oh, bother my hat! I want Virginia!" cried the little Duke, laughing, and they galloped on to the railway station. There Mr. Otis inquired of the station-master if anyone answering the description of Virginia had been seen on the platform, but could get no news of her. The station-master, however, wired up and down the line, and assured him that a strict watch would be kept for her, and, after having bought a hat for the little Duke from a linen-draper, who was just putting up his shutters, Mr. Otis rode off to Bexley, a village about four miles away, which he was told was a well-known haunt of the gypsies, as there was a large common next to it. Here they roused up the rural policeman, but could get no information from him, and, after riding all over the common, they turned their horses' heads homewards, and reached the Chase about eleven o'clock, dead-tired and almost heart-broken. They found Washington and the twins waiting for them at the gate-house with lanterns, as the avenue was very dark. Not the slightest trace of Virginia had been discovered. The gypsies had been caught on Brockley Meadows, but she was not with them, and they had explained their sudden departure by saying that they had mistaken the date of Chorton Fair, and had gone off in a hurry for fear they might be late. Indeed, they had been quite distressed at hearing of Virginia's disappearance, as they were very grateful to Mr. Otis for having allowed them to camp in his park, and four of their number had stayed behind to help in the search. The carp-pond had been dragged, and the whole Chase thoroughly gone over, but without any result. It was evident that, for that night at any rate, Virginia was lost to them; and it was in a state of the deepest depression that Mr. Otis and the boys walked up to the house, the groom following behind with the two horses and the pony. In the hall they found a group of frightened servants, and lying on a sofa in the library was poor Mrs. Otis, almost out of her mind with terror and anxiety, and having her forehead bathed with eau-de-cologne by the old housekeeper. Mr. Otis at once insisted on her having something to eat, and ordered up supper for the whole party. It was a melancholy meal, as hardly anyone spoke, and even the twins were awestruck and subdued, as they were very fond of their sister. When they had finished, Mr. Otis, in spite of the entreaties of the little Duke, ordered them all to bed, saying that nothing more could be done that night, and that he would telegraph in the morning to Scotland Yard for some detectives to be sent down immediately. Just as they were passing out of the dining-room, midnight began to boom from the clock tower, and when the last stroke sounded they heard a crash and a sudden shrill cry; a dreadful peal of thunder shook the house, a strain of unearthly music floated through the air, a panel at the top of the staircase flew back with a loud noise, and out on the landing, looking very pale and white, with a little casket in her hand, stepped Virginia. In a moment they had all rushed up to her. Mrs. Otis clasped her passionately in her arms, the Duke smothered her with violent kisses, and the twins executed a wild war-dance round the group.

"Good heavens! child, where have you been?" said Mr. Otis, rather angrily, thinking that she had been playing some foolish trick on them. "Cecil and I have been riding all over the country looking for you, and your mother has been frightened to death. You must never play these practical jokes any more."

"Except on the ghost! except on the ghost!" shrieked the twins, as they capered about.

"My own darling, thank God you are found; you must never leave my side again," murmured Mrs. Otis, as she kissed the trembling child, and smoothed the tangled gold of her hair.

"Papa," said Virginia quietly, "I have been with the ghost. He is dead, and you must come and see him. He had been very wicked, but he was really sorry for all that he had done, and he gave me this box of beautiful jewels before he died."

The whole family gazed at her in mute amazement, but she was quite grave and serious; and, turning round, she led them through the opening in the wainscoting down a narrow secret corridor, Washington following with a lighted candle, which he had caught up from the table. Finally, they came to a great oak door, studded with rusty nails. When Virginia touched it, it swung back on its heavy hinges, and they found themselves in a little low room, with a vaulted ceiling, and one tiny grated window. Imbedded in the wall was a huge iron ring, and chained to it was a gaunt skeleton, that was stretched out at full length on the stone floor, and seemed to be trying to grasp with its long fleshless fingers an old-fashioned trencher and ewer, that were placed just out of its reach. The jug had evidently been once filled with water, as it was covered inside with green mould. There was nothing on the trencher but a pile of dust. Virginia knelt down beside the skeleton, and, folding her little hands together, began to pray silently, while the rest of the party looked on in wonder at the terrible tragedy whose secret was now disclosed to them.

"Hallo!" suddenly exclaimed one of the twins, who had been looking out of the window to try and discover in what wing of the house the room was situated. "Hallo! the old withered almond tree has blossomed. I can see the flowers plainly in the moonlight."

"God has forgiven him," said Virginia gravely, as she rose to her feet, and a beautiful light seemed to illumine her face.

"What an angel you are!" cried the young Duke, and he put his arm round her neck and kissed her.

7

Four days after these curious incidents a funeral started from Canterville Chase at about eleven o'clock at night. The hearse was drawn by eight black horses, each of which carried on its head a great tuft of nodding ostrich-plumes, and the leaden coffin was covered by a rich purple pall, on which was embroidered in gold the Canterville coat-of-arms. By the side of the hearse and the coaches walked the servants with lighted torches, and the whole procession was wonderfully impressive. Lord Canterville was the chief mourner, having come up specially from Wales to attend the funeral, and sat in the first carriage along with little Virginia. Then came the United States Minister and his wife, then Washington and the three boys, and in the last carriage was Mrs. Umney. It was generally felt that, as she had been frightened by the ghost for more than fifty years of her life, she had a right to see the last of him. A deep grave had been dug in the corner of the churchyard, just under the old yew-tree, and the service was read in the most impressive manner by the Rev. Augustus Dampier. When the ceremony was over, the servants, according to an old custom observed in the Canterville family, extinguished their torches, and, as the coffin was being lowered into the grave, Virginia stepped forward and laid on it a large cross made of white and pink almond-blossoms. As she did so, the moon came out from behind a cloud, and flooded with its silent silver the little churchyard, and from a distant copse a nightingale began to sing. She thought of the ghost's description of the Garden of Death, her eyes became dim with tears, and she hardly spoke a word during the drive home.

The next morning, before Lord Canterville went up to town, Mr. Otis had an interview with him on the subject of the jewels the ghost had given to Virginia. They were perfectly magnificent, especially a certain ruby necklace with old Venetian setting, which was really a superb specimen of 16th century work, and their value was so great that Mr. Otis felt considerable scruples about allowing his daughter to accept them.

"My lord," he said, "I know that in this country mortmain is held to apply to trinkets as well as to land, and it is quite clear to me that these jewels are, or should be, heirlooms in your family. I must beg you, accordingly, to take them to London with you, and to regard them simply as a portion of your property which has been restored to you under certain strange conditions. As for my daughter, she is merely a child, and has as yet, I am glad to say, but little interest in such appurtenances of idle luxury. I am also informed by Mrs. Otis, who, I may say, is no mean authority upon Art—having had the privilege of spending several winters in Boston when she was a girl— that these gems are of great monetary worth, and if offered for sale would fetch a tall price. Under these circumstances, Lord Canterville, I feel sure that you will recognise how impossible it would be for me to allow them to remain in the possession of any member of my family; and, indeed, all such vain gauds and toys, however suitable or necessary to the dignity of the British aristocracy, would be completely out of place among those who have been brought up on the severe, and I believe immortal, principles of republican simplicity. Perhaps I should mention that Virginia is very anxious that you should allow her to retain the box as a memento of your unfortunate but misguided ancestor. As it is extremely old, and consequently a good deal out of repair, you may perhaps think fit to comply with her request. For my own part, I confess I am a good deal surprised to find a child of mine expressing sympathy with mediaevalism in any form, and can only account for it by the fact that Virginia was born in one of your London suburbs shortly after Mrs. Otis had returned from a trip to Athens."

Lord Canterville listened very gravely to the worthy Minister's speech, pulling his gray moustache now and then to hide an involuntary smile, and when Mr. Otis had ended, he shook him cordially by the hand, and said, "My dear sir, your charming little daughter rendered my unlucky ancestor, Sir Simon, a very important service, and I and my family are much indebted to her for her marvellous courage and pluck. The jewels are clearly hers, and, egad, I believe that if I were heartless enough to take them from her, the wicked old fellow would be out of his grave in a fortnight, leading me the devil of a life. As for their being heirlooms, nothing is an heirloom that is not mentioned in a will or legal document, and the existence of these jewels has been quite unknown. I assure you I have no more claim on them than your butler, and when Miss Virginia grows up I daresay she will be pleased to have pretty things to wear. Besides, you forget, Mr. Otis, that you took the furniture and the ghost at a valuation, and anything that belonged to the ghost passed at once into your possession, as, whatever activity Sir Simon may have shown in the corridor at night, in point of law he was really dead, and you acquired his property by purchase."

Mr. Otis was a good deal distressed at Lord Canterville's refusal, and begged him to reconsider his decision, but the good-natured peer was quite firm, and finally induced the Minister to allow his daughter to retain the present the ghost had given her, and when, in the spring of 1890, the young Duchess of Cheshire was presented at the Queen's first drawing-room on the occasion of her marriage, her jewels were the universal theme of admiration. For Virginia received the coronet, which is the reward of all good little American girls, and was married to her boy-lover as soon as he came of age. They were both so charming, and they loved each other so much, that every one was delighted at the match, except the old Marchioness of Dumblton, who had tried to catch the Duke for one of her seven unmarried daughters, and had given no less than three expensive dinner-parties for that purpose, and, strange to say, Mr. Otis himself. Mr. Otis was extremely fond of the young Duke personally, but, theoretically, he objected to titles, and, to use his own words, "was not without apprehension lest, amid the enervating influences of a pleasure-loving aristocracy, the true principles of republican simplicity should be forgotten." His objections, however, were completely overruled, and I believe that when he walked up the aisle of St. George's, Hanover Square, with his daughter leaning on his arm, there was not a prouder man in the whole length and breadth of England.

The Duke and Duchess, after the honeymoon was over, went down to Canterville Chase, and on the day after their arrival they walked over in the afternoon to the lonely churchyard by the pinewoods. There had been a great deal of difficulty at first about the inscription on Sir Simon's tombstone, but finally it had been decided to engrave on it simply the initials of the old gentleman's name, and the verse from the library window. The Duchess had brought with her some lovely roses, which she strewed upon the grave, and after they had stood by it for some time they strolled into the ruined chancel of the old abbey. There the Duchess sat down on a fallen pillar, while her husband lay at her feet smoking a cigarette and looking up at her beautiful eyes. Suddenly he threw his cigarette away, took hold of her hand, and said to her, "Virginia, a wife should have no secrets from her husband."

"Dear Cecil! I have no secrets from you."

"Yes, you have," he answered, smiling, "you have never told me what happened to you when you were locked up with the ghost."

"I have never told anyone, Cecil," said Virginia gravely.

"I know that, but you might tell me."

"Please don't ask me, Cecil, I cannot tell you. Poor Sir Simon! I owe him a great deal. Yes, don't laugh, Cecil, I really do. He made me see what Life is, and what Death signifies, and why Love is stronger than both."

The Duke rose and kissed his wife lovingly.

"You can have your secret as long as I have your heart," he murmured.

"You have always had that, Cecil."

"And you will tell our children some day, won't you?"

Virginia blushed.

He Walked By Day

JULIUS LONG

He couldn't rest because there was still work he had to do. So instead of walking by night. . . .

He Walked By Day

FRIEDENBURG, OHIO, sleeps between the muddy waters of the Miami River and the rusty track of a little-used spur of the Big Four. It suddenly became important to us because of its strategic position. It bisected a road which we were to surface with tar. The materials were to come by way of the spur and to be unloaded at the tiny yard.

We began work on a Monday morning. I was watching the tar distributer while it pumped tar from the car, when I felt a tap upon my back. I turned about, and when I beheld the individual who had tapped me, I actually jumped.

I have never, before or since, encountered such a singular figure. He was at least seven feet tall, and he seemed even taller than that because of the uncommon slenderness of his frame. He looked as if he had never been warmed by the rays of the sun, but confined all his life in a dank and dismal cellar. I concluded that he had been the prey of some insidious, etiolating disease. Certainly, I thought, nothing else could account for his ashen complexion. It seemed that not blood, but shadows passed through his veins.

"Do you want to see me?" I asked.

"Are you the road feller?"

"Yes."

"I want a job. My mother's sick. I have her to keep. Won't you please give me a job?"

We really didn't need another man, but I was interested in this pallid giant with his staring, gray eyes. I called to Juggy, my foreman.

"Do you think we can find a place for this fellow?" I asked.

Juggy stared incredulously. "He looks like he'd break in two."

"I'm stronger'n anyone," said the youth.

He looked about, and his eyes fell on the Mack, which had just been loaded with six tons of gravel. He walked over to it, reached down and seized the hub of a front wheel. To our utter amazement, the wheel was slowly lifted from the ground. When it was raised to a height of eight or nine inches, the youth looked inquiringly in our direction. We must have appeared sufficiently awed, for he dropped the wheel with an abruptness that evoked a yell from the driver, who thought his tire would blow out.

"We can certainly use this fellow," I said, and Juggy agreed.

"What's your name, Shadow?" he demanded.

"Karl Rand," said the boy, but "Shadow" stuck to him, as far as the crew was concerned.

We put him to work at once, and he slaved all morning, accomplishing tasks that we ordinarily assigned two or three men to do.

We were on the road at lunchtime, some miles from Friedenburg. I recalled that Shadow had not brought his lunch.

"You can take mine," I said. "I'll drive in to the village and eat."

"I never eat none," was Shadow's astonishing remark.

"You never eat!" The crew had heard his assertion, and there was an amused crowd about him at once. I fancied that he was pleased to have an audience.

"No, I never eat," he repeated. "You see"—he lowered his voice—"you see, I'm a ghost!"

We exchanged glances. So Shadow was psychopathic. We shrugged our shoulders.

"Whose ghost are you?" gibed Juggy. "Napoleon's?"

"Oh, no. I'm my own ghost. You see, I'm dead."

"Ah!" This was all Juggy could say. For once, the arch-kidder was nonplussed.

"That's why I'm so strong," added Shadow.

"How long have you been dead?" I asked.

"Six years. I was fifteen years old then."

"Tell us how it happened. Did you die a natural death, or were you killed trying to lift a fast freight off the track?" This question was asked by Juggy, who was slowly recovering.

"It was in the cave," answered Shadow solemnly. "I slipped and fell over a bank. I cracked my head on the floor. I've been a ghost ever since."

"Then why do you walk by day instead of by night?"

"I got to keep my mother."

Shadow looked so sincere, so pathetic when he made this answer, that we left off teasing him. I tried to make him eat my lunch, but he would have none of it. I expected to see him collapse that afternoon, but he worked steadily and showed no sign of tiring. We didn't know what to make of him. I confess that I was a little afraid in his presence. After all, a madman with almost superhuman strength is a dangerous character. But Shadow seemed perfectly harmless and docile.

When we had returned to our boarding-house that night, we plied our landlord with questions about Karl Rand. He drew himself up authoritatively, and lectured for some minutes upon Shadow's idiosyncrasies.

"The boy first started telling that story about six years ago," he said. "He never was right in his head, and nobody paid much attention to him at first. He said he'd fallen and busted his head in a cave, but everybody knows they ain't no caves hereabouts. I don't know what put that idea in his head. But Karl's stuck to it ever since, and I 'spect they's lots of folks round Friedenburg that's growed to believe him—more'n admits they do."

That evening, I patronized the village barber shop, and was careful to introduce Karl's name into the conversation. "All I can say is," said the barber solemnly, "that his hair ain't growed any in the last six years, and they was nary a whisker on his chin. Nor, sir, nary a whisker on his chin."

This did not strike me as so tremendously odd, for I had previously heard of cases of such arrested growth. However, I went to sleep that night thinking about Shadow.

The next morning, the strange youth appeared on time and rode with the crew to the job.

"Did you eat well?" Juggy asked him.

Shadow shook his head. "I never eat none."

The crew half believed him.

Early in the morning, Steve Bradshaw, the nozzle man on the tar distributer, burned his hand badly. I hurried him in to see the village doctor. When he had dressed Steve's hand, I took advantage of my opportunity and made inquiries about Shadow.

"Karl's got me stumped," said the country practitioner. "I confess I can't understand it. Of course, he won't let me get close enough to him to look at him, but it don't take an examination to tell there's something abnormal about him."

"I wonder what could have given him the idea that he's his own ghost," I said.

"I'm not sure, but I think what put it in his head was the things people used to say to him when he was a kid. He always looked like a ghost, and everybody kidded him about it. I kind of think that's what gave him the notion."

"Has he changed at all in the last six years?"

"Not a bit. He was as tall six years ago as he is today. I think that his abnormal growth might have had something to do with the stunting of his mind. But I don't know for sure."

I had to take Steve's place on the tar distributer during the next four days, and I watched Shadow pretty closely. He never ate any lunch, but he would sit with us while we devoured ours. Juggy could not resist the temptation to joke at his expense.

"There was a ghost back in my home town," Juggy once told him. "Mary Jenkens was an awful pretty woman when she was living, and when she was a girl, every fellow in town wanted to marry her. Jim Jenkens finally led her down the aisle, and we was all jealous—especially Joe Garver. He was broke up awful. Mary hadn't no more'n come back from the Falls when Joe was trying to make up to her. She wouldn't have nothing to do with him. Joe was hurt bad.

"A year after she was married, Mary took sick and died. Jim Jenkins was awful put out about it. He didn't act right from then on. He got to imagining things. He got suspicious of Joe.

" 'What you got to worry about?' people would ask him. 'Mary's dead. There can't no harm come to her now.'

"But Jim didn't feel that way. Joe heard about it, and he got to teasing Jim.

" 'I was out with Mary's ghost last night,' he would say. And Jim got to believing him. One night, he lays low for Joe and shoots him with both barrels. 'He was goin' to meet my wife!' Jim told the judge."

"Did they give him the chair?" I asked.

"No, they gave him life in the state hospital."

Shadow remained impervious to Juggy's yarns, which were told for his special benefit. During this time, I noticed something decidedly strange about the boy, but I kept my own counsel. After all, a contractor can not keep the respect of his men if he appears too credulous.

One day Juggy voiced my suspicions for me. "You know," he said, "I never saw that kid sweat. It's uncanny. It's ninety in the shade today, and Shadow ain't got a drop of perspiration on his face. Look at his shirt. Dry as if he'd just put it on."

Everyone in the crew noticed this. I think we all became uneasy in Shadow's presence.

One morning he didn't show up for work. We waited a few minutes and left without him. When the trucks came in with their second load of gravel, the drivers told us that Shadow's mother had died during the night. This news cast a gloom over the crew. We all sympathized with the youth.

"I wish I hadn't kidded him," said Juggy.

We all put in an appearance that evening at Shadow's little cottage, and I think he was tremendously gratified. "I won't be working no more," he told me. "There ain't no need for me now."

I couldn't afford to lay off the crew for the funeral, but I did go myself. I even accompanied Shadow to the cemetery.

We watched while the grave was being filled. There were many others there, for one of the chief delights in a rural community is to see how the mourners "take on" at a funeral. Moreover, their interest in Karl Rand was deeper. He had said he was going back to his cave, that he would never again walk by day. The villagers, as well as myself, wanted to see what would happen.

When the grave was filled, Shadow turned to me, eyed me pathetically a moment, then walked from the grave. Silently, we watched him set out across the field. Two mischievous boys disobeyed the entreaties of their parents, and set out after him.

They returned to the village an hour later with a strange and incredible story. They had seen Karl disappear into the ground. The earth had literally swallowed him up. The youngsters were terribly frightened. It was thought that Karl had done something to scare them, and their imaginations had got the better of them.

But the next day they were asked to lead a group of the more curious to the spot where Karl had vanished. He had not returned, and they were worried.

In a ravine two miles from the village, the party discovered a small but penetrable entrance to a cave. Its existence had never been dreamed of by the farmer who owned the land. (He has since then opened it up for tourists, and it is known as Ghost Cave.)

Someone in the party had thoughtfully brought an electric searchlight, and the party squeezed its way into the cave. Exploration revealed a labyrinth of caverns of exquisite beauty. But the explorers were oblivious to the esthetics of the cave; they thought only of Karl and his weird story.

After circuitous ramblings, they came to a sudden drop in the floor. At the base of this precipice they beheld a skeleton.

The coroner and the sheriff were duly summoned. The sheriff invited me to accompany him.

I regret that I cannot describe the gruesome, awesome feeling that came over me as I made my way through those caverns. Within their chambers the human voice is given a peculiar, sepulchral sound. But perhaps it was the knowledge of Karl's bizarre story, his unaccountable disappearance that inspired me with such awe, such thoughts.

The skeleton gave me a shock, for it was a skeleton of a man *seven feet tall!* There was no mistake about this; the coroner was positive.

The skull had been fractured, apparently by a fall over the bank. It was I who discovered the hat near by. It was rotted with decay, but in the leather band were plainly discernible the crudely penned initials, "K.R."

I felt suddenly weak. The sheriff noticed my nervousness. "What's the matter, have you seen a ghost?"

I laughed nervously and affected nonchalance. With the best off-hand manner I could command, I told him of Karl Rand. He was not impressed.

"You don't——?" He did not wish to insult my intelligence by finishing his question.

At this moment, the coroner looked up and commented: "This skeleton has been here about six years, I'd say."

I was not courageous enough to acknowledge my suspicions, but the villagers were outspoken. The skeleton, they declared, was that of Karl Rand. The coroner and the sheriff were incredulous, but, politicians both, they displayed some sympathy with this view.

My friend, the sheriff, discussed the matter privately with me some days later. His theory was that Karl had discovered the cave, wandered inside and come upon the corpse of some unfortunate who had preceded him. He had been so excited by his discovery that his hat had fallen down beside the body. Later, aided by the remarks of the villagers about his ghostliness, he had fashioned his own legend.

This, of course, may be true. But the people of Friedenburg are not convinced by this explanation, and neither am I. For the identity of the skeleton has never been determined, and Karl Rand has never since been seen to walk by day.

When The
Night Wind Howls

W. S. GILBERT

When The
Night Wind Howls

When the night wind howls in the chimney cowls,
    And the bat in the moonlight flies,
And inky clouds, like funeral shrouds,
    Sail over the midnight skies;
When the footpads quail at the night bird's wail,
    And the black dogs bay the moon,
Then is the spectres' holiday,
    Then is the ghosts' high noon!

    As the sob of the breeze sweeps over the trees,
        And the mists lie low in the fen,
    From grey tombstones are gathered the bones
        That once were women and men;
    And away they go, with a mop and a mow,
        To the revel that ends too soon,
    For cock crow limits our holiday,
        The dead of the night's high noon!

        And then each ghost, with his lady toast,
            To their churchyard beds take flight,
        With a kiss, perhaps, on her lantern chaps,
            And a grisly grim "Goodnight."
        Till the welcome knell of the midnight bell
            Rings forth its jolliest tune,
        And ushers in our next high holiday,
            The dead of the night's high noon!

Mr. Whitcomb's Genie

WALTER BROOKS

A genie can be very handy around the house . . . except in time of war when civilians have to do without many things so that the boys in the Army can have whatever they need. That's how Mr. Whitcomb found that war-time rationing and a very efficient genie create unusual problems. . . .

Mr. Whitcomb's Genie

THERE WAS this old couple and their names were Mr. and Mrs. Jethro Whitcomb. They had a small farm up back in the hills with a few cows and some chickens and usually a pig. They sold most of the milk and eggs, but they smoked and pickled the pig. They had a garden and some fruit trees and every summer Mrs. Whitcomb put up three hundred cans of vegetables and fruit. So they always had plenty to eat and the milk and eggs bought them coffee and tea and flour and gas for the old truck. Of course, they rolled up a total of working hours per week that would have put the average industrial worker on the ash heap in a couple of months. But it seemed a comfortable life to them, though naturally no fiesta.

Every spring, Mr. Whitcomb plowed up the garden and harrowed it and then Mrs. Whitcomb took over and put in her vegetables. And one day she was setting out cabbage plants when the piece of broomstick she used to poke the holes for the plants struck something hard just under the surface.

A stone, she thought, and, feeling for the edge of it with her stick, pried it out. But it wasn't a stone. It seemed to be a very low oval pitcher with an odd up-curved snout and a handle at the opposite side. Under the crusted dirt it showed green like corroded brass, and a long scratch—probably made by a harrow tooth—gleamed yellow. So she threw it over in the grass and went on with her planting.

By and by she went in to get dinner and she took the brass thing with her and left it on the back steps, but she didn't think of it again until as she was washing up the dishes Mr. Whitcomb came back into the house and asked her what it was.

187

She told him where she'd found it. "I thought I'd try to shine it up," she said. "It would look real pretty on the parlor mantel."

Mr. Whitcomb said maybe it was some kind of Indian relic because the spring above their garden had once been the site of an Indian encampment and he had turned up a number of arrowheads there through the years. "Though I didn't suppose they had brass," he said.

"They might have got it in trade," said Mrs. Whitcomb, "though for the life of me I don't see what anybody could use it for. Such an unhandy shape."

On fine evenings the Whitcombs always sat out on the porch after supper until the sun went down and then they went to bed because they had to get up early to milk. This evening Mr. Whitcomb brought out the vinegar cruet and rag and went to work on the pitcher. He never liked to be idle unless he was asleep. But he had hardly given more than a few hard rubs with the rag when around the corner of the house came the tallest and swarthiest man they had ever seen. He was just a trifle over eight feet from the soles of his sandals to the top of his turban and all he had on between was a white loincloth. He stood there before them on the grass, blotting out the sunset, and he bowed, touching his breast and his forehead with the fingers of his right hand, and then folded his arms and just stood there.

Without even a growl old Shep jumped up from where he had been lying beside Mrs. Whitcomb's chair and slunk into the house. Mr. Whitcomb sat up straight and his mouth fell open and his pipe dropped on the porch floor, but he didn't even notice it.

Mr. Whitcomb was not scared of much, but Mrs. Whitcomb was not scared of anything and she stopped rocking and said severely, "You ought to be ashamed of yourself going around like that! Go put some clothes on!"

"To hear is to obey," said the man in a voice that rumbled like thunder under the porch roof, and he turned and vanished. But in no time at all he was back and now he had on a loose white robe belted with a green sash through which was thrust a huge scimitar.

The Whitcombs looked at each other uneasily. Then Mr. Whitcomb turned again to the visitor. "Who are you?" he asked and the man said, "I am the slave of the lamp."

"What lamp?" said Mr. Whitcomb and the man said, "The lamp that thy wife found and that lies before thee on the floor."

"Are you a Quaker?" Mr. Whitcomb asked and Mrs. Whitcomb said, "That isn't a lamp—it's a pitcher."

"Wait a minute," said Mr. Whitcomb. "Maybe it's a lamp like they used in ancient times. I've seen pictures of them somewhere. Can you show us how it works?"

The man picked up the pitcher in his huge hand and passed the other hand over it and now they saw that it was filled with oil and from the spout protruded half an inch of wick on which a little flame flickered.

"Great earth and seas!" said Mrs. Whitcomb and Mr. Whitcomb said, "How in the world did you do that?" But the man just put the lamp down in front of them and folded his arms again.

For a minute no one spoke. The Whitcombs fixed their eyes on the lamp, for somehow they felt a great reluctance to look at their guest, and to look at each other was to demand an explanation of things they didn't want to think about.

"Burns nicely," said Mr. Whitcomb. "Well enough," Mrs. Whitcomb replied, "but it's a poor contraption to what we have nowadays." Then she took a deep breath and raised her eyes to the dark face that she could happily not see too clearly because behind it the sky was flaming into orange and gold. "I suppose you are a magician," she said. "Are you with a—a circus?"

"Circus hasn't been through these parts in five years, mother," said Mr. Whitcomb, "and anyway it's too early in the season." Then he looked at the visitor. "That was a good trick with the lamp," he said. "Can you do any others?"

"Whatever you desire, master," said the man.

"Well," said Mr. Whitcomb, "I've always heard a lot about that Indian rope trick."

"You wish me to do it?" the man asked and Mr. Whitcomb said, "Well, if it isn't too much trouble." And he was going on to say that, of course, they couldn't afford to pay for a performance, but they'd be glad to give him some supper if he was hungry. But the man had turned away.

He drew his scimitar and cut down the clothesline that stretched over to a pole across the yard and Mrs. Whitcomb half rose to protest, but before she could say anything he had thrown one end of the line up into the air. And it stayed there. The edge of the porch roof cut off sight of the upper end of the line and Mr. Whitcomb supposed that it must have caught on the telephone wire. But then the man caught hold of the line and began to climb up hand over hand. No telephone wire would support such a weight. Up he went, the scimitar flashing red and gold in the sunlight. The turban disappeared above the edge of the porch roof, then the robe, and last the sandaled feet. They both hurried to the porch railing and looked up. And as they did so the clothesline rustled limply down into the grass. And the man had disappeared.

Mr. Whitcomb laughed shakily. "That was a neat way of getting rid of him, mother," he said.

"I wouldn't have believed it," said Mrs. Whitcomb emphatically. "I wouldn't have believed it if I hadn't seen it."

"Do you believe it?" said Mr. Whitcomb. "I don't."

They looked at each other. There didn't seem to be anything to say. "I think I'd better go in and make a good strong pot of coffee," said Mrs. Whitcomb at last.

"I guess so," said Mr. Whitcomb.

He picked up the lamp and blew it out and then gave it an absent-minded rub with the rag which he still held in his hand. And suddenly there was their visitor again, bowing and touching finger tips to breast and forehead.

"Oh, good land!" said Mr. Whitcomb, but Mrs. Whitcomb paused in the doorway and said, "We promised him supper, Jethro." She measured the man with her eye. "We'll never get him into that kitchen," she said. "I'll fix something and bring it out. You entertain him."

"Entertain him!" said Mr. Whitcomb under his breath. But he went slowly back to his chair. "Sit down," he said. "Mrs. Whitcomb will have something for you in a few minutes."

So the man sat down cross-legged in the grass and, after Mr. Whitcomb had picked up his pipe and taken six matches to relight it, he asked him politely where he came from and the man said, "From the East, master."

"I see," said Mr. Whitcomb, "but how do you come to be in this part of the country?"

"I am the slave of the lamp," said the man, "and I come to do your bidding."

"Well, Mr. Whitcomb saw that he wasn't getting anywhere with his questions and he thought, "Maybe he doesn't understand English very well and I suppose he's just sticking to the regular line of talk he gives his audiences." So he talked about the wet spring and the prospects for a good hay crop and pretty soon Mrs. Whitcomb came out with a tray which she put down on the steps. "Maybe you can manage here," she said. "You're too big to sit in these chairs." And as the man just looked at it, "Eat it! Eat it!" she said.

Well, he ate it. He ate four fried eggs and eight slices of bacon and half a cherry pie, and washed it down with coffee; and when that was gone he ate all the bread and a whole pound of margarine.

"Good grief," said Mrs. Whitcomb, "the man must have been starving!" And she went in and brought out some cold boiled potatoes and a slice of ham and a big plate of doughnuts and the man ate them all to the last crumb.

Mrs. Whitcomb looked rather dismayed, for there was now hardly enough left in the house for breakfast. But she laughed and said, "Well, this has got to stop somewhere and I guess this is the place. I don't suppose you'll be going on any farther tonight?" she said. "We'd like to offer you a bed, but there isn't a bed big enough for you—nor a room either. But you can sleep in the barn if you don't mind. In the hay." And as the man didn't answer she said, "Jethro, you take him out and show him." But first she said, "Give me that sword—you won't need that." So the man handed her the scimitar and then followed Mr. Whitcomb off to the barn.

Well, the Whitcombs sat up later than usual that night talking about the strange visitor. "I told him to go to sleep in there and he lay down and went right to sleep," said Mr. Whitcomb. "He don't act as if he had anywhere to go."

"He doesn't and that's a fact," said Mrs. Whitcomb. "If he didn't have such an almighty appetite it would be nice if he stayed for a while and helped with the chores. He seems willing."

Mr. Whitcomb said, "You aren't afraid of him?" and Mrs. Whitcomb said, "No, I've got a feeling about him that he's harmless. In spite of his never smiling or saying thank you."

"Well, mother, you're usually right about such things," Mr. Whitcomb said, "so we'll see in the morning. But he's a queer customer and no mistake."

So in the morning after he'd milked and turned the cows out he went into the barn, but the man was gone. So he went in to breakfast.

Mrs. Whitcomb said, "I'm just as well pleased, for it would take a lot of work to keep up with that appetite and he would have eaten us out of house and home."

Mr. Whitcomb blew on his coffee and started to drink and then he set it down and said, "Funny about that trick, though—and that lamp business. You don't suppose——"

"I certainly don't," said Mrs. Whitcomb firmly, "and you'd better not go getting ideas, Jethro."

"Just the same——" said Mr. Whitcomb, and he picked up the lamp which Mrs. Whitcomb had put in the middle of the table and gave it a rub with his sleeve. And immediately a shadow fell across the open doorway and that deep voice said, "I am here, master."

"Oh, good Lord!" said Mr. Whitcomb and he went quickly to the door and looked out. "You'd better make about ten stacks of pancakes, mother," he said. "Meanwhile I'm going to try something." And he went out to where the man was standing with his arms folded and said, "Your breakfast will be about half an hour. So see that crowbar? Well, take it over in the garden and see if you can lever that big rock out that sticks up there where Mrs. Whitcomb is planting her cabbages. There," he said when he went back, "I guess that'll keep him busy. 'Twouldn't budge for me the other day." And he sat down at the table.

When Mrs. Whitcomb had the man's breakfast ready she went to the door to call him, but he wasn't anywhere in sight. "Guess you discouraged him that time," she said. "He didn't even touch your crowbar."

So Mr. Whitcomb went to the door and, sure enough, there was the crowbar still leaning against the house and he started to say something and then stopped and grabbed Mrs. Whitcomb by the shoulder and said, "Look!" And they both looked and didn't say anything. For up in the garden where the rock had been there was a big hole. But the rock was gone.

Mr. Whitcomb shook his head. "Can't understand it," he said. "The thing must have weighed half a ton."

But Mrs. Whitcomb turned around and walked determinedly back to the house. Mr. Whitcomb followed more slowly. When he came in the door she said quietly, "Sit down and drink your coffee, Jethro."

He sat down, but he didn't drink—he just peered into his cup for a while and then he said slowly, "I don't know just how far this thing'll go, but I'm going to find out." And he reached out his hand for the lamp.

But Mrs. Whitcomb pulled it away. "If you'll take my advice you'll take this thing out and bury it somewheres." She shook her head angrily. "It just don't bear thinking of!"

"Maybe it don't," said Mr. Whitcomb, "but if it comes to that, there's a lot of things don't bear thinking of. We don't have to think of 'em—we accept 'em. Well, I'm accepting this." He picked up the lamp and rubbed it, and when the shadow fell across the doorway he took the tray Mrs. Whitcomb had set and carried it out. "Eat this," he said, "and then go down to the lower pasture. You'll see some places where the wall needs mending. Fix that so the cows can't get out and then if you have time patch up the roof of the old barn down in the corner of the pasture. You'll find everything you need in the tool house." And he turned and went back indoors.

Well, the Whitcombs went about their work all day as usual and they saw nothing of their peculiar visitor. After supper they walked down to the lower pasture. On two sides the wall had been, for years, just a rubble of loose stones topped with brush to keep the cows in. For they had a mean neighbor on that side who would sue you for damages if you dropped a match on his land. The Whitcombs had been trying for years to get a right-of-way through this Mr. Covell's farm because if they could use his lane it would shorten their route to the village by more than half. But he wouldn't give it to them.

But now the brush on the wall had disappeared and the entire wall had been rebuilt to a height of five feet. It was laid up as straight and even as if half a dozen masons had worked on it for a week. But it was the old barn that they could not believe. Its weather-beaten sides were as loose and warped as they had always been and you could throw a cat through them anywhere, but the roof was a brand-new roof of glistening white shingles.

They looked at the wall and the roof and then they looked at each other. There was really nothing to say. But as always Mr. Whitcomb couldn't leave it at that. He sat down wearily on a rock. "But, mother," he said. "How . . . ? Why . . . ?" And Mrs. Whitcomb, who always talked less, but said more, interrupted him. "We don't know the how or why of anything, Jethro," she said, "and the thing we want to think about now is the what. What do we want done? Come—I'm going back to the house."

Mrs. Whitcomb was always more practical than Mr. Whitcomb and she went straight back and got the lamp and rubbed it and when the man appeared she said slowly as if consulting a list in the back of her mind: "Get me six new aprons and a damask tablecloth and a cut-glass water pitcher and—let me see—a sack of flour and two pounds of butter and a box of raisins and a pail of—no, we don't need any lard. Dear me, I can't think. . . . Well, I guess that will be all. No, wait!" she said, and she hesitated a minute and said, "Get me six ripe pomegranates."

"I hear and obey," said the man as she turned back into the house.

Mr. Whitcomb had heard, too, and he started to protest, but he had hardly begun to speak when there was a thump on the back steps and they looked out and there were all the things they had ordered. Mrs. Whitcomb brought them in and Mr. Whitcomb didn't protest any more when he saw how happy she was and how she stroked the fine tablecloth with her worn old fingers and how she held up the water pitcher to the light so that fire and flame danced in it as if it were filled with diamonds. So then they ate one of the pomegranates and didn't like it much and after that they were pretty tired, so they went to bed. But Mrs. Whitcomb took the water pitcher up and put it on the table where it would be the first thing she saw when she opened her eyes in the morning.

Well, Mr. Whitcomb was pretty uneasy and I guess he would have liked to wash his hands of the whole thing, but at breakfast next morning when he saw how Mrs. Whitcomb's eyes sparkled when she looked at the new water pitcher he just ate what was set before him and then went out to work without saying a word. And as soon as he was gone Mrs. Whitcomb summoned the slave of the lamp and ordered eight rolls of wallpaper with rosebuds on it. For she had wanted to repaper the dining room for ten years, but they had never had enough extra money to do it. She got a couple of sawhorses and laid a plank across them and started to mix the paste and then she thought, "What a ninny I am to do this myself!" and she summoned the genie and told him to paper the room. And she went out and sat in her rocker on the porch.

When Mr. Whitcomb came in for dinner at noon he found the table set in the dining room with a snowy damask tablecloth and the cut-glass water pitcher sparkling in the middle. So he put his arms around Mrs. Whitcomb and hugged her and said, "My, my, it certainly freshens the old place up, doesn't it?" And he pulled up his chair.

That afternoon Mrs. Whitcomb sat out on the porch with her mail-order catalogue and made out a list and when Mr. Whitcomb came in after milking he found a whole row of things on the porch. They were all the things that they had seen pictures of and wished they had, and Mr. and Mrs. Whitcomb just sat down among them like children among their presents on Christmas morning and picked up now one thing and now another and talked in quiet voices about how they'd use it. And then they put their arms around each other and cried a little.

After a while Mrs. Whitcomb jumped up and took Mr. Whitcomb's hand and led him out to the barn and there was a brand-new tractor and beside it stood a new plow with two shares so that it could turn two furrows at once.

"Great earth and seas!" said Mr. Whitcomb, but he had used up most of his astonishment on all the other things and in a minute he climbed into the seat and fussed around till he got it started and then after a little experimenting in the barnyard he made Mrs. Whitcomb get up and stand on the rear axle and hold on to the fenders and he took her on a grand tour of the whole farm.

Well, the lamp altered a good many things in the next few weeks. As Mrs. Whitcomb pointed out, they could just as easily have lived in a palace with a hundred servants and eaten off gold dishes. But what is sometimes called New England caution, but is probably just the ordinary horse sense that is pretty thoroughly distributed through the rural sections of the country—this caution kept them from overdoing it.

"There's only so much work in a horse," said Mr. Whitcomb, "and if you drive him too hard he drops dead on you. This genie ain't any different." So when they had put in a bathroom, with a windmill and a tank to supply it with water, and a hot-water heater and a few other domestic luxuries like that, they limited their demands to such things as a new dress or a pound of the best tea or some good plug tobacco. Except on Mrs. Whitcomb's birthday when Mr. Whitcomb surprised her by having the genie serve a ten-course dinner complete, from caviar canapés, which they didn't like, to little pink candies in silver dishes, which they did. It was served in the front parlor and the last course was an enormous birthday cake with pink icing and seventy candles. But they both ate too much and were uncomfortable afterwards!

They would have liked to put electricity in, but Mr. Whitcomb didn't know how the genie could arrange with the company and anyway he didn't quite trust him to do a safe job of wiring. But he had him help with the farm work. He liked to have somebody to talk to when he was working and the genie was good company because he hardly ever said anything at all. When Mr. Whitcomb told him to do something he just said, "Yes, master."

This form of speech bothered Mr. Whitcomb. "You must talk as we do, Gene," he said. He called the genie Gene.

"O.K., boss," said the genie.

Well, it got along towards haying time and Mr. Whitcomb thought it would be nice to have a new barn, because the old one was no great shakes and the one in the lower pasture was just a small one. So he figured what he needed and then ordered the genie to bring it and in five minutes there was all the lumber—beams and joists and siding and shingles—stacked up neatly in a huge pile, along with kegs of nails and cans of paint and all the hardware and fittings in boxes. And Mr. Whitcomb went right to work.

The slave of the lamp dug a trench and they began laying up the foundation wall.

Well, they had a pretty good start when John Covell drove into the yard. This Mr. Covell was the mean neighbor who had the right of way the Whitcombs wanted. Covell's was the next farm below Whitcomb's, which was at the head of the valley, and it had everything Whitcomb's didn't, including hired help and two hundred cows which were milked by machine. But it did not have a genie. And so Mr. Covell's little eyes blinked rapidly when he saw the building materials and he said, "You aimin' to build, Jethro?"

"New barn," said Mr. Whitcomb.

"How'd you manage priorities?" said Mr. Covell, and Mr. Whitcomb, who hadn't thought about that, began to mumble something when the genie in his working clothes, which were the loincloth and turban, came out from where he had been mixing mortar behind the lumber pile.

"Great roarin' Jehoshaphat!" said Mr. Covell and started for his car.

But Mr. Whitcomb laughed and said, "Wait, John, it's only my new hired man, Gene," so Mr. Covell came back slowly and Mr. Whitcomb introduced them and the genie said, "Pleased to meet you."

Mr. Covell said, "H'm," and fluttered his eyelids slyly as he looked the genie over, and Mr. Whitcomb thought, "He's wondering if he can hire him away from me. He'd give his eyeteeth for such a man if he had them, which he hasn't." But Mr. Covell just said, "Where'd you get him?"

"He just stopped by," said Mr. Whitcomb.

"You like it here?" Mr. Covell asked the genie.

" 'Tain't bad," the genie said.

"He feed you well?" asked Mr. Covell, who never bothered to be tactful with his poorer neighbors.

"Good enough," said the genie.

"Well," said Mr. Covell with a sort of giggle, "if he don't eat more'n he talks it don't cost you much to feed him, Jethro. But I'm surprised the Army didn't get him."

Well, Mr. Whitcomb didn't have anything to say to that, so he said, "What did you want to see me about, John?" and Mr. Covell said he'd started haying and would Mr. Whitcomb come over and lend a hand.

Well, at haying time, with the shortage of labor, you had to help even your enemies, and Mr. Whitcomb said he would, but he didn't have the prudence to leave it at that, but succumbed to the sin of pride and said he'd bring his new tractor if they could use it. Mr. Covell blinked more than ever, but he didn't ask any questions and pretty soon he drove off.

So that afternoon Mr. Whitcomb started out on his tractor. But before he went he told the slave of the lamp to continue work on the new barn. Remembering how quickly the stone wall had been rebuilt, he thought the foundation would be finished long before suppertime. But he started in utter amazement when he drove into the yard at six o'clock and saw the barn standing there complete to the last shingle and door hinge. But what really made Mr. Whitcomb uneasy was that it was all painted. And the paint was dry. He was thoroughly scared.

Well, of course Mr. Whitcomb was not the first man to be scared of a genie. Yet in all such cases it is not the genie who is the real cause for alarm. For the slave of the lamp was not malevolent. But Mr. Covell was. And one day old Tom Pratt, who was a cousin of Mrs. Whitcomb's aunt's second husband, phoned and said, "Jethro, our OPA board's been meetin' in the village and I understand they're coming out to ask you some questions today. I thought I ought to let you know."

"Questions about what?" said Mr. Whitcomb and Mr. Pratt said, "That new barn and those new tires on your tractor that haven't got any serial numbers onto them, and so on. I tell you, Jethro," he said, "there's some of 'em down here on the ration board—John Covell and Henry Sloan 'mongst 'em—that's been fixing to cause you trouble."

"Well, they're the board," said Mr. Whitcomb. "They've got a right to ask."

"Yah! That John Covell!" said Mr. Pratt. "He's had a gretch against you ever since he found out you was eight years older than him and had all your teeth. Talked about it all last winter. And he's been tryin' to get priorities for some lumber, too, and couldn't do it. So instead of bein' open and aboveboard about it he stirs up Henry to put in a complaint. I held out agin 'em as long as I could, Jethro."

"I know you would, Tom, I know you would," Mr. Whitcomb said.

"And there's something about getting the draft board after your hired man, too," Mr. Pratt said. "I hope you can explain it, Jethro."

"I hope so, too," said Mr. Whitcomb and hung up.

Well, by and by, Mr. Covell and Mr. Sloan and another man named Mark Pierce drove into the yard. Mr. Covell sort of hung back, but the others went up to the porch where the Whitcombs were sitting, and Mr. Sloan said, "Well, Jethro, we've got to ask you some questions about that new barn you built."

"What barn?" said Mr. Whitcomb.

Mr. Sloan looked around, but all he saw was the little white-painted house and the old rambling barn that had certainly not been built within the last half century. And he said in a puzzled way, "Why, I understood——"

"Maybe you had reference to that barn," said Mrs. Whitcomb, and she pointed down the valley. For the genie had moved the new barn down into Mr. Covell's woodlot.

So Mr. Sloan turned to Mr. Covell and said, "Why, John, ain't that on your land?"

"Wh-where'd that barn come from?" demanded Mr. Covell and his eyelids blinked so rapidly that you could hardly see them.

"I guess you'd better answer that one, John," said Mr. Pierce, and he looked at Mr. Covell suspiciously.

But Mr. Covell turned and ran for his car and after a second the others followed him. Mr. Whitcomb went along, too. But Mrs. Whitcomb smiled and leaned back in her rocking chair and had the genie bring her a good strong cup of tea and a slice of fruitcake.

Well, the four men drove down to Covell's and got out and followed Mr. Covell up to the woodlot and, sure enough, there right in among the trees was the fine new barn.

"Guess you're the one that's got to explain about priorities, John," said Mr. Pierce.

"But it's Jethro's barn!" shrieked Mr. Covell, who was now almost out of his mind, with rage and bewilderment. "I tell you I saw it being built and night before last I walked up on the hill to look over and see how far Jethro'd got with it and there it was all built—right to the east of the house."

"Yeah," said Mr. Sloan sarcastically, "and I suppose Jethro put it in his wheelbarrow and brought it over here to make you a present of it!"

But Mr. Covell was beyond speech now and he just sat down on a log and gibbered at them, and Mr. Sloan and Mr. Pierce didn't say any more, but just looked worried and took Mr. Covell by the arms and led him back to the house and told his wife to put him to bed. And then they all walked back to Whitcomb's.

So they sat down on the porch and Mrs. Whitcomb brought out some cider and doughnuts and Mr. Pierce said it was a pity Mr. Covell's mind had all give way at once like that. "Accusing you of getting black-market lumber, Jethro," he said, "when he must have been buying it himself."

"And what a crazy notion," said Mr. Sloan, "to build his barn up in the woodlot! I never see anything to beat it."

"Thought nobody'd see it up there, I expect," said Mr. Pierce. "You can't see it from the road."

So they talked for a while and the Whitcombs persuaded them not to take any action against Mr. Covell at least until his mind cleared, and they apologized for causing the Whitcombs trouble and went home. And then Mr. Whitcomb had the genie move the barn back again.

But Mr. Covell was a pretty shrewd citizen and I suspect that maybe in his day he had had some traffic with the supernatural himself, for, a couple of days later, he came up to Whitcomb's again. He got out of his car and hardly glanced at the new barn, but came up and sat down as if nothing had happened and said, "Jethro, you know what they're saying about me down to the village?"

"No," said Mr. Whitcomb, "but I can imagine."

"They're saying I'm stark staring mad—that's what they're saying," said Mr. Covell. His eyes blinked rapidly and he blew hard through his nose and said. "It's all this hanky-panky of yours with the barn. I don't know how you did it, but ain't you harassed and mortified me enough?"

"Well, John," said Mr. Whitcomb, "you've harassed and mortified me plenty in the past."

"You mean that right of way?" said Mr. Covell and Mr. Whitcomb said, "Yes, and I mean setting the OPA onto me. And the draft board, too, I understand."

"I only did my patriotic duty," said Mr. Covell, "for you've got a young able-bodied hired man which there aren't any records of his ever having registered at the local board———"

"Young?" interrupted Mr. Whitcomb. "Why, Gene's older than the hills."

"Nonsense!" Mr. Covell snapped. "I guess you forget that I saw him with my own eyes. Why, he ain't over———"

"Just a minute," said Mr. Whitcomb and he went in the house and rubbed the lamp. When the genie appeared he looked just the same as he had before when Mr. Covell had seen him except that he had a long white beard.

Mr. Covell's eyelids were like a couple of agitated butterflies, only not as pretty, and he went over and climbed up on the porch rail where his face was on a level with the incredible whiskers and examined them and even tugged at them gingerly and then he got down and said wearily, "All right, Jethro, you win. Now what do you want of me?"

Well, Mr. Whitcomb said that all he wanted was just common neighborly consideration.

"You mean that right of way?" said Mr. Covell and Mr. Whitcomb said "Yes."

"All right," Mr. Covell said, "you can have it, provided you can persuade Henry and Mark that the whole barn thing was maybe just a joke. Though what they're going to say the next time they come up and see there isn't any barn in the woodlot———"

"Leave it to me," said Mr. Whitcomb. "I'll guarantee there won't be any talk."

"Well," said Mr. Covell doubtfully, "if you think you can pull the wool over their eyes———"

"You saw me pull it over Gene's chin," said Mr. Whitcomb with a chuckle. "You leave it to me."

Well, the offices of the draft and ration boards were in the town hall and by 10:30 next morning the population of about the entire village was gathered in front of that building. For, piled up between the sidewalk and the front steps, was a miscellany of rationed and high priority goods, and each item had a tag on it addressed to either Mr. Sloan or Mr. Pierce.

Obviously the ignorance these gentlemen expressed as to the origin of the goods was met with deep suspicion. Mr. Sloan and Mr. Pierce were kept much too busy for a while to bother about a little thing like a disappearing barn.

Well, late one afternoon the Whitcombs were sitting on the porch. The genie was in the barn, milking. More and more of the farm work had been turned over to him until now Mr. Whitcomb hardly had anything to do at all and could sit on the porch in his old rocking chair and rock from dawn to dusk except when it rained. And then he took the rocker inside. But this afternoon he was restless. He would get up and go to the edge of the porch and look at the sky and then he would go indoors and wander around aimlessly and at last Mrs. Whitcomb said, "Land sakes, Jethro, what ails you lately? You're as restless as an old gander with the earache."

"Well, I am!" said Mr. Whitcomb crossly, and then he sat down and looked worried and said, "There ain't anything to do!"

Mrs. Whitcomb nodded. "Yes," she said, "I expect that's it. Maybe you've noticed I never have Gene wash the dishes or feed the chickens or cook the meals." She rocked a few minutes in silence and then she said, "Jethro, why don't we get rid of him?"

Well, Mr. Whitcomb brightened up a lot when she said that, but he rocked for quite a while, too, before he said, "Yes, mother. Yes, I guess you've hit it. 'Taint natural the way we've been living. And what ain't natural ain't right."

"I don't know about the right and wrong of it," Mrs. Whitcomb said, "but it isn't what we're accustomed to. And we're too old to change."

Mr. Whitcomb allowed that was true. But there were all those fine things that the genie had brought them.

"I'm not saying a word against them," Mrs. Whitcomb said. "But enough's enough. And some of it has pretty near been too much. That barn pretty near brought us trouble, Jethro. And some day if we keep on we'll find ourselves in a fix we can't get out of. Things you don't pay for don't do you much good."

Well, they talked it over for a long time and at last they agreed that they would wait a week. During that time they would make a list of all the things they thought they ever might want and then they would dismiss the slave of the lamp. They would tell him to take it to Greenland or some-where, because it would do no good just to bury it—they'd be sure to dig it up again some day when they wanted a spool of thread or a bottle of ketchup without the bother of waiting to go to the village.

So at the end of the week Mr. Whitcomb said, "Well, mother, have you got that list?"

"There's nothing on it," said Mrs. Whitcomb. "I couldn't think of anything else I wanted."

"Well, now!" said Mr. Whitcomb and he laughed. "There's nothing on mine, either." So he took the lamp and rubbed it and the genie appeared.

"Well, Gene," Mr. Whitcomb said, "we've about decided that we don't need you any longer."

The genie stood before the porch looking down on them with the fires of the sunset blazing in the sky behind him just as he had the first time they saw him. The swarthy face under the white turban was indistinct, but across it passed something they had never seen on it before—the shadow of a smile.

"What are you smiling at?" said Mr. Whitcomb and the slave said, "At my thoughts, master."

"Tell me your thought," said Mr. Whitcomb and the genie said, "I smile that with all the riches of the world at your feet you turn away."

"Others have had the lamp," said Mr. Whitcomb. "Didn't any of them ever give it up willingly?"

"Sooner or later all were glad to rid themselves of it," said the genie. "None kept it longer than a few months. I have served you longer than most, for you have been wiser than most. But no man is so wise that he can bear to own a world."

"H'm," said Mrs. Whitcomb. "I wouldn't have given them credit for so much sense."

"Well," said Mr. Whitcomb, "before you go we each want to hold back one wish. I expect you know what I mean. We can't think of anything else we want right now, but we want to have one wish that we can use at some time in the future. Is that possible?"

"Yes, master," said the genie, "you each have one wish."

"Very well," said Mr. Whitcomb, "and now before we change our mind take the lamp and go."

"I hear and obey," said the genie and vanished, and when they looked around the lamp was gone.

Well, half an hour later when Mrs. Whitcomb was getting supper she said, "Drat that fire—I wish it would burn properly!" And immediately the fire burned up bright and clear. "Good land, Jethro!" she said, "I've gone and used up my wish already!"

They were pretty upset about it for a while and Mr. Whitcomb realized that he would have to be pretty careful not to express any wish at all until he found the one that he really wanted to come true.

In the next few months it bothered him a good deal. For he didn't think of anything that he really wanted a lot and he had to watch everything he said so carefully that he hardly dared open his mouth. And at last one day he was out in the new barn and he was looking around and thinking how fine it was and how he really had everything he wanted except one thing— the freedom to say he wished for something without expecting to get it. And he said suddenly, "I wish I didn't have any wish coming to me."

And then, of course, he didn't any more. And he went in and told Mrs. Whitcomb and she hugged him and they went out after supper and sat on the porch and wished for everything they could think of just for the fun of not getting anything at all. And I guess they were completely happy.

The Water Ghost

JOHN KENDRICK BANGS

Every Christmas Eve she came, dank and dismal, to make life miserable for the distracted master of Harrowby Hall. . . .

The Water Ghost

THE TROUBLE with Harrowby Hall was that it was haunted, and, what was worse, the ghost did not content itself with merely appearing at the bedside of the afflicted person who saw it, but persisted in remaining there for one mortal hour before it would disappear.

It never appeared except on Christmas Eve, and then as the clock was striking twelve. The owners of Harrowby Hall had done their utmost to rid themselves of the damp and dewy lady who rose up out of the best bedroom floor at midnight. They had tried stopping the clock, so that the ghost would not know when it was midnight; but she made her appearance just the same, and there she would stand until everything about her was thoroughly soaked.

Then the owners of Harrowby Hall calked up every crack in the floor with the very best quality of hemp, and over this were placed layers of tar and canvas. The walls were made waterproof, and the doors and windows likewise, but even this did not help. The following Christmas Eve she appeared as promptly as before, and frightened the occupant of the room quite out of his senses by sitting down alongside of him and gazing with her cavernous blue eyes into his. In her long, bony fingers bits of dripping seaweed were entwined, the ends hanging down, and these ends she drew across his forehead until he swooned away, being found unconscious in his bed the next morning by his host, simply saturated with sea-water and fright.

The next year the master of Harrowby Hall decided not to have the best spare bedroom opened at all, thinking that perhaps the ghost would be satisfied by haunting the furniture. The ghost appeared as usual in the room—that is, it was supposed she did, for the hangings were dripping wet the next morning, and in the parlor below the haunted room a great damp spot appeared on the ceiling. But finding no one there, she set out to haunt the owner of Harrowby himself. She found him in this own cosy room, congratulating himself upon having foiled her. Suddenly the curl went out of his hair and his clothing was soaking wet. He saw before him the lady of the cavernous eyes and seaweed fingers. The sight was so terrifying that he fainted, but immediately came to, because the water in his hair, trickling down over his face, restored him to consciousness.

Now it so happened that the master of Harrowby was a brave man, and he was not to be daunted by an apparition. He had paid the lady the compliment of fainting from the effects of his first surprise, but now he intended to find out a few things he felt he had a right to know. He would have liked to put on a dry suit of clothes first, but the ghost refused to leave him for an instant until her hour was up. Every time he moved she followed him, with the result that everything she came in contact with got a soaking. In an effort to warm himself up he approached the fire, an unfortunate move that brought the ghost directly over the flames, which were immediately extinguished. At this, he turned with some anger to the ghost, and said:

"Far be it from me to be impolite to a woman, madam, but I wish you'd stop your infernal visits to this house. Go sit out on the lake, if you like that sort of thing; but do not, I implore you, come into a gentleman's house and soak him and his possessions in this way!"

"Henry Hartwick Oglethorpe," said the ghost, in a gurgling voice, "you don't know what you are talking about. You do not know that I am compelled to haunt this place year after year by a dreadful fate. It is no pleasure to me to enter this house, and ruin and mildew everything I touch. I never wanted to be a shower-bath, but it is my doom. Do you know who I am?"

"No, I don't," returned the master of Harrowby. "I should say you were the Lady of the Lake."

"No. I am the Water Ghost of Harrowby Hall, and have been for two hundred years to-night."

"How the deuce did you ever come to get such a messy job?" asked the master.

"Through a mistake," replied the specter. "I am the ghost of that fair maiden whose picture hangs over the mantelpiece in the drawing-room.

"It was my father's fault. He built Harrowby Hall, and the haunted chamber was to have been mine. My father had it furnished in pink and yellow, knowing that blue and gray was the only combination of colors I could bear. He did it merely to spite me, and I declined to live in the room. My father said I could live there or on the lawn, he didn't care which. That night I ran from the house and jumped over the cliff into the sea."

"That was a bit hasty," said the master of Harrowby.

"So I've heard," returned the ghost. "But I really never realized what I was doing until after I was drowned. I had been drowned a week when a sea-nymph came to me and informed me that I was to be one of her followers forever afterwards, adding that it should be my doom to haunt Harrowby Hall for one hour every Christmas Eve throughout the rest of eternity. I was to haunt that room on such Christmas Eves as I found it occupied; and if it should turn out not to be occupied, I was to spend the allotted hour with the head of the house."

"I'll sell the place."

"That you cannot do, for it is also required of me that I must appear to any purchaser, and divulge to him the awful secret of the house."

"Do you mean to tell me that on every Christmas Eve that I don't happen to have somebody in that guest-chamber, you are going to haunt me, extinguishing my fire, and soaking me to the skin?" demanded the master.

"Exactly, Oglethorpe. And what is more," said the water ghost, "it doesn't make the slightest difference where you are, if I find that room empty, wherever you may be I shall douse you with my spectral pres—"

Here the clock struck one, and immediately the apparition faded away. It was perhaps more of a trickle than a fade, but as a disappearance it was complete.

"By St. George and his Dragon!" cried the master of Harrowby, wringing his hands. "Next Christmas there will be an occupant in the spare room, or I spend the night in a bathtub!"

But the master of Harrowby, when Christmas Eve came again, was in his grave. He never recovered from the cold he caught that awful night. Harrowby Hall was closed, and the heir to the estate was in London. There to him in his apartment came the same experience that his father had gone through, except that being younger and stronger, he survived the shock. Everything in his rooms was ruined—his clocks were rusted; a fine collection of water-color drawings was entirely washed out. What was worse, the apartments below his were drenched by the water soaking through the floors, a damage for which he was compelled to pay, and which caused his landlady to ask him to leave immediately.

The story of the family ghost got around, and no one would invite him out to any function on Christmas save afternoon teas and receptions. Fathers of daughters declined to permit him to remain in their houses later than eight o'clock at night.

So the heir of Harrowby Hall resolved, as his ancestors for several generations before him had resolved, that something must be done.

His first thought was to have the fireplace in the room enlarged, so that he might evaporate the ghost. Then he remembered what his father had told him—that no fire could withstand the lady's extreme dampness. Next he thought of steam-pipes. These, he remembered, could lie hundreds of feet deep in water, and still retain sufficient heat to drive the water away in vapor. So the haunted room was heated by steam to a withering degree.

The scheme was only partially successful. The water ghost appeared at the specified time, but hot as the room was, it shortened her visit by no more than five minutes, during which time the nervous system of the young master was well-nigh shattered, and the room itself was cracked and warped to an extent which required a large sum of money to repair. And worse than this, as the last drop of the water ghost was slowly sizzling itself out on the floor, she whispered to him that there was still water in great plenty where she came from, and that next year would find her as extremely wet as ever.

It was then that, going from one extreme to the other, the ingenious heir of Harrowby hit upon the means by which the water ghost was ultimately conquered, and happiness once more came within the grasp of the house of Oglethorpe.

The heir provided himself with a warm suit of fur underclothing. Donning this with the furry side in, he placed over it a tight-fitting rubber garment. On top of this he put another set of underclothing made of wool, and over this was a second rubber garment like the first. Upon his head he placed a light and comfortable diving helmet; and so clad, on the following Christmas Eve, he awaited the coming of his tormentor.

It was a bitterly cold night that brought to a close this twenty-fourth day of December. The air outside was still, but the temperature was below zero. Within, all was quiet, the servants of Harrowby Hall waiting with beating hearts the outcome of their master's campaign against his supernatural visitor.

The master himself was lying on the bed in the haunted room, when—

The clock clanged out the hour of twelve.

There was a sudden banging of doors, a blast of cold air swept through the halls, the door leading into the haunted chamber flew open, a splash was heard, and the water ghost was seen standing at the side of the heir of Harrowby. Rivulets of water streamed from him, but deep down under the various garments he wore, he was as dry and as warm as he could have wished.

"Ha!" said the young master of Harrowby. "I'm glad to see you."

"You are the most original man I've met, if that is true," returned the ghost. "May I ask where did you get that hat?"

"Certainly, madam," returned the master, courteously. "It is a little portable observatory I had made for just such emergencies as this. But, tell me, is it true that you are doomed to follow me about for one mortal hour—to stand where I stand, to sit where I sit?"

"That is my fate," returned the lady.

"We'll go out on the lake," said the master, standing up.

"You can't get rid of me that way," returned the ghost. "The water won't swallow me up; in fact, it will just add to my present bulk."

"Nevertheless," said the master, firmly, "we will go out on the lake."

"But, my dear sir," returned the ghost, "it is fearfully cold out there. You will be frozen hard before you've been out ten minutes."

"Oh no, I'll not," replied the master. "I am very warmly dressed. Come!" This last in a tone of command that made the ghost ripple.

And they started.

They had not gone far before the water ghost showed signs of distress.

"You walk too slowly," she said. "I am nearly frozen. My knees are so stiff now I can hardly move. Please hurry!"

"I should like to oblige a lady," returned the master, courteously, "but my clothes are rather heavy, and a hundred yards an hour is about my speed. Indeed, I think we should sit down on this snowdrift, and talk matters over."

"No! No! Do not do so, I beg you!" cried the ghost. "Let me move on. I feel myself growing rigid as it is. If we stop here, I shall be frozen stiff."

"That, madam," said the master slowly, seating himself on an ice-cake, "that is why I have brought you here. We have been on this spot just ten minutes; we have fifty more. Take your time about it, madam, but freeze, and that is all I ask of you."

"I cannot move my right leg now," cried the ghost, in despair, "and my overskirt is a solid sheet of ice. Oh, good, kind Mr. Oglethorpe, light a fire, and let me go free from these icy fetters."

"Never, madam. It cannot be. I have you at last."

"Alas!" cried the ghost, a tear trickling down her frozen cheek. "Help me, I beg. I congeal!"

"Congeal, madam, congeal!" returned Oglethorpe, coldly. "You have drenched me and mine for two hundred and three years, madam. Tonight you have had your last drench."

"Ah, but I shall thaw out again, and then you'll see. Instead of the comfortably warm, genial ghost I have been in my past, sir, I shall be iced-water," cried the lady, threateningly.

"No, you won't, either," returned Oglethorpe; "for when you are frozen quite stiff, I shall send you to a cold-storage warehouse, and there shall you remain an icy work of art forever more."

"But warehouses burn."

"So they do, but this warehouse cannot burn. It is made of asbestos and surrounding it are fireproof walls, and within those walls the temperature is now and shall forever be 416 degrees below zero; low enough to make an icicle of any flame in this world—or the next," the master added, with a chuckle.

"For the last time let me beseech you. I would go on my knees to you, Oglethorpe, were they not already frozen. I beg of you do not doo—"

Here even the words froze on the water ghost's lips and the clock struck one. There was a momentary tremor throughout the ice-bound form, and the moon, coming out from behind a cloud, shone down on the rigid figure of a beautiful woman sculptured in clear, transparent ice. There stood the ghost of Harrowby Hall, conquered by the cold, a prisoner for all time.

The heir of Harrowby had won at last, and today in a large storage house in London stands the frigid form of one who will never again flood the house of Oglethorpe with woe and sea-water.

Three Ghost Stories
For Christmas Eve

JEROME K. JEROME

When are spooks not spooks? When a
spook is a spoof, that's when!

WEEPING
HOURS
10PM-4AM

10PM-2AM
SATURDAYS

The Faithful Ghost

I WAS little more than a lad when I first met with Johnson. I was home for the Christmas holidays, and, it being Christmas Eve, I had been allowed to sit up very late. On opening the door of my little bedroom to go in, I found myself face to face with Johnson, who was coming out. It passed through me, and uttering a long low wail of misery, disappeared out of the staircase window.

I was startled for the moment—I was only a schoolboy at the time, and had never seen a ghost before—and felt a little nervous about going to bed. But, on reflection, I remembered that it was only to sinful people that spirits could do any harm, and so tucked myself up, and went to sleep.

In the morning I told my father what I had seen.

"Oh, yes, that was old Johnson," he answered. "Don't you be frightened of that; he lives here." And then he told me the poor thing's history.

It seemed that Johnson, when it was alive, had loved, in early life, the daughter of a former owner of our house, a very beautiful girl, whose Christian name had been Emily. Father did not know her other name.

Johnson was too poor to marry the girl, so he kissed her good-bye, told her he would soon be back, and went off to Australia to make his fortune.

But Australia was not then what it became later on. Travelers through the bush were few and far between in those early days; and, even when one was caught, the portable property found upon the body was often of hardly sufficiently negotiable value to pay the simple funeral expenses rendered necessary. So that it took Johnson nearly twenty years to make his fortune.

The self-imposed task was accomplished at last, however, and then,

213

having successfully eluded the police, and gotten out of the Colony, he returned to England, full of hope and joy, to claim his bride.

He reached the house to find it silent and deserted. All that the neighbors could tell him was that, soon after his own departure, the family had, on one foggy night, unostentatiously disappeared, and that nobody had ever seen or heard anything of them since, although the landlord and most of the local tradesmen had made searching inquiries.

Poor Johnson, frenzied with grief, sought his lost love all over the world. But he never found her, and, after years of fruitless effort, he returned to end his lonely life in the very house where, in the happy bygone days, he and his beloved Emily had passed so many blissful hours.

He had lived there quite alone, wandering about the empty rooms, weeping and calling to his Emily to come back to him; and when the poor old fellow died, his ghost still kept the business on.

It was there, father said, when he took the house, and the agent had knocked ten pounds a year off the rent in consequence.

After that, I was continually meeting Johnson about the place at all times of the night, and so, indeed, were we all. We used to walk round it or stand aside to let it pass, at first; but when we grew more at home with it, and there seemed no necessity for so much ceremony, we used to walk straight through it. You could not say it was ever much in the way.

It was a gentle, harmless old ghost, too, and we all felt very sorry for it, and pitied it. The women folk, indeed, made quite a pet of it for a while. Its faithfulness touched them so.

But as time went on, it grew to be a bit of a bore. You see it was full of sadness. There was nothing cheerful or genial about it. You felt sorry for it, but it irritated you. It would sit on the stairs and cry for hours at a stretch; and whenever we woke up in the night one was sure to hear it pottering about the passages and in and out of the different rooms, moaning and sighing, so that we could not get to sleep again very easily. And when we had a party on, it would come and sit outside the drawing-room door, and sob all the time. It did not do anybody any harm exactly, but it cast a gloom over the whole affair.

"Oh, I'm getting sick of this old fool," said my father one evening after Johnson had been more of a nuisance than usual, and had spoiled a game of whist, by sitting up the chimney and groaning. "We shall have to get rid of him, somehow or other. I wish I knew how to do it."

"Well," said my mother, "depend upon it, you'll never see the last of him until he's found Emily's grave. That's what he is after. You find Emily's grave, and put him on to that, and he'll stop there. That's the only thing to do."

The idea seemed reasonable, but the difficulty in the way was that we none of us knew where Emily's grave was any more than the ghost of Johnson himself did. Father suggested palming off some other Emily's grave upon the poor thing, but, as luck would have it, there did not seem to have been an Emily of any sort buried anywhere for miles around. I never came across a neighborhood so utterly destitute of dead Emilies.

I thought for a bit, and then I hazarded a suggestion myself.

"Couldn't we fake up something for the old chap?" I queried. "He seems a simple-minded old sort. He might take it in. Anyhow, we could but try."

"By Jove, so we will," exclaimed my father; and the very next morning we had the workmen in, and fixed up a little mound at the bottom of the orchard with a tombstone over it, bearing the following inscription:

SACRED

To The Memory Of

EMILY

Her Last Words Were:

"Tell Johnson I Love Him"

"That ought to fetch him," mused Dad as he surveyed the work when finished. "I am sure I hope it does."

It did.

We lured him down there that very night; and—well, there, it was one of the most pathetic things I have ever seen, the way Johnson sprang upon that tombstone and wept. Dad and old Squibbins the gardener cried like children when they saw it.

Johnson has never troubled us any more in the house since then. It spends every night now sobbing on the grave, and seems quite happy.

There still? Oh, yes. I'll take you fellows down and show you it next time you come to our place—10 P.M to 4 A.M. are its general hours, 10 P.M. to 2 A.M. on Saturdays.

The Ruined Home

Well, you all know my brother-in-law, Joe Parkins (we did not know his brother-in-law, but we said we did, so as to save time), and you know, of course, that he once rented an old mill in Surrey, and went to live there.

Now you must know that, years ago, this very mill had been occupied by a wicked old miser, who died there, leaving—so it was rumored—all his money hidden somewhere about the place. Naturally enough, everyone who had since come to live at the mill had tried to find the treasure; but none had ever succeeded, and the local wisacres said that nobody ever would, unless the ghost of the miserly miller should, one day, take a fancy to one of the tenants, and disclose to him the secret of the hiding-place.

My brother-in-law did not attach much importance to the story, and, unlike his predecessors, made no attempt whatever to discover the hidden gold.

"Unless business was very different then from what it is now," said my brother-in-law, "I don't see how a miller could very well have saved anything, however much of a miser he might have been: at all events, not enough to make it worth the trouble of looking for it."

Still, he could not altogether forget that treasure.

One night he went to bed. There was nothing very extraordinary about that, I admit. He often did go to bed of a night. What *was* remarkable, however, was that exactly as the clock of the village church chimed the last stroke of twelve, my brother-in-law woke up with a start, and felt himself quite unable to go to sleep again.

Joe sat up in bed, and looked around.

At the foot of the bed something stood very still, wrapped in shadow.

It moved into the moonlight, and then my brother-in-law saw that it was the figure of a wizened little old man, in knee-breeches and a pigtail.

In an instant the story of the hidden treasure and the old miser flashed across his mind.

"He's come to show me where it's hidden," thought my brother-in-law; and he resolved that he would not spend all this money on himself, but would devote a small percentage of it toward doing good to others.

The apparition moved toward the door; my brother-in-law put on his trousers and followed it. The ghost went downstairs into the kitchen, glided over and stood in front of the hearth, sighed and disappeared.

Next morning, Joe had a couple of bricklayers in, and made them haul out the stove and pull down the chimney, while he stood behind with a potato-sack in which to put the gold.

They knocked down half the wall, and never found so much as a four-penny bit. My brother-in-law did not know what to think.

The next night the ghostly old man appeared again, and again led the way into the kitchen. This time, however, instead of going to the fireplace, it stood more in the middle of the room, and sighed.

"Oh, I see what he means now," said my brother-in-law to himself; "it's under the floor. Why did the old idiot go and stand up against the stove, so as to make me think it was up the chimney?"

They spent the next day in taking up the kitchen floor; but the only thing they found was a three-pronged fork, and the handle of that was broken.

On the third night, the ghost reappeared, quite unabashed, and for a third time made for the kitchen. Arrived there, it looked up at the ceiling and vanished.

"Umph! he don't seem to have learned much sense where he's been to," muttered Joe, as he trotted back to bed; "I should have thought he might have done that at first."

Still, there seemed no doubt now where the treasure lay, and the first thing after breakfast they started pulling down the ceiling. They got every inch of the ceiling down, and they took up the boards of the room above.

They discovered about as much treasure as you would expect to find in an empty soda bottle.

On the fourth night, when the ghost appeared, as usual, my brother-in-law was so wild that he threw his boots at it; and the boots passed through the body, and broke a looking-glass.

On the fifth night, when Joe awoke, the ghost was standing in a dejected attitude, looking very miserable. There was an appealing look in its large sad eyes that quite touched my brother-in-law.

"After all," he thought, "perhaps the silly chap's doing his best. Maybe he has forgotten where he really did put it, and is trying to remember. I'll give him another chance."

The ghost appeared grateful and delighted at seeing Joe prepare to follow him, and led the way into the attic, pointed to the ceiling, and vanished.

"Well, he's hit it this time, I do hope," said my brother-in-law; and next day they set to work to take the roof off the place.

It took them three days to get the roof thoroughly off, and all they found was a bird's nest; after securing which they covered up the house with tarpaulins, to keep it dry.

You might have thought that that would have cured the poor fellow of looking for treasure. But it didn't.

He said there must be something in it all, or the ghost would never keep on coming as it did; and that, having gone so far, he would go on to the end, and solve the mystery, cost what it might.

Night after night he would get out of his bed and follow that spectral old fraud about the house. Each night the old man would indicate a different place; and, on each following day, my brother-in-law would proceed to break up the mill at the point indicated, and look for the treasure. At the end of three weeks there was not a room in the mill fit to live in. Every wall had been pulled down, every floor had been taken up, every ceiling had had a hole knocked in it. And then, as suddenly as they had begun, the ghost's visits ceased; and my brother-in-law was left to rebuild the place at his leisure, and expense.

What induced the old image to play such a silly trick upon a family man and taxpayer? Ah! that's just what I cannot tell you.

Some said that the ghost of the wicked old man had done it to punish my brother-in-law for not believing in him at first; while others held that the apparition was probably that of some deceased local plumber or carpenter, who would naturally take an interest in seeing a house knocked about and spoiled. But nobody knew anything for certain.

The Ghost of
The Blue Chamber

"I don't want to make you fellows nervous," began my uncle in a peculiarly impressive, not to say blood-curdling, tone of voice, "and if you would rather that I did not mention it, I won't; but, as a matter of fact, this very house, in which we are now sitting, is haunted."

"You don't say that!" exclaimed Mr. Coombes.

"What's the use of your saying I don't say it when I have just said it?" retorted my uncle somewhat annoyed. "You talk so foolishly. I tell you the house is haunted. Regularly on Christmas Eve the Blue Chamber" (they call the room next to the nursery the "Blue Chamber," at my uncle's) "is haunted by the ghost of a sinful man—a man who once killed a Christmas carol singer with a lump of coal."

"How did he do it?" asked Mr. Coombes, eagerly. "Was it difficult?"

"I do not know how he did it," replied my uncle; "he did not explain the process. The singer had taken up a position just inside the front gate, and was singing a ballad. It is presumed that, when he opened his mouth for B flat, the lump of coal was thrown by the sinful man from one of the windows, and that it went down the singer's throat and choked him."

"You want to be a good shot, but it is certainly worth trying," murmured Mr. Coombes thoughtfully.

"But that was not his only crime, alas!" added my uncle. "Prior to that he had killed a solo cornet player."

"No! Is that really a fact?" exclaimed Mr. Coombes.

"Of course it's a fact," answered my uncle testily. "At all events, as much a fact as you can expect to get in a case of this sort."

219

"The poor fellow, the cornet player, had been in the neighborhood barely a month. Old Mr. Bishop, who kept the 'Jolly Sand Boys' at the time, and from whom I had the story, said he had never known a more hard-working and energetic solo cornet player. He, the cornet player, only knew two tunes, but Mr. Bishop said that the man could not have played with more vigor, or for more hours a day, if he had known forty. The two tunes he did play were 'Annie Laurie' and 'Home, Sweet Home'; and as regarded his performance of the former melody, Mr. Bishop said that a mere child could have told what it was meant for.

"This musician—this poor, friendless artist—used to come regularly and play in this street just opposite for two hours every evening. One evening he was seen, evidently in response to an invitation, going into this very house, *but was never seen coming out of it!*"

"Did the townsfolk try offering any reward for his recovery?" asked Mr. Coombes.

"Not a penny," replied my uncle.

"Another summer," continued my uncle, "a German band visited here, intending—so they announced on their arrival—to stay till the autumn.

"On the second day after their arrival, the whole company, as fine and healthy a body of men as one would wish to see, were invited to dinner by this sinful man, and, after spending the whole of the next twenty-four hours in bed, left the town a broken and dyspeptic crew; the parish doctor, who had attended them, giving it as his opinion that it was doubtful if they would, any of them, be fit to play an air again."

"You—you don't know the recipe, do you?" asked Mr. Coombes.

"Unfortunately I do not," replied my uncle; "but the chief ingredient was said to have been railway dining room hash.

"I forget the man's other crimes," my uncle went on; "I used to know them all at one time, but my memory is not what it was. I do not, however, believe I am doing his memory an injustice in believing that he was not entirely unconnected with the death, and subsequent burial, of a gentleman who used to play the harp with his toes; and that neither was he altogether unresponsible for the lonely grave of an unknown stranger who had once visited the neighborhood, an Italian peasant lad, a performer upon the barrel-organ.

"Every Christmas Eve," said my uncle, cleaving with low impressive tones the strange awed silence that, like a shadow, seemed to have slowly stolen into and settled down upon the room, "the ghost of this sinful man haunts the Blue Chamber, in this very house. There, from midnight until cock-crow, amid wild muffled shrieks and groans and mocking laughter and the ghostly sound of horrid blows, it does fierce phantom fight with the spirits of the solo cornet player and the murdered carol singer, assisted at intervals by the shades of the German band; while the ghost of the strangled harpist plays mad ghostly melodies with ghostly toes on the ghost of a broken harp."

Uncle said the Blue Chamber was comparatively useless as a sleeping apartment on Christmas Eve.

"Hark!" said my uncle, raising a warning hand toward the ceiling, while we held our breath, and listened: "Hark! I believe they are at it now—in the Blue Chamber!"

I rose up and said that *I* would sleep in the Blue Chamber.

"Never!" cried my uncle, springing up. "You shall not put yourself in this deadly peril. Besides, the bed is not made."

"Never mind the bed," I replied. "I have lived in furnished apartments for gentlemen, and have been accustomed to sleep on beds that have never been made from one year's end to the other. I am young, and have had a clear conscience now for over a month. The spirits will not harm me. I may even do them some little good, and induce them to be quiet and go away. Besides, I should like to see the show."

They tried to dissuade me from what they termed my foolhardy enterprise, but I remained firm and claimed my privilege. I was "the guest." "The guest" always sleeps in the haunted chamber on Christmas Eve; it is his right.

They said that if I put it on that footing they had, of course, no answer, and they lighted a candle for me and followed me upstairs in a body.

Whether elevated by the feeling that I was doing a noble action or animated by a mere general consciousness of rectitude is not for me to say, but I went upstairs that night with remarkable buoyancy. It was as much as I could do to stop at the landing when I came to it; I felt I wanted to go on up to the roof. But, with the help of the banisters, I restrained my ambition, wished them all good-night and went in and shut the door.

Things began to go wrong with me from the very first. The candle tumbled out of the candlestick before my hand was off the lock. It kept on tumbling out again; I never saw such a slippery candle. I gave up attempting to use the candlestick at last and carried the candle about in my hand, and even then it would not keep upright. So I got wild and threw it out the window, and undressed and went to bed in the dark.

I did not go to sleep; I did not feel sleepy at all; I lay on my back looking up at the ceiling and thinking of things. I wish I could remember some of the ideas that came to me as I lay there, because they were so amusing.

I had been lying like this for half an hour or so, and had forgotten all about the ghost, when, on casually casting my eyes round the room, I noticed for the first time a singularly contented-looking phantom sitting in the easy-chair by the fire smoking the ghost of a long clay pipe.

I fancied for the moment, as most people would under similar circumstances, that I must be dreaming. I sat up and rubbed my eyes. No! It was a ghost, clear enough. I could see the back of the chair through his body. He looked over toward me, took the shadowy pipe from his lips and nodded.

The most surprising part of the whole thing to me was that I did not feel in the least alarmed. If anything I was rather pleased to see him. It was company.

I said: "Good evening. It's been a cold day!"

He said he had not noticed it himself, but dared say I was right.

We remained silent for a few seconds, and then, wishing to put it pleasantly, I said: "I believe I have the honor of addressing the ghost of the gentleman who had the accident with the carol singer?"

He smiled and said it was very good of me to remember it. One singer was not much to boast of, but still every little helped.

I was somewhat staggered at his answer. I had expected a groan of remorse. The ghost appeared, on the contrary, to be rather conceited over the business. I thought that as he had taken my reference to the singer so quietly perhaps he would not be offended if I questioned him about the organ grinder. I felt curious about that poor boy.

"Is it true," I asked, "that you had a hand in the death of that Italian peasant lad who came to the town once with a barrel-organ that played nothing but Scotch airs?"

He quite fired up. "Had a hand in it!" he exclaimed indignantly. "Who has dared to pretend that he assisted me? I murdered the youth myself. Nobody helped me. Alone I did it. Show me the man who says I didn't."

I calmed him. I assured him that I had never, in my own mind, doubted that he was the real and only assassin, and I went on and asked him what he had done with the body of the cornet player he had killed.

He said: "To which one may you be alluding?"

"Oh, were there any more then?" I inquired.

He smiled and gave a little cough. He said he did not like to appear to be boasting, but that, counting trombones, there were seven.

"Dear me!" I replied, "you must have had quite a busy time of it, one way and another."

He said that perhaps he ought not to be the one to say so; but that really, speaking of ordinary middle-class society, he thought there were few ghosts who could look back upon a life of more sustained usefulness.

He puffed away in silence for a few seconds while I sat watching him. I had never seen a ghost smoking a pipe before, that I could remember, and it interested me.

I asked him what tobacco he used, and he replied: "The ghost of cut cavendish as a rule."

He explained that the ghost of all the tobacco that a man smoked in life belong to him when he became dead. He said he himself had smoked a good deal of cut cavendish when he was alive, so that he was well supplied with the ghost of it now.

I thought I would join him in a pipe, and he said, "Do, old man"; and I reached over and got out the necessary paraphernalia from my coat pocket and lit up.

We grew quite chummy after that, and he told me all his crimes. He said he had lived next door once to a young lady who was learning to play the guitar, while a gentleman who practiced on the bass-viol lived opposite. And he, with fiendish cunning, had introduced these two unsuspecting young people to one another, and had persuaded them to elope with each other against their parents' wishes, and take their musical instruments with them; and they had done so, and before the honeymoon was over, *she* had broken his head with the bass-viol, and *he* had tried to cram the guitar down her throat, and had injured her for life.

My friend said he used to lure muffin-men into the passage and then stuff them with their own wares till they burst. He said he had quieted eighteen that way.

Young men and women who recited long and dreary poems at evening parties, and callow youths who walked about the streets late at night, playing concertinas, he used to get together and poison in batches of ten, so as to save expense; and park orators and temperance lecturers he used to shut up six in a small room with a glass of water and a collection-box apiece, and let them talk each other to death.

It did one good to listen to him.

I asked him when he expected the other ghosts—the ghosts of the singer and the cornet player, and the German band that Uncle John had mentioned. He smiled, and said they would never come again, any of them.

I said, "Why, isn't it true, then, that they meet you here every Christmas Eve for a row?"

He replied that it was true. Every Christmas Eve, for twenty-five years, had he and they fought in that room; but they would never trouble him or anybody else again. One by one had he laid them out, spoiled and made them utterly useless for all haunting purposes. He had finished off the last German band ghost that very evening, just before I came upstairs, and had thrown what was left of it out through the slit between the window sashes. He said it would never be worth calling a ghost again.

"I suppose you will still come yourself, as usual?" I said. "They would be sorry to miss you, I know."

"Oh, I don't know," he replied; "there's nothing much to come for now; unless," he added kindly, "*you* are going to be here. I'll come if you will sleep here next Christmas Eve."

"I have taken a liking to you," he continued; "you don't fly off, screeching, when you see a party, and your hair doesn't stand on end. You've no idea," he said, "how sick I am of seeing people's hair standing on end."

He said it irritated him.

Just then a slight noise reached us from the yard below, and he started and turned deathly black.

"You are ill," I cried, springing toward him; "tell me the best thing to do for you. Shall I drink some brandy, and give you the ghost of it?"

He remained silent, listening intently for a moment, and then he gave a sigh of relief, and the shade came back to his cheek.

"It's all right," he murmured; "I was afraid it was the cock."

"Oh, it's too early for that," I said. "Why, it's only the middle of the night."

"Oh, that doesn't make any difference to those cursed chickens," he replied bitterly. "They would just as soon crow in the middle of the night as at any other time—sooner, if they thought it would spoil a chap's evening out. I believe they do it on purpose."

He said a friend of his, the ghost of a man who had killed a tax collector, used to haunt a house in Long Acre, where they kept fowls in the cellar, and every time a policeman went by and flashed his searchlight down the grating, the old cock there would fancy it was the sun, and start crowing like mad, when, of course, the poor ghost had to dissolve, and it would, in consequence, get back home sometimes as early as one o'clock in the morning, furious because it had only been out for an hour.

I agreed that it seemed very unfair.

"Oh, it's an absurd arrangement altogether," he continued, quite angrily. "I can't imagine what our chief could have been thinking of when he made it. As I have said to him, over and over again, 'Have a fixed time, and let everybody stick to it—say four o'clock in summer, and six in winter. Then one would know what one was about.' "

"How do you manage when there isn't any clock handy?" I inquired.

He was on the point of replying, when again he started and listened. This time I distinctly heard Mr. Bowles' cock, next door, crow twice.

"There you are," he said, rising and reaching for his hat; "that's the sort of thing we have to put up with. What *is* the time?"

I looked at my watch, and found it was half-past three.

"I thought as much," he muttered. "I'll wring that blessed bird's neck if I get hold of it." And he prepared to go.

"If you can wait half a minute," I said, getting out of bed, "I'll go a bit of the way with you."

"It's very good of you," he replied, pausing, "but it seems unkind to drag you out."

"Not at all," I replied; "I shall like a walk." And I partially dressed myself, and took my umbrella; and he put his arm through mine, and we went out together, the best of friends.